MR

D0265857

CLASS	AF	LOCATION	(R)
AUTHOR	MacALISTER, Katie		
TITLE	Up in smoke.		

THIS BOOK IS TO BE RETURNED ON OR BEFORE THE
LAST DATE STAMPED BELOW

ACCESS

FL39

X720

15 FEB 2011

24 JAN 2017 O

4247

X484
X715
X296
B161
X1168
X730
F116

X714

X863

E165

11 MAY 2012

X752

F96
FL52

X484

23. JUL 14

STIRLING COUNCIL LIBRARIES

5256

SILVER DRAGONS

UP IN SMOKE

A NOVEL OF THE SILVER DRAGONS

KATIE MACALISTER

THORNDIKE
CHIVERS

This Large Print edition is published by Thorndike Press, Waterville, Maine, USA and by BBC Audiobooks Ltd, Bath, England.
Thorndike Press, a part of Gale, Cengage Learning.
Copyright © Katie MacAlister, 2008.
The moral right of the author has been asserted.

The text of this Large Print edition is unabridged.
Other aspects of the book may vary from the original edition.
Set in 16 pt. Plantin.
Printed on permanent paper.

LIBRARY OF CONGRESS CATALOGING-IN-PUBLICATION DATA

MacAlister, Katie.
  Up in smoke : a novel of the silver dragons / by Katie MacAlister. — Large print ed.
    p. cm. — (Thorndike Press large print romance)
  Originally published: New York : Signet, 2008.
  ISBN-13: 978-1-4104-1318-5 (alk. paper)
  ISBN-10: 1-4104-1318-7 (alk. paper)
  1. Large type books. I. Title.
PS3613.A227U6 2009
813'.6—dc22   2008045357

BRITISH LIBRARY CATALOGUING-IN-PUBLICATION DATA AVAILABLE

Published in 2009 in the U.S. by arrangement with NAL Signet, a member of Penguin Group (USA) Inc.
Published in 2009 in the U.K. by arrangement with The Penguin Group (USA) Inc.

U.K. Hardcover: 978 1 408 43297 6 (Chivers Large Print)
U.K. Softcover: 978 1 408 43298 3 (Camden Large Print)

Printed in the United States of America
1 2 3 4 5 6 7 13 12 11 10 09

To Dave Morace and Aimee Schmelter, with many thanks for making me giggle at inappropriate moments, and for letting me refer to them as Lintyblobs and Iddykins.

CHAPTER ONE

"Beautiful in is beautiful out; that's what they taught us at Carrie Fay, and I absolutely believe it's true. I mean, think about it — the sort of person you are doesn't just stay inside you, now, does it?"

Before I could sort through that odd bit of logic, a cold, wet blob smelling of earth and minerals was slathered across my mouth. "Mmm-hmm," I contented myself with answering.

"I'll wipe off your lips, but no talking, sugar. We can't have you moving your mouth as the mask dries. Anyway, it's absolutely true. Just look at you, for instance!"

The petite, blond, perky woman in front of me who had been applying an olive green clay mask to my face stepped back to consider me; she held a small bowl in one hand, and her other hand was sheathed in a latex glove covered in the same gloop. She waved at me with the bowl. "You don't look evil in the least, and yet here you are, about to wed a demon lord!"

"Sally, I'm not marrying Magoth —" I started to say, but she cut me off with a frown.

"No talking, sugar! I just told you that! Where were we? Oh, yes, how appearances can be deceiving." Her frown deepened somewhat as she eyeballed me. I squirmed in the chair, never comfortable being the center of anyone's attention . . . with one notable exception.

My heart gave a little quiver as a familiar ache started within me at the vision that rose in my mind's eye — a man laughing with utter delight, dimples set in his beautiful latte-colored skin, his eyes flashing like quicksilver. Just the thought of him had my heart speeding up even as I mourned the fact that I hadn't seen Gabriel in more than a month.

"You look like a normal woman — although I have to say that the 1920s flapper hairstyle you seem to enjoy is a bit less than mainstream. But other than that, you look perfectly normal, kind almost, not at all like you were to become Mrs. Demon Lord."

"I'm not marrying Magoth," I said, trying not to move my lips.

"Oh, well, consort, marrying . . . it's all the same thing, isn't it? Just a smidgen more on your forehead, sugar. You need a lot of exfoliating there. Whatever have you been using on your face? No, don't answer; let the mask dry. Here, do you want to see yourself?" Sally put down her things and peeled off the glove, admiring her handiwork for a moment before offering me a mirror.

I kept my jaw clamped shut as I said slowly, moving my mouth as little as possible, "No, thanks. I'm a doppelganger. We don't have reflections."

"You don't? I never noticed that."

"It's not something that most people know."

"Must make plucking your eyebrows difficult." She admired her own image in the mirror for a moment, fluffing up a strand of extremely styled blond hair before setting down the mirror and giving me a big, sharky smile. "Even if you can't use the mirror, you have to admit that all this is awfully romantic."

"Romantic?" I asked, my thoughts immediately turning to the dragon in human form who made my knees weak.

"Yes! Terribly so!" She must have seen the look of confusion in my eyes because she continued as she packed away into a small pink duffel bag a good fifty pounds of cosmetics and accompanying items. "Magoth making you his consort and giving you access to all that goes with such a position, I mean. It's so incredibly romantic that he wants you so much he's willing to overlook the fact that you're not at all suited for the position. It just goes to show that even a demon lord has his soft side."

I rolled my eyes. "Magoth has no soft side, and he doesn't want me. Nor have I said I'd become his consort. I'm a wyvern's mate, and that is where my heart lies, not here in Abaddon with Magoth."

Sally's jaw sagged a little. "You're a wyvern's mate? The dragon kind of wyvern? The leader of, what do they call them, a dragon sept?"

"That's it," I answered, still trying not to move my mouth at all. The mask was drying, pulling my flesh taut, which didn't make it easy.

"A wyvern's mate!" She looked thoughtful for a moment. "Then what are you doing here?"

I sighed. "It's a long story, too long to tell you now, but the abridged version is that when my twin created me, I was bound to Magoth as his servant. Because I'm a doppelganger, he used me to steal items he wanted. One day I ran across Gabriel — he's the wyvern for the silver dragons — and we discovered I was his mate. Magoth found out about it and demanded I steal a priceless dragon artifact for him, the Lindorm Phylactery. I refused and gave it to Gabriel, instead."

Her eyes, kind of a muddy green, almost popped out of her head. "You *refused?* You went dybbuk?"

I nodded.

"Sins of Bael! But . . . you're still alive. And whole. Not to mention the fact that Magoth told me you agreed to be his consort. Why would he say that, let alone allow you to live *without* being in perpetual torment, if you went dybbuk?"

"Magoth is a bit . . . different," I said, only barely stifling the wry smile that hovered on my lips. "I guess he knows that being his consort is more of a perpetual torment than anything he could do to me physically."

"You find him unattractive?" she asked, shaking her head in disbelief. "He's gorgeous!"

"Physically, I think he's very attractive. What woman could resist those smoldering dark looks? Certainly the women of the last century couldn't. And didn't. You know he was a silent film star, yes?"

11

"Well, I know he looks kind of familiar." She thought for a moment, then mentioned a name.

"That's him. The resemblance to his film self is more noticeable when he wears his hair slicked back. But regardless of his handsome exterior, it's the interior that gives me nightmares." I grabbed at her sleeve as she wandered past, continuing to gather up her things. "Sally, I know you're spending time in Abaddon as part of your application for the empty demon lord position, but I don't think you really understand what things here are really like, what the demon lords are. They may appear to be human, but they lost all shreds of humanity long, long ago, and Magoth is no different from any of the others . . . well, except he may be slightly more airheaded than the rest."

"Not the biggest garbanzo in the three-bean salad?" she asked with a smile.

I gave her a wary look. "Not even close to it, no."

"That's all right." She patted my hand for a moment, then turned to preen in front of the blackdraped mirror that sat in the room Magoth had (unwillingly) assigned to me. "I like my men a bit dim. Makes them easier to handle."

It was my turn to stare in disbelief, and stare I did. "It's true I don't know anything about your background other than you felt it important, for some reason that is completely beyond my comprehension, to try and obtain the currently vacant position of prince of Abaddon, but that aside, I think you are grossly underestimating just what exactly is Magoth's true nature. He's manipulative, greedy, self-centered, ruthless to the extreme, and he brings new meaning to the word 'diabolical.' In short, he is everything evil you can possibly imagine . . . and so much more."

"Sweet, sweet May . . . singing my praises to the delicious Sally, are you? How thoughtful."

The voice that spoke held a note of amusement that didn't lull me into a sense of comfort. Magoth in a normal (read: evil) mood I could handle, but a playful, amused Magoth was especially dangerous.

"I'm simply telling her the truth about you," I said cautiously, turning to eye him. As a mortal, Magoth had been an incredibly handsome man, with sinfully black hair and eyes and a seductive manner that had left women over the centuries sighing . . . those who survived his attentions, that is. Although demon lords could change their appearances to suit their whims, Magoth had never altered his, finding that his true form suited his purposes just fine.

He leaned with languid grace against the door frame to my room, a wicked light dancing in his black eyes, his hair once again slicked back, making obvious the resemblance to his movie-star self of some ninety years before. "May I enter?" he asked now with a slightly raised eyebrow at my slowness.

"Sins of the saints, you make him ask to come into your room?" Sally's little gasp of surprise drew Magoth's attention to her as he oiled his way into the room.

"It is a little game we play, my sweet May and I — she insists that I not enter her so charming chamber without her express consent, and I pretend to go along with it. And speaking of games, shall we indulge in a threesome?" Magoth flung himself down on my bed and patted the mattress with a seductive look pointed at me. "I'll have to let May go first, since she will be my consort, but you may feel free to indulge in your wildest fantasies with me, Sally. I'm sure May won't protest if you ride me like a rented mule."

"Oh!" Sally said, shooting me a quick glance, but I was unsure if she was startled by the thought of indulging in a threesome, or by the fact that I would apparently not be bothered by my so-called lover's infidelities. "I don't . . . um . . ."

"She's not interested any more than I am," I said, coming to Sally's rescue. I would have added a frown at Magoth for lounging around on my bed, but the mask was now so tight, it prohibited movement . . . not to mention the fact that Magoth wasn't in the least concerned whether or not I frowned at his actions. "Did you want something in particular?"

"If I said 'you', would you hold it against me?" he asked with a waggle of his eyebrows. "And by *it,* I mean your delectable self. Naked? And dabbed with just a light touch of that edible jasmine oil I had made for you?"

I crossed my arms over my chest. "Take a look at my face, Magoth. What do you see?"

"I see a woman who is trying desperately to make herself beautiful for me, and yet, I already find you attractive. Did you want me to bed you wearing the facial mask? It's rather kinky, although not nearly so kinky as having you slathered in pig's grease and bound to that delightful little device I showed you in my playroom —"

I held back a shudder. "Your playroom

could double as a torture museum, not that I'm going to enter it again."

"But, my sweetest of all sweet Mays, I assure you that a little tingle of electricity in clamps placed on well-oiled nipples can be stimulating in ways —"

"Will you stop?" I interrupted in a loud voice, not wanting to get him wound up again. "I am not going to sleep with you. Not now, not ever, and certainly not when there are pig's grease and nipple clamps around."

Sally sucked in another startled breath, no doubt in response to the manner in which I had addressed Magoth. "May, honeychild, you must take a little smidgen of advice from one who is wiser and very, very slightly older — an attitude of respect, tinged with a tiny little morsel of humility, can go a long way when dealing with those in authority."

Magoth laughed and rose from the bed, waving a hand that had his clothing melting right off his body. "Perhaps you just need to be reminded of what it is you are so callously and ignorantly spurning, my queen?"

"I'm not your queen," I said evenly, holding back my temper.

"Oh, my!" Sally's eyes just about bugged out as she took in Magoth in all his glory. "You're . . . er . . . aroused."

He leered at her as I said, "He's *always* aroused."

"My sweet one speaks the truth," he said, glancing down with pride at his penis. "I have incredible sexual prowess and can give pleasure for hours on end."

"Hours?" Sally asked, sounding a little breathless. Her eyes went a bit misty as she gave him a very thorough visual once-over.

"His idea of pleasure isn't the same as yours and mine," I said softly, leaning in toward her.

"How do you know what I find pleasurable?" she shot back, and for a moment, there was a glimpse of something in her eyes that might explain why a woman who appeared perfectly normal would suddenly decide she wanted to become a demon lord.

"I don't," I admitted. "But Magoth's form of pleasure usually holds a sting. Sometimes it's fatal."

"I haven't killed a woman with sex in days," he said with another leer, cocking a hip so his penis, tattooed with a curse put there by an unhappy lover, waved at me.

I shot him a horrified glance. He laughed again. "May, my adorable one, you're like putty in my hands. A silky-skinned, blue-eyed vixen sort of putty, but putty nonetheless. I take it my suggestion of a threesome is out?"

"Way out," I agreed.

"Ah." He glanced down at his penis in mock regret. "Perhaps the lady prefers a different color scheme? Maybe this would be more to your favor?"

His form shimmered for a moment, blurring slightly before settling into that of a tall man with skin the color of my favorite latte, his hair growing into shoulder-length dreadlocks, a close-cropped goatee and mustache framing lips that were firm, yet so very sensitive. My heart leaped in my chest, thudding madly as I beheld the vision of the man for whom I had sacrificed so much. I fisted my hands, fighting to control the urge to strike Magoth for his cruelty, knowing that he was fishing for just such a reaction from me. It took a moment, but at last I mastered my emotions and leveled him a gaze that by rights should have struck him down.

"You're not even a fraction of the man Gabriel is," I told him.

"Ah, but he's not a man at all," Magoth answered, looking down at himself. He shuddered delicately and returned to his normal appearance, thankfully complete with clothing. "I tell myself that one day I will understand your preference for the silver wyvern over me, but I begin to wonder if it is not just some perverse obstinacy on your part."

I took a deep breath, ignoring the need to lash out. My voice was as bland as I could make it as I asked, "Was there something you wanted, a threesome aside?"

"How about a threesome *astride?*" he asked hopefully.

I tightened my lips.

"That dragon has ruined you," he said with a sigh, shaking his head. "You used to be such fun. As it happens, I did have a bit of news about which I wish to inform you —"

I never heard the rest of the sentence. A faint tingling sensation swept over me for the space between seconds; then suddenly I was yanked out of the room, out of Magoth's house, clear out of Abaddon, and plopped down in the center of a familiar room.

My vision, which had blurred for a few seconds, resolved itself. A black woman with a white stripe in her shoulder-length hair leaned forward and peered at me through red glasses. "Are you all right?" she asked, concern evident in her warm brown eyes.

"I . . . yes. I think." As I was about to ask

who the woman was — and more importantly, how she'd gotten me out of Abaddon
— a flicker of movement at the edge of my
peripheral vision had me spinning around,
my heart suddenly singing at the sight of
the man who stood there.

"Gabriel!" I shouted, and flung myself
into his arms as he ran forward to catch me.

CHAPTER TWO

"I knew you'd find a way to get me out of Abaddon," I said in between pressing kisses to Gabriel's face. He was warm and solid, and the wonderful woodsy scent that seemed to cling to him wrapped itself around me, sinking into my pores like rain on a parched desert. "I knew you would understand what I couldn't say in front of Magoth. I didn't think it would take you quite this long to get me out, but given that I didn't manage to extricate myself from Magoth's grip, I can't complain. Not when we're together again."

Gabriel's bright silver eyes seemed to see through me to the depths of my soul, lighting up all the little dark corners, shining into me with a white-hot heat that immediately set my body alight. "Little bird, I am . . . why is your face green?"

"Oh." I touched my cheek, picking off a piece of dried clay. "It's a facial mask."

"I see. I'm —"

Before he could finish the sentence, I was summarily yanked from his arms and spun through a sickening miasma of blackness that blossomed into red pain when I was dropped on a cold marble floor.

"Ow. What the —" I looked up from the floor, rubbing the part of my forehead where it had struck the marble. A little circle of green clay dust marked the spot. My heart shriveled into a minuscule ball of misery when I beheld the sight of a frowning Magoth, with Sally peering out from behind him.

"Who summoned you, May?"

"I don't know," I said, but Magoth was no fool. His gaze turned even blacker as I got to my feet and dusted off my pants. "You can stop looking daggers at me — or whatever hideous torture device you'd like to use — I don't know who summoned me." That was strictly the truth; I had no idea who the woman was who Gabriel had hired to summon me, but whoever she was, I wanted to sing her praises.

Magoth was not amused by my attempts at prevarication. "It was your dragon!"

"Gabriel was there, yes. But he didn't summon me. Dragons can't summon either minions or servants of dark lords, and since

I'm considered one of the latter grou—"

Before the word left my lips, I was jerked back through the fabric of time and being, and deposited back in a familiar room.

"Mayling!"

"Hello again. Um . . . am I here to stay this time?" I asked as Gabriel pulled me into his arms. "I sure hope I am, because that look in your eyes really makes me want to . . ."

A gentle cough alerted me to the fact that we had an audience.

"It's a pleasure to see you again, May, facial mask and all," a woman said, and I turned in Gabriel's arms to smile at Aisling. She stood leaning against her husband, a dark-haired, green-eyed wyvern named Drake.

"Oh, man, did you have to interrupt her? I wanted to hear what it was she was gonna do to Gabriel. I bet it involved tongues. And possibly peanut butter and a cake spatula. At least I *hope* the spatula was involved." The large shaggy black Newfoundland that sat next to Aisling might look like a normal dog, but I knew better.

"No peanut butter or spatulas of any variety, Jim. And it's nice to see you all again, too, Aisling, although I imagine you're about ready to have that baby."

She sighed and rubbed her large belly. "Another six weeks, the midwife says. I sure hope that's all, because I'm getting a bit tired of being treated like I'm made of glass. Do you know that Drake wouldn't even let me summon you by myself? He insisted my mentor, Nora, do the actual work. Oh, you haven't met Nora, have you? Nora Charles, this is May Northcott, who you might have guessed is Gabriel's mate."

"It's a pleasure to meet you," the woman with the red glasses said with a warm smile, offering me her hand.

I reached out to take it but fell into a black pit instead, crashing with a complete lack of grace onto the black marble floor of Magoth's main hall.

"What is going on? Who keeps summoning you from me? I will not have this, May! I absolutely will not have this! You are my consort! Who dares to pull you from my side?" Magoth stormed.

I sighed and got to my feet again, brushing off the remaining dried bits of clay that had mostly been knocked from my face. "I was summoned by Nora Charles."

Magoth's frown turned somewhat puzzled. "I do not know this name. Who is this person?"

"She's a Guardian, I suspect," I answered,

picking my words carefully. My standard operating policy was that the less information Magoth had, the happier I was, and although the fact that I had been bound to him at my creation meant I had to answer his questions truthfully, it didn't mean I had to blab *everything* to him.

"Oh, dear; all that talking has destroyed the mask," Sally said, her hands fluttering around vaguely. "Now it won't do the least bit of good."

"I'm sure my pores will survive, assuming the rest of me does as well." I disappeared down the hall to the bathroom attached to my room, quickly scrubbing off the remains of the mask. Magoth and Sally both followed.

"I sense that you're unhappy with me, May. This distresses me. I so hoped we'd be good friends," Sally said, fretting with the pale pink lace that clung to the wrists of her darker pink cashmere sweater. "I know that as a demon lord, I won't be expected to notice, let alone converse with, a minion of a fellow demon lord, but I've found that a little honey can make every situation easier, and I'd like us to be friends."

There wasn't much I could say that wasn't outright rude, so I said nothing, returning to my bedroom.

"This Guardian — your dragon must have hired her to steal you from me," Magoth said, his face clearing. "I suspected he would do something like this, but it is easily stopped. I will simply tell him that if he tries it again, I will torture you."

I ignored the word "torture" (not to mention the light of enjoyment that suddenly dawned in Magoth's black eyes) and confined myself to the important point. "Oh? And how do you expect to tell Gabriel that? It's not possible for you to leave Abaddon — you don't have the power or ability to do so — and Gabriel is certainly not foolish enough to come here and place himself in your power."

Magoth's jaw worked for a moment. Sally, who had plopped herself down in a chair and was browsing through my journal, looked up. "You know, one of the things that they taught us at the Carrie Fay Academy of Allurement and Attraction was to never say something was impossible. Surely there must be *some* way you can leave Abaddon, Magoth?"

"Hmm." Magoth stopped looking like he was about to rain down death and destruction (not in the least bit unlikely) as he thought that over.

I wondered what the penalty was for throttling a demon-lord candidate.

"I could have sworn — if you'll forgive me for chiming in here when you haven't asked my advice, and Bael only knows that you have far, far more experience in this field than I have — but I could have sworn that I read something in the Doctrine of Unending Conscious about methods of leaving Abaddon."

Magoth stared at her as if she had suddenly sprouted a halo and a pair of wings.

"Aren't you familiar with the Doctrine?" she asked, shooting a confused look my way before returning to him. "It's a set of laws governing Abad—"

"I know what the Doctrine is." He interrupted her with an abrupt gesture. "I wrote the chapter on suitable methods of punishment for unruly minions, a fact my sweet May seems to have forgotten."

"I'm here, aren't I?" I said with blithe disregard. "I haven't forgotten."

"I can't imagine anyone thinking that time spent with you is a punishment," Sally told him with a smile that really did seem to have more teeth than was humanly possible. "You're by far the nicest of all the demon lords I've met."

Magoth all but shimmied over to her, both hands on her boobs as he undulated against her. "And you have much insight and a true understanding of what it is to be such a sublime being as myself, but alas, until my sweet May consents to being my consort, I cannot bed you as is your due."

"Where on earth did *that* come from?" I asked, astounded by that little tidbit.

He shrugged and reluctantly stopped fondling Sally's boobs. I noted acidly to myself that she didn't protest the groping at all. "I am wooing you to be my consort. Until you agree to that, I must concentrate my full energies on you. But if you consented, then we might have a deliciously wicked threesome in which one of you —"

"I've already told you that is not happening," I interrupted before he went into graphic detail. Magoth loved to go into graphic detail. It didn't matter whether it was punishment or sex; he would happily spend hours describing both.

"Which, the threesome or the consort?" Sally asked.

"Both." I turned to Magoth. "I accepted the punishment of being bound to your side for going dybbuk, but I am *not* going to be your consort."

"Did I tell you that the position comes with access to my powers?" he asked, strolling toward me. Magoth didn't have the same smooth, sinuous, coiled-power sort of movements that Gabriel had, but I couldn't deny that he came darned close. He stopped next to me, so close he was almost touching me, his body leeching all the warmth from the air. I shivered, due to either his proximity or nerves.

"Er . . . no, you didn't. What sort of power?" For a moment I toyed with the idea of accepting Magoth's offer of consort, imagining myself in a position of power whereby I could escape his clutches and return to Gabriel.

"Well . . ." He smiled and drew a finger down the line of my jaw, his touch sending icy little shivers down my back. "Let us just say that in Abaddon, a consort is viewed as an extension of the demon lord. You would be treated with respect by the other princes."

I thought for a moment, taking a step backwards as I did so. "Would I have the ability to banish you to the Akasha?"

"The Akasha!" Sally gasped. "You would send dear Magoth to limbo? May, dear, I know you are new to this position just as I am new to it all, but to even joke about such a thing —"

"No one has that power," Magoth cut her off as if she hadn't been speaking, his dark eyes lit with pleasure as he tipped my chin up, his thumb brushing frigid strokes across my lips.

"Aisling does."

Magoth jerked his hand away, his eyes narrowing for a moment. "Aisling Grey, the prince?"

"Former prince," I answered, having heard the tale of how Aisling had managed to escape her unwanted membership in the prince of Abaddon club. "She was tricked into destroying one of you demon lords, after which Bael made her fill the position."

"She was expulsed, excommunicated," he answered, but his nostrils flared a couple of times, and he didn't make another move to touch me. "Stripped of all her powers."

"Just her prince of Abaddon ones. I know this because Aisling is a good friend of Gabriel," I added. "And me."

Magoth watched me closely for a moment, his gaze trying to strip away all my layers of protection to see deep into my thoughts, but if I had done nothing else during the six weeks since I'd gone dybbuk, I had learned how to hide my true thoughts.

Even so, he relaxed and gave me a genuine smile. "Your friend would find it difficult to send me to the Akasha. Such a feat could not be conducted without a great cost to herself, and I believe the dragon to whom she is bound would not allow such a sacrifice. No, my sweet May, I have no fear of your friends any more than I do of you."

"Me?" I gave a soft, bitter little laugh. "I pose no danger to you."

"Indeed you do not — if it was otherwise, you would not be standing here with your skin on," he said simply. I shuddered at the truth evident in his voice. "However, the delicious Sally has brought to mind something that I had forgotten — written in the Doctrine are many rules that govern us, one of which is simple, but very pertinent."

"What's that?" I asked warily.

"Oh, I know!" Sally said, raising her hand and waving it to get our attention. "I remember now what I was trying to think of a moment ago. It's in the section of the Doctrine dealing with consorts. It says that just as a consort has access to the world of the demon lord, so the lord has access to the consort's world. It's sort of a reciprocal effect."

A deep sense of horror gripped me. For nearly the past hundred years Magoth had lacked both the power and the resources to step foot in the mortal world, something for which I was profoundly grateful. If I had even for a moment considered becoming his consort, the fact that doing so would leave the world open to him was enough to kill that thought entirely.

"Exactly," Magoth said. Some of the horror I felt must have slipped through the normally tight rein I held on my emotions, because he slid his arm around me and attempted to pull me against him. "Don't look so distraught, sweet May! We'll have fun together in the mortal world! Mayhem, destruction, perhaps some good old-fashioned pillaging and rapine — it'll be just like the old days, back when I could come and go in the mortal world at will."

"I can't begin to name the deities to which I offer my soul-deep gratitude for the fact that you haven't been able to do that for almost a century," I answered, rubbing the goose bumps on my arms as I stepped out of his chilly embrace.

"Come. We shall take care of this matter right now." Magoth grabbed my wrist and started to haul me out of the room. "We will formally announce to the other princes that you will be made my consort in . . . how long will it take you to prepare for the ceremony?"

"A millennium?" I asked, feeling a familiar tingle start at my toes and work upward. "I think I'm being summoned again, just so you know."

He let go of my hand, surprising me with an expression of pleasure. "It must be your dragon again. Excellent. You have my permission to tell him of the impending consorthood. In fact, tell him he's invited to the ceremony. All the dragons are! You may have five minutes to explain everything, after which I will expect you to return to me. I will begin the proceedings while you are doing that."

His image shimmered for a moment, then was gone, no doubt on his way to the room he called his library, although it resembled a porn museum more than any collection of literature.

"Gee, thanks," I told Sally.

"Oh, I'm sorry, sugar; did I overstep my bounds?" she asked, sincerity filling her face, but I wasn't fooled one bit.

"You'll make a grade-A demon lord, you know."

She flashed a smile at me. "Why, thank you, May! That's very sweet of you to say . . ."

Sally faded as I was yanked out of Magoth's domain and back into the real world.

"Aw, her face isn't green anymore. And I got the digital camera out and everything! I was going to send Cecile a piccy to show

33

her what doppelgangers were looking like these days," a voice complained as I shook away the dizziness that came with such transitions.

"Cecile?" I asked somewhat woozily as my vision returned.

Everyone stood in the same positions as the last time I had seen them, Aisling leaning on Drake, Jim sitting at her feet (with a digital camera), Nora the Guardian, and behind me . . .

"Magoth has given me five minutes, which I think should just about be enough time to kiss the living fire right out of you," I told Gabriel.

His dimples flashed as he held his arms open. I didn't hesitate, just threw myself on him, my soul singing as his warmth and scent and presence sank into me. "It'll take a lifetime for that to happen, little bird. But before you have your wanton way with me, there is something I must first tell you."

"Perhaps we should give them a little privacy," Nora murmured behind me.

"We'll be in the sitting room if you need us," Aisling said.

"I want to stay. Look, Gabriel's got his hands on her butt, and it looks like May is going to — ow! I'm calling the demon-abuse hotline!"

Jim's voice faded as Aisling hauled the demon out with her.

Gabriel's bright eyes flickered away from me for a moment. "This won't take long," he told Drake, who had paused after ushering Aisling and her demon out.

One of Drake's eyebrows quirked upward, but he said nothing, just bowed to me and left the room, closing the door quietly behind him.

"Much as I would love to argue with you that it will, in fact, take a long, long time, I suspect you aren't talking about lovemaking. Not to mention the fact that Magoth would end up summoning me back before we could do much of anything." I slid my hands over the soft black linen shirt Gabriel wore. Although most dragons wore clothing that reflected the color of their septs, Gabriel dressed just as often in black as he did in silver and gray, something I took as a nod to the origins of the silver dragon sept.

A speculative glint lightened Gabriel's eyes. He cast a quick glance to the side, where a long chaise held sway in the corner of the room, but sanity quickly returned to him. His chest rose beneath my hands as he gave a heavy sigh. "I'm quick, but not that quick. A mutual seduction will have to wait until we have more time, Mayling."

"Agreed, although you know how fast you can make me . . . No, you're right, we'll wait. It'll be better if we aren't rushed. What was that little look to Drake all about? And how did you get Nora to summon me? I'm not a demon."

"No, but you are a minion, and as such can be summoned just as easily as a demon. Mayling, I have missed you."

His lips were warm against mine as he spoke. My entire body answered the unspoken desire in his eyes. "I can't begin to tell you how much I've missed you, although I don't have time to. Magoth will be sure to recall me in" — I consulted my watch — "four and a half minutes. Oh, to hell with it. It's been a long, long six weeks . . ."

His fingers dug into my hips as he hoisted me up so he could kiss me without bending down. I wrapped my legs around him, twining my tongue around his as he swept into my mouth.

"Fire, please," I whispered, giving his lower lip a quick nip to remind him just how much I loved the feeling of sharing his dragon fire.

"Such a demanding little bird," he chuckled, then groaned when I swept my hands under his shirt, around his ribs, stroking the lovely long lines of muscle in his back. He gave me what I wanted, his fire spilling from him to me as he kissed me with a yearning that echoed deep within me.

I gave in to the passion that swept me up in its fiery grip, emotion that was joined by joy, sorrow, and the fear that despite the fact that we were fated to be together, there might not be a way to overcome that which separated us.

"I told you when you left me that I do not give up what is mine, and you, my raven-haired mate, are most definitely mine." Gabriel's words were as soft as the whisper of his beard against my jaw as he kissed a burning line over to my ear.

"I didn't leave you," I pointed out, moaning just a little when he hit a spot that made me shiver in his arms. I turned my attention to nibbling his neck, pushing aside the soft dreadlocks to suck his earlobe, something I knew drove him wild. "I sacrificed myself for your happiness."

Gabriel stopped kissing the shivery spot and pulled back just enough to give me a chastising look.

"Oh, all right," I told the look, kissing the one eyebrow that had risen in question. "I didn't sacrifice myself per se, I simply did what I had to do in order to buy us a little time. I take it that since you had Aisling's friend summon me, it means that you found a way to get me out of Abaddon?"

"In a manner of speaking." He kissed me again, then reluctantly let me slide down his body until I was on my feet again. "I've had everyone working on the situation with you and Magoth. Through Aisling's auspices, I've consulted the Guardians' Guild, a number of oracles, and even a seer. All of them told me the same thing — there is no way to force a demon lord into giving up a minion bound to him."

I said nothing but watched him closely, sure that he wouldn't let the matter end there.

His dimples emerged. "So then I went back to Aisling and asked her what she would do if she was in my position."

A little pang of jealousy gave me a moment of irritation. Before I had met Gabriel, he had been what I assume was moderately smitten with Aisling, evidently considering stealing her from Drake. That he gave up the idea when he found out Aisling was pregnant said much, but I wouldn't be female if it didn't annoy me just a smidgen that he turned to her for help.

"Jealousy becomes you," he said, his dimples flashing even deeper.

"I sure wish I knew why you can read my

mind at times, and I can't read yours at all," I answered, giving him a hearty pinch on his attractive behind. "I'm not jealous. I'm just . . . Oh, move on. We don't have time for me to explain my emotions."

"I look forward to the time when you can explain," he answered with a wicked glint in his quicksilver eyes. The amusement in them faded as he continued. "Aisling thought about the situation for several weeks but in the end had only one suggestion: that you barter for your freedom."

"Barter? Barter what? Not the phylactery, I hope."

"No, not that," he said, the lines of his face deepening. "I would not part with that, not after what it cost you."

"Good, because I didn't give it to you lightly. I knew you would keep it safe, keep it from Kostya or Magoth or anyone else misusing its power. Er . . . where is it?"

"Safe," he answered.

I searched his face but was satisfied with the honesty I found there. Gabriel knew what it had cost me to go dybbuk by giving him the phylactery — he wouldn't give it up to anyone. "Do you have something I can barter with, then? Because I'm at a loss as to what you think I have," I said, casting my mind over my meager possessions. "If I had anything valuable, Magoth would have long ago demanded I hand it over."

He shook his head. "I have many treasures that the demon lord would no doubt covet, but I do not give up anything I hold." His thumb swept across my lower lip. I bit it. "That includes you, little bird."

"Then, what am I supposed to barter with?"

"You."

"Me?" A horrible thought came to mind, one that I instantly dismissed as being too ludicrous for words.

Gabriel looked offended. "Do you seriously believe I would allow you to sell your body —"

"Of course I don't! And stop being indignant over the idea. If you hadn't read my mind, you wouldn't know that the thought had even occurred to me. It's just . . . what exactly about me do you think will sway Magoth?"

"Your origins, Mayling. You're a doppelganger, yes, but you live in the mortal world. Aisling tells me that of all the princes of Abaddon, only one has the ability to frequent this world, something that irritates the other lords."

Enlightenment dawned on me at that moment. "*Agathos daimon* — you want to

40

release Magoth on the mortal world? Gabriel, I can't begin to tell you what a very, very bad idea that is. There's no one who wants to be out of Abaddon more than me, but not at the cost of endangering mortals."

"But they would not be endangered, not if Magoth is granted access via you. Aisling has a copy of a book that sets down the rules of Abaddon."

"The Doctrine of Unending Conscious, yes," I said, nodding. "I'm familiar with it. You're talking about the part that says if I agree to become Magoth's consort, he will have access to my world of origin, but I say again: that's not a good idea."

"You are not as familiar with it as you might be," he said, his hands warm on my waist as he gently pulled me up against his chest, his breath brushing my face. "The book also says that when a demon lord accesses the world in such a manner, it is in a diminished capacity."

"Diminished?" I bit my lip and thought about that for a moment. It made sense — a demon lord's abilities came from the dark power that had its source in Abaddon, which was why so few of them ever established a presence in the mortal world. Only the very strongest of all the demon lords, the head prince of Abaddon himself, was known to possess enough power to walk among mortals and immortals alike. The others had appeared briefly now and again, but only Bael could maintain a presence here.

"Aisling and her mentor, Nora, researched the matter most thoroughly, I can assure you, and they both agree that Magoth would enter the mortal world with little power, nothing that can't be controlled by keeping him under surveillance. And I have arranged to do just that."

"But what if that's wrong? What if he comes through with more power than anyone expects?"

"How could he do so?" Gabriel asked.

I wrapped my arms around him and leaned against him, my mind working over what he asked. "I don't know. I guess he couldn't. I don't have any power he can share — his origins are dark, so he can't go into the shadow world like we can. I guess I just hate to give him what he wants."

"I understand, little bird, and I wish the situation was different. But I cannot think of another way to free you from his control other than to give him something he wants more than you."

What he said made sense — it made absolute sense — but still, it irked me.

"All right, then," I said with dull acceptance. "Since it doesn't bother you to have your mate made the consort of a demon lord, I'll give Magoth what he wants."

Gabriel moved faster than I could see. He spun me around so that I was pressed up against the window, the glass icy cold against my back as he burned my front with eyes that spat silver fire. "Do not ever say that it doesn't bother me, May. You are mine, my mate, the only woman who will ever be such, and I do *not* share what is mine. But just as you sacrificed yourself at the time for the better good, so I will ignore the pain that is caused by knowing my mate is technically the consort of a demon lord."

"I'm sorry," I said softly, unable to keep from stroking the hard line of his jaw.

He continued to pin me back with a heated look that left me in no confusion about his emotions, then turned his head slightly and kissed my palm, tracing out on it a smaller symbol of a hand bearing a crescent moon. It was the symbol of the silver dragons and was identical to the small brand I wore on my upper back. "We have been too long apart. It is not your fault that you have not yet accepted that you are everything to me."

"Oh, gods, how I missed you," I said, kissing him with all the passion I had.

"There is nothing —"

The world spun drunkenly, yanking me from Gabriel's arms before he could finish his sentence, sending me plummeting with a gut-wrenching feeling into an abyss of darkness.

CHAPTER THREE

"This is the most exciting thing that has ever happened to me! Will I be asked to speak, do you think? You know, something like toasting the bride and groom?" Sally asked as she posed in front of a full-length mirror, tugging at the neckline of a Pepto-Bismol pink dress. "Oh, I'm sorry; I'm hogging the mirror. I'm sure you want to check yourself."

"That's not necessary," I said absently, turning in my hands a scanty bit of lamé and leather that Magoth had produced as proper consort wear. "He has to be kidding. This isn't enough to cover a hamster, let alone a woman."

"Well, you are positively tiny," Sally said, turning around so she could examine her backside in the mirror. "Do you think the bow at the derriere is too much? I think it adds a sort of jaunty touch, but if you think it's out of line with the gravity of the moment, I can snip it off."

I shook out the consort garment in hopes it would magically enlarge, sighing when it remained a pathetic little contraption made up of leather straps and what I assumed were strategically placed bits of cloth. "I don't think it's really going to matter. Thank god I didn't tell Gabriel that Magoth wanted him for the consort ceremony. I'd really rather he not see me in this. Magoth went way over the line this time."

"Oh, I'm sure it's not that bad," Sally called after me as I escaped to the privacy of the bathroom to don the skimpy outfit. "I've found that he has exceptionally good taste. He absolutely loves this dress!"

It took me a minute to struggle into the skintight leather-strap outfit that Magoth had created for me, and then another couple of minutes to steel my nerve to step out of the bathroom. I knew without even seeing my reflection that I looked like a cross between a bondage princess and a stripper, buckled leather straps the only things covering my naked torso. The straps continued down my legs, ending in a pair of stilettos that would quite possibly leave me lame. There was a bit of cloth at the crotch, but other than that, it was all leather straps. "I think this little item puts the question of

Magoth's supposed good taste to an end."

"I wonder if I should change into a strapless bra for this dress," Sally murmured, fluffing her cleavage and leaning down to examine the results in the mirror. "Sorry? Did you say someth . . . Oh, my."

"Don't say it," I told her, only *just* keeping from looking down at myself to make sure one of my breasts hadn't popped out of its restrictive strap.

"You . . . That's very . . . Oh, my."

"Uh-huh." I picked up a spiked dog collar and pursed my lips at it for a moment as I contemplated canceling the whole thing, but the image of a silver-eyed dragon rose in my mind. I strapped the dog collar onto my neck and nodded to Sally. "All right, demon of honor, let's get this done."

"Don't you want to . . . er . . . check your outfit?" she asked, waving a hand toward the mirror. The look on her face was a nearly indescribable mixture of horror and amusement.

"I wouldn't if I could," I said, giving the mirror a quick frown. "Magoth really is perverse."

She eyed me as I slipped my familiar dagger into the sheath at my ankle. "It's hard to deny a statement like that when faced with your ensemble, but perhaps he didn't know what it would look like on you?"

I opened the door, adjusted the large leather strap that ran across my breasts so it hid my nipples, tugged down the minuscule bit of cloth on my rump, and prayed the upcoming ceremony was going to be brief. "That isn't actually what I was referring to, although it certainly applies. I was talking about the mirror."

"The mirror? You're still going on about that? And you know, I'm not really a demon, so the term 'demon of honor' isn't technically correct. I think I'd prefer the term 'counsel,' since I'm here to give you the benefit of my experiences with both the Carrie Fay world and Abaddon."

It was on the tip of my tongue to ask her what was the difference, but I managed to stifle that urge. "Magoth had that huge mirror put in my room simply out of perverse pleasure. He insists on pretending he can't remember that I don't have a reflection even though we both know better."

We emerged into a vast open hall, high Gothic arches soaring over our heads. The air was cold, just as it was in all of Magoth's domain, my room excepted. I rubbed the goose bumps on my bare arms, wishing for a space heater or thick down comforter.

"Which room did he say the ceremony was being held in?"

Sally gave me a look that spoke volumes. "I've never been one to offer unsolicited advice, but I feel compelled by the bonds of our friendship, and the fact that I will soon be a colleague of your master, to break that rule just this once. You are about to become Magoth's consort, recognized by all members of Abaddon as such, and bestowed with powers and responsibilities appropriate to such a lofty position. Given all that, you really should make more of an effort to listen to him when he speaks."

"I tried that once. It gave me a migraine." I narrowed my eyes as I thought. "Library?"

"Oratory," she said with a shake of her head.

"Figures. He loves that room. He used to act out all of his old movies in there because the acoustics are so good. I have no doubt he'll ham it up this time, as well."

Sally didn't say anything to my flip comment, but censure was heavy in the air.

Like the rest of Magoth's domain in Abaddon, the oratory — which reflected more the original interpretation of the word (a place where one speaks) as opposed to the religious interpretation — was built with chilly walls of black basalt, and floors of even colder marble. I hadn't been to any other parts of Abaddon, but I assumed the cold was just one of Magoth's personal quirks and not a reflection of the general temperature of the place many mortals thought of as Hell.

Taking a deep breath before the double doors that led to the oratory, I lifted my head and threw open the doors, hoping against hope that none of the other demon lords had decided to come to the ceremony.

The room was packed, standing room only.

"Agathos daimon," I murmured under my breath at the mass of bodies filling the room.

"My Latin is a bit rusty, but doesn't that mean 'good spirit'?" Sally asked, peering over my shoulder at the crowd. "Oh! How lucky! It looks like everyone has shown up."

" 'Lucky' isn't quite the word I was going to — oh, gods."

Despite my hope that the ceremony was going to be as unobtrusive as possible, the sight of the room full of people didn't depress me. After all, I reasoned, what did it matter if all the demon lords and their minions watched while — clad in a scanty outfit straight out of Magoth's twisted sexual dreams — I formally agreed to be his consort? Once the ceremony was over,

I'd return to the mortal world, give Magoth a lecture about behaving himself, and send him on his way before flinging myself into Gabriel's arms.

That was the first thought that ran through my sorely abused brain when I saw the crowd. But then I got a better look at who stood on the far side of the room, and I stopped dead in my tracks, wanting to turn around and run back to my room. "That bastard."

"Pardon?"

"Magoth. He invited the dragons."

She pursed her lips as she gave me a critical once-over. "Didn't he say he wanted your dragon here?"

"Yes, but he was so damned happy about the prospect of getting access to the mortal world, he agreed to not invite the dragons for the ceremony. And just look — he not only brought in Gabriel and his two bodyguards; Drake is there with his men, and those guys in blue have to be the blue dragons. That bastard lied to me!"

"Well, he *is* a demon lord. Oh, one moment — let me just spritz you with a little bit of this delicious mist. We call it Sunset Afterglow, and it has the most wonderful iridescent sparkly things in it. You'll love it. There! You're perfect! Or as perfect as we can make you."

Sally stood aside with a pleased smile. I batted away the iridescent cloud and took a deep breath. No one had noticed us at the door of the oratory, the room being filled to capacity with demon lords, demons, and other minions of Abaddon. Across from them, the dragons stood together, warily watching the rest of the audience. My happiness upon seeing Gabriel dissolved into a horrified feeling of embarrassment and shame. "Magoth really is grinding my face in it," I muttered. "It's not enough I agreed to be his consort so he can finally access the mortal world; oh, no, he has to bring in every dragon he could find to witness this horrible event."

"Carrie Fay always says that nothing is really horrible unless it eats away your face," Sally said with sublime disregard.

That pulled me up short.

"You have to admit, she has a point," Sally said in answer to my look of disbelief.

"Right. This promises to be one of the most humiliating moments in my life, but the reward at the end of it is worth it a thousand times over, so let's just get this done, shall we?"

"When I was a corporate motivational speaker, I used to tell my clients that attitude is everything," Sally advised as I pushed past her into the crowd of low-level demons. "If you believe you're going to have fun, you will have fun! Unless, of course, Magoth requires you to undergo the ritual of burning flesh as part of the ceremony, in which case you'll probably just writhe on the ground in the most intense agony you could ever imagine, but at least you'd be providing entertainment to others, so even *that* isn't all bad."

The demons, most of which were in human form, refused to allow me through their throng until I elbowed them, poked them, or in a few cases, whapped them upside the head with my spiked necklace wrapped around my hand. Almost all of them were bigger than me, which made for slow going until I had the bright idea of shoving the larger Sally in front of me and letting her do the hard work.

"My hair!" she squawked when I shoved her at a clump of level-five demons in dirty black leather jackets with "Satins Minyuns" scrawled in blood across their respective backs. "My dress!"

"Just pretend they're a bunch of Microsoft yuppies, and give them your standard motivational speech. That ought to make them cringe and cower."

The look she shot me confirmed my suspicion that she would fit right in with this place, but I didn't have long to dwell on her rightness with things demonic before she managed to beat her way through the demons to the raised stone dais where Magoth stood chatting with a smallish, ordinary-looking man. Gabriel, Drake, and the rest of the dragons stood just beyond them. I tried to keep my gaze averted from Gabriel's, rather hoping to miss his expression upon first seeing me in my nearly non-existent ensemble, but it was asking too much of my aching heart.

I caught the first expression of joy in his silver eyes before a form of indignation flashed in their depths as I cleared the crowd and moved toward Magoth. That was soon followed by sheer rage, but luckily, that faded and was replaced by a slight deepening of the indentations on his cheeks that marked his dimples.

I relaxed a smidgen, relieved that I wasn't going to have to intervene in a battle between Gabriel and Magoth, and gave the former a small smile to let him know I appreciated him seeing the humor of the situation.

"There she is!" Magoth said, springing at me. "How delightful you look almost wearing that outfit. My lord Bael, I should like to present for your approval my consort, the sweet and deliciously nubile May, a doppelganger who has been bound to me since the moment of her creation, and one who, I am delighted to say, has served my many and varied personal needs to my utmost satisfaction."

I thought about telling Magoth to knock it off, that Gabriel was going to see through such obvious tactics, but the presence of the premier prince of Abaddon kept my tongue behind my teeth. Bael gave me a thorough once-over as I made a little bow, but unlike Magoth's, his visual examination was not the least bit sexual. Power sparked off him in a palpable corona, leaving me with a sick feeling in my stomach as he seemed to strip away my facade and look deep into my soul. It was a nerve-shattering experience, but I drew comfort from the fact that Gabriel was there, and managed to keep from cowering before Bael.

He dismissed me with a gesture that indicated he was less than impressed. "Let the ceremony proceed. I have more important things to do than watch you preen."

Magoth didn't like that, but as the lowest of all the demon lords, he knew better than to lip off. He simply nodded and held his hand out for me, his eyes on Gabriel as he paraded me around the perimeter of the dais. "Fellow demon lords, members of my legions, and minions of all sorts, today at long last I take a consort. Behold the sweet and succulent May Northcott, servant and doppelganger, whom I bestow with not only the pleasures to be found in my body, but all rights and honors due me. *Venisti remanebis donec denuo compeltus sis, decus et tutamen, dulce et utile.*"

I kept my lips from curling in a grimace at his words. The Latin Magoth spoke was a phrase I'd seen in the Doctrine of Unending Conscious and was loosely translated as "From whence you came, you shall remain, until you are complete again, an ornament and a safeguard, a sweet and useful thing." It was Magoth's way of granting me the position of his consort, while reminding me that such a position was pretty much in name only. All the rights and honors he'd spoken of came to about nothing, which was fine with me. The less I had to do with the workings of Abaddon, the happier I'd be.

Magoth stopped in front of Bael and waited for my response. I knew what I was supposed to say — the standard form of the consort's agreement was also in Latin, society in Abaddon preferring to cling to the old ways — but I couldn't bring myself to speak the words that would praise Magoth above all others.

"Duae tabulae rasae in quibus nihil scriptum est," I improvised.

Magoth's jaw dropped just a smidgen.

"I saw that at the studio back when you were making movies," I whispered, my gaze flickering over to Gabriel.

His dimples flared briefly to life, telling me he spoke Latin. "Two minds, not one single thought" had been used in a Stan Laurel movie, the set of which I'd visited many decades before. As an acknowledgment of my newfound status, it was less than polite, but it suited the situation.

"Hic et nunc," Bael said, putting his official seal of approval on the ceremony. "I will leave you to enjoy your new consort."

Magoth bowed low to Bael as he shimmered in the air, then disappeared, turning back to me with a wicked glint in his eyes.

"Thank god that's over," I said, yanking my hand from his, fully intending to run to Gabriel.

"I agree — it was a tedious ceremony, but alas, one has to observe the formalities. Still, it was worth it to have access to your precious mortal world. I assume you are desirous of leaving? Excellent. As am I."

Before I could take two steps from him, Magoth grabbed my wrist, rent the fabric of space, and jerked me through after him as he plunged into the mortal world for the first time in almost ninety years.

"Don't! Wait! Gabrieeeee—" The words spiraled into a scream as I was hauled after him, my last view that of Gabriel leaping toward me.

I hit the pavement hard enough to stun me for a few seconds. My hands and knees stung as I pushed myself off the ground, shaking my head to clear it before glaring at Magoth. "A little warning would have been nice. What on earth are you doing?"

Magoth stood with his hands on his hips, his head tipped back, his eyes closed as he sucked in deep breaths. "Can't you smell it?"

I eyed the nearby trash can as I got to my feet. We were in some sort of an alley, assumedly in Paris if the garbage that littered the ground was anything to go by. "I'd have to be dead to not smell it. The garbage collectors are probably on strike again."

"No, foolish consort. The humanity. Can't you smell the humanity? All that delicious fear and anger and hatred floating in delightful layers upon the air — oh, it takes me back; it truly does. How I have missed the mortal world. Well! There's no time to waste in conversation with you. I have deeds to accomplish and tasks to undertake. I bid you adieu, sweet May."

Magoth turned and started down the alley toward a busy street.

"That's it? You're leaving? No thank-you for agreeing to be your consort? No explanation of where you're going?"

"Miss me already, darling?" He heaved a faux sigh. "Much as I would like to introduce you to the pleasures that only I can give you, unfortunately that must wait until I have taken care of more pressing business."

I limped over to him, angry, but aware that I couldn't let that get the better of me. Magoth in the mortal world might effectively have little power, but there was no guarantee that I wouldn't end up back in Abaddon with him before such time as Gabriel and I managed to break my bond to him. I picked my words carefully. "You know full well I am not interested in the least in a carnal relationship with you. But you have been away from the mortal world for almost a century, and I thought you might want to consult me now and again if you find something that confuses you."

The look he gave me would have been

comical if it had its origins in anyone but Magoth. "Sweet May, you are not in the least subtle. I would suggest that you cease trying to be, and simply say what it is you wish to say." He held up a hand as I was about to protest. "Do not insult either of us by pretending you do not wish to keep tabs on me."

My lips tightened in a thin line for a moment before I answered, "Fine. But you can't be surprised that I'm worried about you running around the mortal world."

He shrugged and flicked a minute bit of lint off his arm. "Your dragon no doubt informed you that accessing this world via you strips me of most of my power. You may tell him from me that he is correct . . . and that despite the situation, I will have no difficulty in escaping any surveillance he attempts to use upon me."

"You can try," was all I said as I followed him out to the street. He stood looking up and down the road, rubbing his hands with pleasure, his black eyes positively dancing with happiness.

"Magoth —" I said, but before I could complete the warning I intended on giving, I realized just where it was we were. I spun around to gaze in growing horror at the large cream-stone building behind us. "Dear gods — that's Suffrage House."

"Yes," he said absently, whipping out a pair of designer sunglasses and positioning them carefully on his face. "I thought it too much of an irony to miss that my first steps into this world should be undertaken from the headquarters of the Otherworld. You do not approve?" He shrugged again. "Adieu, my adorable one. I have no doubt we shall meet again, but until then, think of me often."

A taxi pulled up as Magoth was speaking, depositing a man on the sidewalk. I didn't pay him much attention as he paid the driver, but just as I was going to unburden myself to Magoth of a few choice thoughts, the man glanced our way, did a double take, and froze for a few seconds on the steps leading up to the building.

I may not win a Nobel Prize for overall intelligence, but I did have a few wits about me. Although my first instinct was to assume the man was simply reacting to my unusual outfit, it didn't take me a second to realize his interest was focused on *me* rather than the few shreds of clothing strapped to my body. I turned to bolt, but Magoth was in my way, causing me to lose a few precious seconds.

"Change your mind about the threesome?" he asked as I slammed into him.

"Mei Ling!"

I ducked under the arm Magoth was reaching toward me, hoping I could get far enough away from the man to slip into the shadow world, but my hope was in vain. Before Magoth had the chance to utter an indignant squawk at the elbow I shoved in his belly in order to get him to move aside, the man leaped on me, throwing me to the ground.

"Mei Ling! You dare show your face here? Dr. Kostich will be very happy to see you. Guards! Guards! I have the thief Mei Ling! I have captured the thief!" the man bellowed as he hauled me to my feet, one arm twisted behind me, the other wrapped around my neck.

CHAPTER FOUR

"You could help me," I snarled to Magoth as my captor, most likely a thief taker, dragged me toward the front doors of the building.

Magoth raised one ebony eyebrow in a perfect gesture of disbelief. "And ruin the fun you'll have escaping this latest predicament? I wouldn't think of depriving you of that enjoyment, sweet May."

I grabbed the hand that had a death grip on my throat, and threw myself to the side, trying to pull the man off balance, but he must have had martial arts training, for he stayed solidly on his own feet as he dragged me step by painful step closer to the entrance of Suffrage House. "I'm going to remember this, Magoth."

"The memory of our parting will stay forever green in my mind, as well," he said, deliberately misinterpreting me. "You may wish to watch out," he added to my attacker.

"She bites."

I was just in the process of twisting my head to try and get a grip on the man's arm, but paused to glare at Magoth, who simply blew me a kiss and sauntered off down the sidewalk.

"You're only making things harder on yourself," the man grunted as he heaved me up two steps. I bucked as best I could, and tried to twist away from him. I even shadowed for a second, hoping that my apparent disappearance would throw him off guard, but he must have been alerted to the fact that I was a doppelganger. "If you keep this up, we will be forced to subdue you to unconsciousness," he warned.

"Been there, done that, got the T-shirt," I growled as I suddenly switched tactics and spun around in his hold, simultaneously bringing my knee up into his groin and smashing my fist into his nose.

He gurgled in pain and reacted with an instinct of self-preservation, clutching both his crotch and his face, leaving me free for a fraction of a second.

I flung myself to the side, racing down three steps, and had just hurdled a low cement barrier wall when something slammed into my back and sent me crashing to the ground a second time.

"This is really getting old," I muttered to myself as my new unknown assailant jerked both arms behind my back.

"I've got her," a woman's voice bellowed behind my head. I struggled to get up, but this woman, like the thief taker, knew how to keep me from getting any leverage. "Run inside and fetch the watch."

The all-too-cheerful voice left me in no doubt as to its owner.

"Sally!" I hissed with outrage, struggling to get free from her. "What do you think you're doing?"

"Shush! Rescuing you. Play along."

"She's mine!" the thief taker yelled, but there was a thread of pain in his voice that indicated he was still feeling the effects of my escape.

"I'm not trying to take credit for your capture," Sally said with obvious amusement. "I just happened to see her kick you in your happy place. Go get the watch, why don't you? I can tell by this truly horrible outfit that she's wearing that she'll be too much to handle without lots and lots of help."

I turned my head to the side, peering as best I could up the stairs. The thief taker stood in the throes of indecision, clearly wanting to be the one to drag me in and at the same time injured enough that Sally made sense.

"Hurry!" Sally urged, releasing my hands just enough that I was able to almost rise. "She'll get away!"

The thief taker didn't wait; he just whirled around and ran up the stairs. Before the door closed all the way on him, I was jerked to my feet, a not-so-gentle shove between my shoulder blades sending me reeling down the stairs.

"You'd better scoot, sugar. It probably won't take him long to rouse help."

I glanced over my shoulder at the woman behind me, confused by both her actions and the friendly smile on her face. "Why are you helping me?"

"Silly! You're Magoth's consort!"

I hesitated, not buying her sudden turn of heart.

She shoved me again, and this time I moved. She followed on my heels, saying, "Plus, they're the good guys, and I can't stand to see them win."

That, at least, made sense. I dashed down the sidewalk, spinning around the corner to the alley in which Magoth had chosen to enter the mortal world.

Shouts behind us warned that the thief taker had returned to find me missing.

"Run! They're right behind us!" Sally said, following as I dodged garbage bins, emerging on the far side only to dash into another alley.

We raced away through the streets of Paris, using every skill I possessed to avoid leaving a trail that could be easily followed. We ran up fire escapes and through buildings, and took shortcuts through yards and tiny Parisian gardens, until it seemed like my legs were ground down to nothing and my lungs were about to burst.

"I think we've lost them," Sally said after what I could have sworn were eons of running. We collapsed against the entrance of a seedy building. "I just hope you're going to mention this on my evaluation sheet. It should get me beaucoup extra credit."

"Consider yourself credited," I answered, standing up straight in an attempt to ease a stitch in my side. "Where are you going now that Magoth is in this world?"

She straightened up as well, tidying herself via a reflection in a dirty window. "I have another two weeks with you all, so I'll just run him to earth. See you later, sugar."

"But —"

Sally was off before I had a chance to question her more. I watched for a moment as she quickly blended into the lengthening afternoon shadows before I did the same into the slightly different version of reality that was known as the shadow world. I knew of only one safe house in Paris, and it was there that I headed.

"Hello. I'm May Northcott. Is Gabriel here, by any chance?" I asked some forty minutes later as the door before me opened.

The woman who answered the door blinked green eyes a couple of times, then smiled and stepped back, gesturing me into the house. "Welcome back, May. Drake and Gabriel just returned. You'll find them —"

A door leading into the hall burst open. I didn't stop to thank Suzanne, the green dragon who had let me into Drake's Paris house. I just ran for the man who emerged, flinging myself on him with a shameless whimper of joy. "Gabriel," I whispered into his mouth as I tried my best to kiss the breath right out of his lungs.

"Widdel werd," he answered, kissing me in return with such vigorousness that his words were incoherent. He wrapped both arms around me and hoisted me up so our mouths were at the same level. I dug my fingers through the soft, shoulder-length dreadlocks, tugging wordlessly on his hair until he gave me what I wanted. Dragon fire, as hot and potent as his mouth, swirled around us in a dance of light and shadow. The taste of him, the feel of him pressed hard against my body, and his heady scent sinking deep into my being triggered something deep within me that had been locked away the last six weeks.

"Mate," he groaned when the need for air forced our mouths apart.

"You don't know how I've needed that," I said, my tongue running around my mouth, savoring the taste of him. Gabriel always tasted like he had been eating something with cloves in it, partly spicy, partly sweet, and wholly addicting. "And I have so much to tell you. Sally, the candidate for demon lord, actually helped me earlier."

"Later," he said, his face twisting as if he was in pain.

"Are you all right?" I asked, stepping back to see if he had acquired any wounds while making his way out of Abaddon. "Did Magoth's demons do something to hurt you?"

"No. I need you, Mayling."

I smiled and brushed my lips against his. "I missed you, too. So much has happened since you had me summoned. This outfit for one, and that show Magoth insisted I put on. I want you to know that I had nothing to do —"

"You don't understand," he said, his voice,

normally as smooth as silk sliding over satin, tinged with a roughness that seemed to thrum in deep, hidden parts of me. "I *need* you, May. Now."

The look of pain on his face was growing, reminding me of a similar expression he'd worn a couple of months before. I couldn't help but smile as I rubbed my hips against his. "Oh. That kind of need."

He groaned again and allowed me to slide down his body. "You're tormenting me."

"Just a little. Not too much, because I'd be happy to participate in the activities I know you have in mind —"

That's all the agreement it took. Without another word, he scooped me up and started toward the stairs leading to the upper floors.

I glanced over his shoulder to see the tall figure of a dark-haired, green-eyed man. "Hello, Drake. How's Aisling doing?"

Drake made a smooth bow that was almost as good as the kind Gabriel made. "Good afternoon, May. Aisling is resting at the moment. I'll tell her you were asking after her."

"Thank you. I'm looking forward to talking with her again." I glanced at the hard lines of Gabriel's face. "Later."

"Much later." Drake's voice followed us as Gabriel turned left at the top of the stairs and strode toward a room we had occupied earlier. I could swear there was laughter in Drake's voice, but there was no sign of a smile before he disappeared from sight.

"Wait a moment," I said when Gabriel kicked the bedroom door closed behind us. I was still in his arms as he moved over next to the bed. "I know you wyverns have some need to be physically with your mates when they've been taken from you, and *you* know that I'm happy to indulge your need for incredibly steamy, unbridled lovemaking. But since we also both know that such an event makes me lose what few wits I have, maybe we could have a quick conversation to catch up before things get out of hand?"

Gabriel looked at me as if I had suddenly turned into a frog in his arms, his silver eyes so beautiful, I wanted to dive into their mercurial depths.

"It's just that we've been apart for so long. I have so much to tell you, so much I want to ask you. How have you been? Where have you been? How are Maata and Tipene, and all the other silver dragons? Things like that." I put my hand on his cheek. He closed his eyes and leaned into the caress. "I appreciate more than I can say how much you want to physically join, but Gabriel, I want so much more than to just make love to you.

I want to be with you. I want to know what you're thinking, what you've done while I was gone, and I want to tell you about the things that happened to me. Couldn't we have just a smidgen of conversation before things get too carried away?"

"No," Gabriel said simply, and dropped me onto the bed.

I looked up the long length of his body as he silently pulled off his clothing. Gabriel was tall, a foot and then some more than my five foot nothing, with long, muscled legs, a chest that had just enough hair on it to make it sexy without being hirsute, and shoulders broad enough to make me feel very feminine in comparison. I looked at all that and threw conversation to the wind. "OK," I said as I held my arms open.

To my utter surprise, he didn't immediately pounce on me.

"What's wrong?" I asked, confused.

He glanced down at my body lying supine before him.

"If it's about the outfit, that was Magoth's choice, not mine. I had nothing to do with it —"

"No," he interrupted, his gaze molten as it crawled its way up my mostly exposed skin. I did a rather clumsy shimmy to rid myself of the upper part of the outfit, tossing it to a nearby chair with a come-hither look that could probably have steamed a carpet. "It's not that, although I have to admit that Magoth's taste in clothing is . . ."

"Horrendous?" I said as Gabriel's sentence petered off. "Appallingly hideous? Utterly and completely inappropriate?"

"Exceptionally fine," Gabriel said, his fingers giving little spasmodic jerks as he stood naked — and aroused — next to the bed, watching me.

"We'll discuss that point later. What I'd like to know now is why you aren't, at this very moment, pleasuring me like I've never been pleasured before." A thought occurred to me as the memory of a similar experience came to mind. "You're not still worked up about the fact that we never seem to get time to indulge in foreplay, are you? Because I told you the last time this came up" — I eyed his penis, which bobbed merrily at me — "that it really isn't an issue."

A muscle in his jaw worked. "I talked to my mother about you. She agreed that this lack of self-control I exhibit around you is not fair to you."

I sat up, glaring at him. "You talked to your *mother* about our sex life?"

An odd sort of wary look crossed his face. "She sensed something profound had

73

changed my life. I told her about you. She was very pleased that you are my mate, and looks forward to meeting you. Do you have an issue with my mother? You would like her, Mayling. She is not at all like Drake's mother — she would never try to have you killed."

Startled, I got off the bed and marched around it to poke him on his chest. "That's not the point. What is the point is . . . Drake's mom tried to have Aisling killed?"

Gabriel's brows pulled together, his hands on his hips. "Little bird, now is not the time to discuss Aisling and Drake. You have been separated from me for six weeks. I must rejoin with you. It is the way of the dragons."

"I'm not the one who brought up the subject of his mother," I said, pointing at the bed. "I was laid out there like a stuffed turkey, but all you seem to want to do is talk."

We both looked down at his penis.

"It's not that easy," he answered seriously. "There is nothing more I wish to do at this moment than fulfill each and every one of those intriguing fantasies you have about me. The one involving taking you while on the back of a horse might be a little difficult, but with some practice, I think it would be possible."

"And that's another thing — why can you read my smutty thoughts about you, but I can't read your mind?"

"I told you before," he answered, taking the hand I was using to poke him repeatedly in the chest. His fingers stroked mine, lighting my fingernails on fire. "It is a trait I inherited from my mother. I do not know if you can do the same, although I suspect it's possible."

"Let's get back to that point — you asked your *mom* for sex advice?" I had a hard time getting past that point. I pulled my hand from his, spreading my fingers through the hair on his chest. "Gabriel, I know I'm inexperienced, but don't you think we could have discussed what it was that I'm not doing right before you had to consult your mother?"

"You are not doing anything wrong, Mayling. I am the problem, and it is that for which I sought advice from my mother. She is a shaman of much renown. Even if she was not the mate of a dragon, I would consult her, for she knows much of our ways."

"Well, I may not be the most knowledgeable of people when it concerns dragons, but I do know that from where I stand . . . sit . . . lie down . . . there's nothing you need to change. Except maybe this proclivity to stand around staring at me as if I'm a chunk of tenderloin and you're a hungry wolf. More action and less talk, wyvern," I said, kicking off of the loathsome bit of material that was all that remained of my ceremonial outfit. I slid my hands up Gabriel's sides and around to the lovely terrain of his back.

He stiffened, sucking in a good quarter of the air in the room. "My mother told me that I was being selfish in thinking only of my own needs, and that even the most accommodating of women need time and attention to achieve full satisfaction."

I bit his shoulder. "Have I looked unsatisfied with you? Other than this moment, that is?"

"No," he said slowly, his eyes molten with desire. I licked the spot I had bitten. "But you are petite in stature, and dragon matings are not always easy."

I decided that words just weren't going to do the job, leaving actions my only choice. I tipped my head and bit gently on the little brown nub of a nipple peeking through his soft chest hair.

"She also said . . ." Gabriel groaned deep in his chest as I swirled my tongue over his nipple. His hands were on my shoulders now, fingers digging into my flesh, his eyes screwed up tight as he made a face that expressed both rapture and exquisite pain. "She said that my inability to retain control around you could be dangerous and risky, that you see me as a man, and I must go carefully before you see my true depths. I am trying to do so, little bird, but I begin to think it is impossible. You are too much a part of me now."

I stopped tormenting his nipple and looked up, rocked to the bottom of my soul with what he had said.

"You're stopping?" he asked, opening his eyes in surprise.

I put both hands on his cheeks, searching his face for signs of anything that hinted of an untruth. There was nothing, much as I expected. Gabriel might be many things, but he had never lied to me. "Did you mean that?" I asked.

"Mean what?"

"That you can't control yourself around me because I'm so much a part of you? You meant that?"

He picked me up, carrying me over to the bed, spinning me around so I was astride his thighs as he sat. "I wish it was different. I wish I had the ability to retain my control when I'm with you, but I am obviously lacking in character."

"Oh, Gabriel," I said, my heart melting at the look shining from his eyes. "No one has ever said anything so beautiful to me."

"Beautiful?" His dimples flashed to life for a moment as he shook his head. "I have never met a woman like you, May."

"A doppelganger, you mean?" I asked, sliding my hands up his arms.

"No. A woman who finds my lack of self-control an attribute rather than a flaw."

"It means I really matter to you," I said, kissing the corners of his mouth. "So much so that you can't stop yourself from showing your inner dragon when we make love."

"You are my mate, my life. You are bound to me. You do more than matter, little bird — you are my reason for existence."

"That," I said, pushing him backwards onto the bed, "is not the least bit true, and we both know it. However, due to the fact that you are the sexiest dragon I've ever met, and I'm probably going to expire if you don't make love to me in the next ten seconds, I'm willing to let it go for now."

"My mother said," he started to say, but I kissed him to a stop.

"I love you," I said, the words tumbling out unexpectedly.

Gabriel's eyes opened wide. I froze for a second, unsure of what to do or say, but that dilemma ended quickly when he lifted me slightly and shifted me forward, impaling me with a swift upward thrust of his hips. "Foreplay later," he growled, the cords in his neck standing out as his eyes shut for a moment in ecstasy.

The intrusion into my body was fast and hard, but not unanticipated, making me moan with pleasure as he pierced parts that had been too long without him. I leaned forward to kiss him, his hands hard on my hips, urging me to a faster rhythm.

"I want all of you, Gabriel."

His eyes opened to flash with quicksilver brightness, his gaze hot enough to scorch. But his dragon fire came from his mouth as he pulled me down, taking my breast in his mouth, bathing it with fire that danced down my skin until it covered us both. I gasped as he pistoned upward even harder, deeper than he had been before, the sensation of his mouth on my other breast almost pushing me over the edge of sanity. I gripped him hard with my knees, watching with amazement as the taut, brown flesh between my thighs turned iridescent, forming into white scales that rippled upward into a beautiful silver that was almost as bright as Gabriel's eyes. The body beneath me and inside me thickened, lengthening and changing in ways that were both wholly foreign and yet somehow familiar. The hands that gripped my breasts changed as well, the long, brown fingers changing to silver, tipped with curved claws the color of blood.

Part of my brain shrieked to me that it was wrong, that the man I was riding was no man — he was a beast — but my heart knew the truth. The tension inside me built until I flung back my head, arching my back as I was locked in an orgasm, the muscles embracing Gabriel tightening with an ecstasy that was almost painful. Gabriel thrust upward at the same time he roared his pleasure, a primal, terrifying sound that echoed in the room and in my soul. There was a word in that roar, one word: my name. The fire leaped between us, back and forth until there was no ending and no beginning. It just was — and so were we. I knew with every atom of my being, every infinitesimal part that combined to make me, that Gabriel and I were one. Nothing could ever change that — no demon lord with delusions of grandeur, no authority in this world or any other, existed that could take me from him. Gabriel had somehow become an integral part of me, and that thought shook me to my core.

"Mayling!"

I slid off him, collapsing onto my stomach, the blanket beneath me cool on my fevered flesh.

"Little bird, did I hurt you?"

The hand that grasped my shoulder was human again, the fingers long and sensitive. I laid my cheek on the bed, clutching the blanket as my body shook with the aftereffects of both Gabriel's attentions and my own realization.

I was me, May, created wholly formed, and independent of all, even those to whom I was bound. Even when I had accepted my role as Gabriel's mate, when I had agreed that we were fated to be together, it never occurred to me that he would become necessary to the very act of living.

I had just survived a six-week separation from him. And yet I knew at that moment, knew without a shred of doubt, that quite simply I could not exist without him. It was a terrifying realization, one that left me feeling powerless and angry.

The hand on my shoulder slid away. "Did I frighten you?" Gabriel asked, his voice quieter, filled with emotion.

I turned my head to look at him. "Yes," I answered.

Pain was visible in his eyes. "I'm sorry. I

would not frighten you for the world, but I cannot control the shifting —"

"No," I interrupted, sitting up. "It wasn't that. You meant it, didn't you?"

He was silent for a moment, no doubt reading my thoughts. "Yes, I meant it. You are life to me, May."

"But you told me you were born in the seventeen hundreds. How could you live for three hundred years without me?"

He examined my face for a moment before leaning forward, his kiss so sweet it made me want to melt. "Before you, I merely existed. Now I will truly begin to live."

CHAPTER FIVE

"Weh-hell, look what the cat dragged in."

I entered the dining room, determined to keep my face placid despite the fact that everyone in the house had probably heard Gabriel and me the night before. "Good morning."

Jim, demon in Newfoundland dog form, looked up from where it lay on the floor with a copy of a Paris newspaper, cocking one furry eyebrow at me as it examined me from toes to nose. "Wow. I would have thought you'd at least be walking funny or something after all that boink—"

"Jim!" Aisling snapped, grabbing up a magazine and leaning over to whap the demon. She gasped instead, dropping the magazine and grabbing at her belly. Instantly, Drake, who was seated at the other end of the table, was at her side, kneeling next to her.

"*Kincsem,* are you all right?"

"I'm fine; it's just a muscle twinge."

Gabriel, who had been standing behind me, his hand warm on my back, moved around me to Aisling's other side. He put a hand on her belly. "What did it feel like? Have you had any other pain this morning?"

A completely irrational desire to yank him away from her washed over me, a desire I stomped upon as firmly as possible. I may still be struggling with the depth of feelings I felt for Gabriel, but I was not going to let jealousy get the better of me.

"Stop touching my mate!" Drake demanded, scowling at Gabriel's hand on Aisling's very pregnant stomach.

I wholly approved of Drake's demand.

"I am a healer," Gabriel answered, squatting next to Aisling. He pressed gently on different parts of her belly. "If she is in labor, I can help her with the pain."

I moved over to stand directly behind him, nudging him with my knee.

"Guys, I'm not in labor. I just moved too quickly, OK?" Aisling said.

"Take your hands off her," Drake said in a low voice that sounded very much like a growl.

Jim sucked in its breath, sitting up to watch.

"I'm not hurting her," Gabriel answered,

bending over her belly as he continued to gently prod her. "I'm simply trying to ascertain if she's in labor or not. Aisling, is the pain sharp or dull?"

The door opened, and Gabriel's two bodyguards, Tipene and Maata, entered. Behind them came one of Drake's men, a thick-necked, redheaded man named István. The latter picked up on Gabriel's question.

"Aisling is in pain? She is having the baby?"

"I should examine you more fully," Gabriel said, smiling at Aisling as he took her hand. "Do not worry, Aisling. I have delivered many dragons over the centuries. My mother is a very good midwife and has taught me well."

Drake snatched up her other hand. "You will not examine my mate any further! We have an excellent green-dragon midwife who is attending her. Now, get away from her before I have you removed!"

Aisling looked perfectly fine to me. She rolled her eyes, casting a pleading look skyward. I might not have experience in this area, but it was clear to me that she was not in labor. I shot a glare at Gabriel, grinding my teeth just a little at the stupidity of what was normally such a bright man, my fingers itching to pry his hand from Aisling's.

"I will tell you once more — remove your hands from her!" Drake's voice got even more menacing.

"Gabriel, I think she would know if she was in labor," I said, nudging the dragon of my dreams a bit more forcefully.

"A voice of reason at last," Aisling said, giving me a smile. "Guys, I'm not —"

István turned in the doorway and bellowed out of it. "Pál! Call the midwife! Aisling is in labor! I will call Nora and Rene. They wish to be here, yes? Should I boil water?"

He evidently asked the last bit of Maata, who, as the female member of Gabriel's attendants, was obviously expected to know the answer. Maata looked surprised. "Would it make you feel better to boil water?" she asked.

István nodded his head vigorously. "It is done, is it not? The boiling of water? It is important. I saw it in a movie."

"Then, by all means, boil water," she answered.

István nodded again, announced to the room in general, "I boil water!" and rushed out to suit action to word.

Pál, the second of Drake's two redheaded bodyguards, slammed into István as he was leaving, scattering apologies as he dashed

86

into the room, a cell phone in his hand. "The midwife's phone is busy!" he said, offering the phone to Drake as proof.

"Oh, man, if there's going to be baby juice and blood and guck, I'm getting out of here," Jim said, sidling around the clutch of people that surrounded Aisling. "I'm going to Amelie's to be with Cecile. Someone tell me when it's all over."

"Hello, can anyone hear me? I'm not in labor!" Aisling said.

"What should I do?" Pál asked Drake, shaking the phone at him. "It is busy! Busy! How can it be busy?"

A little wisp of smoke escaped Drake's nose as he glared at the phone. "It should not be busy. Go fetch her. There is no business she can have as important as this."

Pál didn't stop to answer; he just bolted from the room.

"Oh, for the love of Pete! I'm not in pain! And unless dragons have some sort of painless labor, a notion your mother vehemently says is false, then I'm not having the baby," Aisling said, but was drowned out by Maata asking if Gabriel needed help at the same time Tipene offered to take over midwife phone duty.

Gabriel stood, putting one arm behind Aisling, obviously about to lift her out of the chair.

"I will take you upstairs to your room and examine you. You could be further along than you think."

"Gabriel," Drake said in a low, mean voice, his eyes narrow slits of emerald. I had the feeling he was a cat about to pounce.

Aisling looked at me. "How do you feel about violence against your loved ones?"

I eyed a nearby silver coffee carafe. It looked heavy enough to dent even the densest of dragon skulls. "I'm starting to see the appeal of it."

"I completely under— oh!" Aisling hunched forward again as Gabriel slid his arm under her legs.

Drake exploded, slamming Gabriel up against the wall, snarling something that sounded vicious, his arm against Gabriel's windpipe.

Maata and Tipene were instantly at his side but at a gesture from Gabriel backed away.

"Drake, let him down. It's just a twinge, nothing more!" Aisling said, waving me toward them. "Stop him, May. Although don't hurt him; I'm rather fond of him as he is, overprotective tendencies and all."

I tapped Drake politely on the shoulder. "Would you mind letting Gabriel down? I promise I won't let him hold Aisling's hand anymore. Or touch her stomach."

Drake eyed Gabriel for a moment. I have to admit that Gabriel surprised me by not fighting back. Having seen him go at it with Drake's black-dragon brother, Kostya, I knew he was not one to remain passive when attacked. But he stayed still, not struggling at all despite the fact that his face was gaining a dull red tint due to lack of oxygen.

"All right," Drake said at last, removing his hold on Gabriel. "But I will hold you responsible for his actions."

Gabriel's eyes flashed in warning, but Aisling bursting into laughter defused the situation enough that he could see the ridiculousness of such a comment.

I touched a faintly swollen spot on Gabriel's neck. "Would you like me to kiss what hurts and make it better?" I asked softly.

He'd been looking at Aisling, obviously about to make some observation about her health, but at my words a new look of interest filled his eyes. "Only if I get to pick what needs kissing."

"I am so glad Jim is not present to hear that, because it would no doubt make all sorts of inappropriate comments that would force me to smack it with a rolled-up magazine, and then we'd be back to Gabriel groping my stomach and Drake having a hissy fit," Aisling said, helping herself to a glass of orange juice. "Please do have some breakfast, you two. Without any ribald intent to the following comment, you both look like you could use a little food. Did you tell May about the *sárkány* yet?"

"The what?" I asked, distracted when Gabriel, in the act of seating me next to Aisling, trailed his fingers across the back of my bare neck.

"*Sárkány.* It's Hungarian, isn't it, sweetie?" she asked Drake.

"*Sárkányok* is the term for Hungarian dragons. A *sárkány* is traditionally a dragon in the form of a multiheaded giant," he answered.

Gabriel took a seat across the table. "The term has been adopted to represent a weyr meeting called to discuss issues pertaining to a specific wyvern or sept."

"Ah. Something about the troublesome Kostya? Is he still petitioning to take over your sept?" I wouldn't have been surprised to hear that Kostya had continued his unauthorized war against the silver dragons. His sept had been wiped out by their own wyvern in a tragic attempt to bring the silver dragons — at one time black dragons, but

90

long since autonomous — back into the fold. "Don't tell me he's been trying to steal the phylactery again."

"No, the phylactery is safe," Drake answered. He frowned and looked over to Gabriel. "It *is* safe?"

"Very," Gabriel answered, his voice once again rich and velvety smooth.

Drake continued to study him. "You don't have it with you?"

"I don't believe I said that," Gabriel said, making a gesture of nonchalance as he buttered a piece of cold toast.

"Where is it?" Drake asked.

"It's safe. Does it matter where it is kept so long as Kostya will not find it?"

Drake's slight frown turned even blacker as he narrowed his eyes at Gabriel. "It matters because it is the Lindorm Phylactery. It is a priceless piece of the dragon heart. To treat it in a cavalier manner —"

"You do not need to lecture me as if I was a young dragon learning his history," Gabriel interrupted, a slight frown of his own pulling his brows together. "I may not have been wyvern as long as you have, but I am not untried, nor am I a fool. I would never treat the phylactery in any manner other than what is it due . . . unlike some dragons."

Drake rose slowly from his chair, a nasty light in his eyes. "Are you implying that I would —"

Aisling's voice cut through the suddenly tense atmosphere. "Don't make me fake a labor pain in order to get you two guys out of what is shaping up to be a really world-class pissing contest."

Drake shot her a glare. She blew him a kiss and motioned him back to his seat. I eyed Gabriel. A muscle that I was coming to view as a barometer of his feelings twitched in his jaw, but he made an effort to relax the grip he held on his knife, and managed to continue buttering his toast.

"I thought you two were friends," I said to him, nodding at Drake. "Don't you go back centuries?"

"Yes," Gabriel said, and applied himself to a thick slab of ham.

Drake said nothing, but sipped an espresso.

"Despite what you're seeing here, they actually are friends," Aisling told me. "It's just that things were a little dicey for a while when Gabriel . . . err . . ."

"When he tried to poison you?" I asked, having heard something of Gabriel's recent experiences with the Guardian.

"I didn't poison her. I saved her life," Gabriel said without meeting my eye. I had a horrible feeling he could sense the unreasonable swell of jealousy that seemed to burst into being whenever I thought about Aisling and him having some sort of relationship that went beyond what was appropriate.

Gabriel's eyes flashed silver at me for a moment before he returned his gaze to his plate, but I could see him fighting to keep his dimples from showing.

The rat.

"You saved her after you betrayed us," Drake said in a deceptively mild voice.

"What matters is that it's all over and done with, and everything is forgiven and forgotten," Aisling said in a loud voice, shooting a meaningful glance at her wyvern. "We're all friends here, no matter how prickly the boys may get now and again."

"Prickly!" Gabriel objected.

"Boys!" Drake added, an outraged look on his face.

Aisling giggled.

"Why did you betray them?" I asked Gabriel.

Silence, heavy and pregnant, fell upon the room. Gabriel studied me for a moment before answering. "Fiat Blu, the wyvern of the blue dragons, used Aisling to strike at

Drake. I tried to reason with him, but Fiat has always been . . ."

"Insane," Aisling offered.

"Unreasonable," Drake said.

". . . difficult," Gabriel finished. "He would not listen to my attempts to defuse the situation, leaving me in an awkward position. I did the best I could to rein him back from the destruction I knew he would inflict, but he was more unbalanced than I thought, and he succeeded in poisoning Aisling before I could stop him."

I sipped my coffee as I mulled over what he was saying. "What happened to the unbalanced Fiat? Didn't you tell me there were two blue wyverns?"

"There can only be one true wyvern at any time," he answered.

"You've been taking answer-avoidance lessons from Drake," Aisling told Gabriel. "I'll tell you what I know, May, although I have to pry every little bit of information from these guys."

"I've noticed that particular trait myself," I murmured.

Aisling gave her husband a long look that he ignored. "I gather that Fiat's uncle Bastian — who, I have to admit, kind of wigs me out because even though he's Fiat's uncle and a hundred years older, he looks the same age as Fiat. Anyway, Bastian was born to be wyvern, but Fiat somehow convinced everyone in his sept that Bastian was insane, and he took over as wyvern instead."

"Bastian tried to usurp Fiat several times, but failed," Gabriel said as he gutted an apple. "There. I have been forthcoming with information not asked of me. Now will you stop shooting annoyed glances at me, little bird?"

I smiled. I couldn't help myself; he was just so completely charming when he dimpled at me.

"A couple of months ago my uncle, my friend Rene, Jim, and I went to free Bastian, and he immediately took over control of the sept as the rightful wyvern. Only he let Fiat escape, and now the blue sept is divided, with some of the dragons following Fiat, and others swearing to support Bastian."

"A civil war? That doesn't sound good," I said, wondering whether that was going to affect the silver dragons. The gods knew Gabriel had enough on his plate without heaping blue-dragon issues on it as well.

"It serves to keep Fiat busy, and away from us," Drake grunted. He stood up, going around to help Aisling out of her chair.

She made a wry face. "Fiat isn't happy with me for what he views as a betrayal, which coming from him is pretty laughable. My money is on Bastian, though. He's been biding his time, and I think he's going to make a great wyvern. But you can judge him for yourself when you see him at the *sárkány,* May. Thanks, sweetie. I need to visit the mothers-to-be room quickly, so don't talk about anything good until I get back."

Gabriel waited until Aisling had left the room before cocking an eyebrow at Drake. "Still haven't told her she's not going to the *sárkány?*"

"No." Drake grimaced. "She's not going to be pleased, but it is too dangerous. She will just have to understand."

Gabriel cast a considering glance my way. "Mayling, if you were in Aisling's shoes, and I forbade you to attend a weyr meeting to which you wished to go, what would you do?"

"I'm a shadow walker. I would simply slip into the shadow world and go anyway. But if I was Aisling herself, I'd probably grab the nearest blunt instrument and smack you upside the head, then go to the meeting."

Drake snorted. "Aisling is not so crass. She would not behave in such a manner." He paused as he walked past me, eyeing for a moment a small stone bust of a woman that sat on an isolated pedestal. He picked up the bust and stuffed it into one of the sideboard cupboards, a set look to his face as Gabriel laughed out loud.

"You have learned, I think."

"I am simply taking an unnecessary precaution, nothing more." He hesitated again, then quickly whisked all the knives from the table, depositing them unobtrusively in an urn on the sideboard just as Aisling opened the door.

"What did I miss?" she asked as Gabriel roared with laughter. "A good joke? I love jokes! Is it the one about the demon and the nun? That one always makes Jim wheeze."

I waited until Drake had helped her into her chair before addressing Gabriel, who was dabbing at his eyes with his napkin. "Who is going to be at this meeting? Bastian or Fiat?"

"Possibly both. The *sárkány* was called by Bastian to address the issue of Fiat, who will probably show up claiming he's the blue wyvern and thus has a right to be there."

"I see. Will Kostya be there, as well?"

"Probably," Gabriel said, "although he has yet to petition the weyr for recognition."

I waited, but he didn't add anything else,

despite seemingly wanting to. I wondered what had been going on between him and Kostya while I was in Abaddon but figured he didn't want to discuss it in front of Drake. While Drake had apparently never been particularly close to his brother, I assumed a blood bond was a hard one to break.

"And the other dragon sept? The red one?"

"Are you finished?" Gabriel asked. I nodded and pushed back my plate. "We have much to do before the meeting this afternoon. The red dragons will likely send a representative, although who that will be is unknown. We are unsure of what the wyvern Chuan Ren's fate was after Aisling cast her into Abaddon."

"That reminds me! I meant to ask you if you'd heard anything about Chuan Ren while you were with Magoth," Aisling said, turning to me. "I have no idea where she ended up, or even if she stayed there long. No one's heard a thing from her, or the red dragons."

I shook my head. "I didn't hear anything about a dragon being imprisoned in Abaddon."

"Well, crap," Aisling said, looking at her

husband. "You don't think she could be dead?"

"I do not know," Drake answered slowly. "It may be that she has yet to return from Abaddon, but that no one has stepped forward to claim her position. She ruled the red dragons for more than a millennium and would have seen to it that any competition within the sept was eliminated before it became dangerous."

"It will be interesting to see who shows up at the *sárkány*," Gabriel agreed, standing and holding out his hand for me. "We will see you there. But first, I promised May I would take her shopping."

I smiled and thanked Aisling again for the loan of her clothes.

"Oh, no problem; nothing fits me now but bedsheets anyway," she said, tugging at an oversized shirt. "I'll see you two at the *sárkány,* later. I'm looking forward to having another mate there!"

"Er . . . about that," Drake said slowly as we exited the room.

Gabriel paused and nodded at the porcelain vase at the opposite end of the room. "You might want to take that out before you tell her," he said brightly. "It looks valuable."

"Before you tell me what?" I heard Aisling

ask. Gabriel quietly closed the door and took my hand to lead me down the hall.

We made it to the front door before we heard the sound of a raised voice, followed shortly by that of porcelain crashing against a hard surface.

"I did warn him," Gabriel said, shaking his head.

"You're a healer," I said as he tried to pull me out the door and into the Parisian sunshine. "Shouldn't you go and see if Drake's all right?"

"There is no treasure that could tempt me into the same room as Aisling right now," he answered, kissing the tip of my nose before trotting down the front stairs to where Tipene was leaning against a car.

I followed him, wondering what it was Aisling could do to instill such respect . . . and whether someday I would be able to command the same.

Chapter Six

Shopping with Gabriel was a slightly stressful experience — not because it was an activity we hadn't done together before, but because he was footing the bill, which meant for the first time in my life I was able to shop without considering a budget, a fact that seemed to amuse him.

"I realize that you have been forced to rely on Magoth for your source of income in the mortal world," he said as he sent the upscale Parisian store saleswoman staggering off to the cash register with her arms piled high with clothing, "but surely your twin has had centuries to build her personal resources. Did she not share them with you?"

"Cyrene may be more than a thousand years old, but that doesn't mean she's managed to save anything. In fact, it's usually the opposite — she hits me up for spending money. I'm lucky that she lives rent-free in an apartment owned by a fellow naiad;

otherwise, I'd probably have her living with me in my little flat," I answered, touching with reverent fingers a lovely silky, nearly transparent midnight gauze blouse embedded with tiny little glittering crystals that sparkled like stars on an ebony sky. The price tag was that of a small used car. I moved on.

Gabriel picked up the blouse, pursed his lips as he eyed his fingers, visible through the sheer material, glanced briefly but speculatively at my breasts, then tossed the blouse onto the mound of clothing at the register. "I am not wealthy by dragon standards, but I can say in all sincerity that I can support both you and your twin without too much of a strain."

I took the blouse back and put it on the rack, giving Gabriel a level look as I did so. "I appreciate the fact that you're willing to help out Cyrene, but that's not necessary. Magoth does pay me, even if it's just barely a living wage. I may have been created some eighty-odd years ago, but I am modern enough to take pride in the fact that I can support myself and Cy, if I have to."

"But you do not have to," Gabriel said, reclaiming the blouse and shoving it into the saleswoman's hands.

"No, and while I'm grateful that you are

generous enough to wish me to live in comfort, I do want to pull my own weight. Or as much as I can, given the fact that Magoth is my employer." I reached for the blouse, but the saleswoman had evidently been watching us, for she hurriedly rang it up, accompanying the process with a defiant toss of her head.

I looked at Gabriel. He grinned. My knees immediately responded by threatening to give way under me. "The only reason I'm allowing you to buy me these things is because everything I own is back in London, and it would take too long to have Cyrene send them here."

"You are *allowing* me to buy you these things because you are my mate, and it is only right and fitting that you are garbed in clothing appropriate to your position," he corrected. "Not to mention that it gives me pleasure to provide you with them. Perhaps you should have two of that see-through one."

"No!" I said quickly, then sighed with mock resignation as he laughed. I placed my hand on his chest so I could feel his heartbeat. My fingernails burst into flame. "Fine, then. Force me to accept an entire wardrobe full of expensive and gorgeous clothing the likes of which I have never had.

Go on, twist my arm."

He laughed again, a velvety sound that seemed to curl around me, stroking my skin in a wholly arousing manner. An answering light of interest shone within his eyes, and I think he would have pulled me into an embrace right there in front of everyone, but just then my phone rang, breaking the spell.

"Oh, good, it's Cyrene," I said, glancing at the caller ID number. "I wondered when she would get back to me. Cy? Yes, it's me, and I'm out."

Gabriel looked for a moment like he wanted to say something but just gave a little head shake and moved off to pay for the clothing.

I took a few steps away to an unoccupied corner of the store, relieved to hear the voice of my twin after such a long absence.

"Mayling! I was so happy to get your voice mail! How did Gabriel get you out of Abaddon? I offered to help him by going to Magoth and begging him to release you, but he said that wasn't necessary, and that he had some plan in the works. Obviously he must have because you're not there now, but I still think that Gabriel might have at least let me try."

"Well, it doesn't really matter because his

plan did work, and I'm here now. How have you been while I've been trapped in Abaddon? You haven't been rescuing anything, have you?"

"Certainly not!" she said with righteous indignation, no doubt hearing the slight tone of censure that had crept into my voice. "I told that dragon of yours that I wouldn't get into trouble while you were gone, and I haven't."

"I'm relieved to hear it." Cyrene attracted trouble the way a flame drew moths. "What have you been doing while you were keeping your nose clean?"

"Oh, this and that," she said airily, and instantly my mental warning sirens went off. "You said you're in Paris?"

"Yes," I said slowly, eyeing Gabriel across the room. I knew he had kept tabs on Cyrene for me while I was out of commission, so surely he would have told me if she'd managed to get herself into some sort of trouble. "What exactly is this and that?"

Silence answered me. It was a silence I was all too familiar with.

"Oh, Cy," I said, slumping into a chair that sat next to the wall. "What have you done now?"

"I haven't done anything! I just got done telling you that! It's . . . er . . . it's just that . . . Oh, Mayling, I'm in trouble! But it's not my fault, I swear!" The sentence ended on a wail, just as I knew it would. It was accompanied by a couple of moist sniffles that meant big tears were rolling down her face.

"What is it now? Something with the committee? Did they find out how you helped me escape confinement?"

"No, it's not them. Kostya said they're not smart enough to figure it out. It's . . . it's something else."

"Kostya?" I leaped on the name that she'd tried to slip past me. "What does the black dragon have to do with your trouble? Is he bothering you, Cy? Because if he is, I'll just tell Drake —"

"No!" she interrupted, her voice thick with tears. "Kostya isn't bothering me — he's wonderful! He's so needy! I know you won't like it, but we've been dating, and oh, May, I think this really may be it! I think he's the one."

I wanted to bang my forehead against the nearest wall, but knew that wouldn't do anyone good. "You're not making the least little bit of sense. When I left you, you had just kneed Kostya in the groin, calling him all sorts of names."

"Oh, that. That was just a little misunderstanding. I've had more than a month to get to know him, really get to know him, and I know now that he's just horribly mistreated by everyone, your wyvern in particular."

I bristled on Gabriel's behalf, but before I could protest, she continued.

"You remember how I said that I thought Gabriel was confused about which of us was really the wyvern's mate, and that since we were twins, I was probably his true mate, and he just thought you were?"

"Um . . ." I didn't want to point out that we had proven beyond all doubt that I was Gabriel's mate. Cyrene tended to be a bit touchy about that subject. Or at least she *had* been . . .

"Well, I started thinking about that, and I figured out why I couldn't handle Gabriel's fire and you could."

"And what did you surmise?" I asked cautiously.

"We're both wyvern's mates!" She giggled. "Mayling, you're breathing like a bulldog. Stop hackling up like I know you are; I'm not going to take your wyvern away from you. That's the beauty of the situation — I have my own! I am clearly meant to be Kostya's mate just like you're meant to be Gabriel's."

I closed my eyes for a moment, and when I opened them, Gabriel stood before me, a quizzical look on his face. "Problems?" he asked.

"Just Cyrene being Cyrene," I said, putting my hand over the mouthpiece. "Can you give me a couple of minutes to try and talk some sense into her?"

He nodded. "Maata's birthday is in two weeks. I'll tell her she may have carte blanche in the store as her present."

I glanced over to where his two guards stood leaning against a wall near the entrance, and nodded. "I'll be as quick as I can."

"I'll tell Maata she has an hour, then," he said with wink before wandering off.

Cyrene, who had continued with a lengthy line of reasoning why she was obviously the best person to be Kostya's mate, drew up short when I interrupted her. "We can talk about the situation with Kostya later. I assume the trouble you referred to earlier is something to do with him? Have the other dragon septs said anything to you?"

"Oh." Her voice, which had been its usual light, burbling self, flattened to a whisper. "No, that's something else. May, it's . . . oh, it's horrible!"

"What?" I asked, my stomach tightening despite long decades of familiarity with the sort of trouble into which she could get herself. "Stop hemming and hawing, and just tell me. You know it's always worse if you try to prepare me for it ahead of time."

"I know, but this time it's especially tricky. It's . . . it's Neptune."

"Who?" I asked, startled.

"Neptune. You know, the head of all us water beings. He rules the sisterhood, not that we like to admit it, because, well, you know how some of the sisters are — they don't like men very much, and Neptune has always been rather condescending toward us naiads, like we're not valuable to the planet or something. As if! We do more work than any of the other elemental beings put together. Anyway." She took a deep breath, her words having slowed down from their initial tumbling rush. "Neptune called me before him, and, May, it wasn't pretty at all."

"I have no doubt of that. How bad is it?"

"Bad. He stripped me!"

"What?" I asked, shocked.

"You and your dirty mind. He stripped me of my title," she wailed. "It was hor-rible!"

I closed my eyes for a moment. "For the

109

love of all that's . . . what exactly happened?"

Ten seconds of silence followed my question. "It's my spring."

"What about it?"

"I've been so busy with Kostya the last month, the spring . . . He was so very needy, you understand, I mean, seriously needy, and he took up vast amounts of my time and attention . . . and the spring . . . well, it just sort of . . . became tainted."

"You let your spring go unattended?" I asked in stark disbelief. Naiads, as water beings, had charge of various freshwater resources. Some protected lakes, others rivers, and some, like Cyrene, personally watched over and preserved springs that fed a number of rivers and underground tributaries. I was familiar enough with the Sisterhood of Hydriades to know just how serious a matter it was to let your charge go without due attention. "Oh, Cy. How could you do that?"

"It was Kostya! He needed me, Mayling! No one has ever needed me the way he has. He . . ." Her voice dropped to an almost inaudible whisper. "He's so incredibly sexy. I just couldn't resist him."

I sighed softly to myself. If there's one thing I've learned in my life, it's that chastisement has little effect on my twin. "Sometimes I wish you'd given up some other trait than your common sense to create me."

"I'm sorry," came the very small reply.

"I know you are. So you were too busy being madly in love with Kostya to watch your spring, and it became tainted. Surely that's not irreversible. Why is Neptune involved?"

"Because Hahn the German sylph wants my position; that's why. Did I ever mention him?"

"No. *Him?* I thought sylphs were female."

"Don't be so behind the times. At the last consortium of elemental beings, they dropped the gender requirements to be more in line with the political correctness of the mundane world. Normally I wouldn't have a problem with a man wanting to join the sisterhood, but Hahn is evil, Mayling, pure evil." Cyrene's voice was filled with righteous indignation. "He wants to become the first male naiad, and duly applied to the sisterhood. When I told him that there wasn't a position open, he claimed we were refusing him based on his gender and threatened to report us to Neptune."

"Wait a minute." Cyrene's life always seemed to be something straight out of a soap opera, so I was used to the usual assortment of odd characters who were attracted to her. But this seemed a bit odd even for her. "Aren't sylphs air elemental beings? Why does he want a job connected with water?"

"I told you — he's evil! No sylph in her right mind would want to switch biases, but Hahn is after notoriety rather than really wanting to preserve the world's freshwater resources, as we naiads do."

I bit back an obvious response.

She continued without the least twinge of guilt. "Well, naturally, we weren't going to let him in after he threw that big scene and threatened to go over our heads, and now it's very clear to me that he thinks that if I get in trouble with Neptune, he'll be a shoo-in for my job. Honestly, how was I to know that a couple of weeks tending to poor Kostya's mental wounds would cause half the crops in Italy to fail?"

"Half the . . . *agathos daimon,* Cy!"

"It's only half! It's not all the crops in Italy, like Hahn claims! But he had to go running to Neptune blabbing that I was abusing my position, and how the mortals were suffering because of it, and you know how Neptune is about mortals."

"I don't, actually. I've never met him."

"Oh, he's gaga about them. He spends all his time going to surfing competitions with them. It's all he thinks about. That and punishing innocent naiads. But that's neither here nor there — you have to help me, Mayling. You have to go to Neptune and explain to him that because of all the trouble with you being dragged off to Abaddon, I didn't have time to take care of the spring."

"Oh, no. You're not going to use me as a scapegoat for the fact that you fell under the charms of a black-eyed dragon. You can just explain the circumstances yourself."

"But he won't listen to me!" she wailed, her voice again thick with unshed tears. "Hahn has filled him with so many lies, Neptune won't believe anything I say."

I rubbed my forehead. "And just why do you expect Neptune to listen to me?"

"He'll listen because you're *you,* Mayling! You're important now! You're a celebrity!"

"What on earth are you talking about?" I rubbed my forehead again. One of the side effects of speaking with Cyrene was a tendency to headaches. "I'm no celebrity."

"Sure you are. You're all they talk about at the clubs — the dragon's mate who is also consort to a demon lord. It's almost as good as what happened to Aisling, although you don't have a demon like she has."

"I have you," I said with irony that I knew would completely bypass Cyrene.

"And obviously that's much more cool," she agreed. "That's why I want you to talk to Neptune. Everyone is talking about you, and he'll listen to you because you don't have an interest at stake. You just want to see justice done."

"Even if he did listen to me, I'm not going to lie, Cyrene. The situation with Magoth and me had nothing to do with the reason you neglected your spring."

"Of course it does! I was so worried about you!" she protested, and I sighed as I heard the sincerity in her voice. I knew that in her mind, she had fully justified her actions by using me as a scapegoat. I thought about arguing the point with her, but long experience with Cyrene had taught me one thing: she was going to win. Somehow, no matter how firm my intentions, I always ended up caving in and helping her. "All right, I'll give him a call. What's his number?"

"You'll have to see him in person," she said brightly, happiness brimming from her voice. "He doesn't believe in cell phones. And you're lucky — he's in Portugal for a big surfing competition, so you won't have far to go to see him."

"*We* won't have far to go," I corrected, a note of steel entering my voice as I spotted Gabriel waiting for me at the entrance of the shop.

"We?" Cyrene asked, her voice almost inaudible.

"Oh, yes. If I have to go see Neptune, you're coming with me."

"But —"

"Where exactly is he?" I interrupted with ruthless determination. I might have to help Cyrene out of yet another sticky situation, but by the twelve gods, I wasn't going to lose any more time with Gabriel than I already had. I'd make a very fast visit to Portugal, convince Cyrene's boss that she was as innocent as she possibly could be, and return to Gabriel's arms.

"The surfing competition is in Faro," Cy answered slowly. "But really, May, I think it would be better —"

"I'll meet you there . . . Let me think . . . I have a dragon meeting today, and although I don't think there's anything pressing on the calendar immediately following it, I would like a little time alone to reacquaint myself with Gabriel. How about we do this in four days?"

"I suppose that would be all right," Cyrene said in a voice tinged with disappointment.

"It's so very kind of you to take time out of your busy life for me."

I gave the phone a wry smile. "You don't do catty well, Cy; you never have."

"I know," she said, sighing. "Four days is all right. I have a few things to do, myself."

"What sort of things?" I asked, suddenly suspicious.

"Oh . . . you'll see."

"Cyrene Northcott, if you are up to anything —"

"I would hate to have a mind as suspicious as yours; I really would," she answered with annoying and completely unreasonable self-righteousness. "I'm not up to anything, as you insist on putting it. But I do have work of my own to do, you know."

"Uh-huh. If you'd been attending to that a little more closely, and fawning over Kostya a little less, I wouldn't have to make time for a trip out to see your surfer dude."

"Yes, Mother."

"Much as I would love to bandy wits, I've got to run. Gabriel is standing all by himself looking utterly delicious, and I have six weeks' worth of kissing to catch up on."

"Mayling —"

"I'll see you on Wednesday. And, Cy, please try to stay out of trouble until then."

"You never used to be this mean to me,"

116

she answered sullenly as I got up and headed for Gabriel. "I don't think the time you spent in Abaddon did your character much good. I just hope you don't think you can talk to me like that all the time and get away with it! I am your twin, you know! You wouldn't be anywhere without me! You should really be thanking me for your existence rather than bullying me."

I gently closed the phone as I stopped in front of Gabriel, who was leaning against the wall with his arms crossed, the molten silver gaze so hot it all but singed. "Finished?" he asked.

"Cyrene isn't, but I am. Take me home?"

He didn't touch me, but he didn't need to. The look in his eyes was all it took to start a fire at my feet. "I'll take you, little bird, but it won't be home."

I smiled. I could get used to being a wyvern's mate.

CHAPTER SEVEN

"So this is a *sárkány.* Would it offend you if I said it looks like any other business meeting?" I whispered to Gabriel as we entered a large ballroom of one of the most prestigious hotels in Paris. The room was filled with people, the vast expanse of chairs that stretched across most of the golden ballroom already occupied. At the far end stood a large conference table, at which were placed only four chairs.

"That's what a *sárkány* is: a gathering of the wyverns to discuss weyr business." Gabriel's hand was reassuring on my back as we stepped off the elevator and entered the large room. "One moment, Mayling. I have something for you."

He tugged me aside into a corner, Maata and Tipene using their bodies to block the view.

"What's all this about?" I asked, confused. Gabriel pulled a chain over his head. On the end of it was a large silverish oval locket, very thick, but finely worked. He put the chain over my head, tucking the locket into my shirt, nudging it down until it was nestled between my breasts.

"Keep it safe," he said, adjusting my shirt slightly to show a little less cleavage.

"What is it?" I asked, touching the silver chain.

"It is the phylactery. I dared not leave it behind, and I hesitate to keep it on my person when Kostya may well show up. He has a tendency to attack first and ask questions later, and I would hate for him to see the phylactery while we were struggling."

"But that's priceless. I don't want to be responsible for something priceless," I said softly, not wanting to attract any attention. I tugged at his sleeve as he scanned the room. "Besides, it's made of gold. Drake smelled it on me before, when I had it in my bodice — he'll smell it on me again."

"Not this time. He didn't smell it this morning, and I wore it all through breakfast. The phylactery is contained in a very special housing made of platinum. He will not notice it."

"But," I protested, following when he started forward. "But platinum is more valuable than gold. He'll just smell that and then everyone will know I've got something priceless on me."

"Nothing is more valuable to a dragon than gold," he answered, nodding as a couple of people greeted him. "Platinum dilutes the scent of gold. No one will know you are wearing it so long as you keep it hidden."

I made a wordless noise of unhappiness, about to launch into a formal objection when he stopped me, leaning close to speak in my ear. "Mayling, the phylactery is beyond price. I could not leave it behind, nor can I wear it at this gathering. It is too dangerous. You must guard it for me until we are finished here."

"But what if someone knows I have it?"

"No one can take it from you," he answered with a flicker of emotion deep in his eyes. "I was not idle while you were in Abaddon. I knew this day would come, and that I must entrust the phylactery to you. That is why the casing has been spelled and warded so that if anyone but a silver dragon touches it, it will cause damage. Should someone try to snatch it from you, they will receive an intense charge of electricity, enough to incapacitate them."

I stared down at my boobs in horror.

"Have no fear, little bird," he said, tipping

my head up to give me a swift, reassuring kiss. "I would not risk your life even for the Lindorm Phylactery. You are my mate, thus you are immune to the spells bound to it."

"I'm glad to hear that," I said, shrugging my shoulders a few times to get used to the metal lodged between my breasts. It warmed quickly to skin temperature but left me feeling very aware that a priceless artifact was stuffed down my bra.

Gabriel flashed his dimples at me and escorted me down an aisle that cut through the chairs, Maata and Tipene following silently. He stopped for a moment when a couple of people rose and greeted him, speaking in a lyrical but unfamiliar language.

I am not a nervous person by nature, but I will admit that the situation gave me a nearly overwhelming desire to slip into the shadows. The room was too brightly lit, however, the lights glittering on gold-paneled walls and matching golden furniture, and even off a gold and old rose carpet. I suspected the dragons chose the room as their meeting place more for the ambiance than for functionality, but none of that made me feel any more comfortable.

Covertly, I brushed a bit of lint off the black wool pants Gabriel had bought me that morning, tweaking the tight cuff of the blouse he had presented me with earlier, saying he'd had it specially made for me. It was a very soft, silky black material he called dragon-weave, heavily embroidered with real silver thread and precious gems in an intricate design of fanciful dragons that leaped and danced around the shirt. It was very pretty, and although I admired it greatly, not to mention worried about wearing what must surely be such an expensive item, I didn't think much about it until I put it on. Then I noticed that the black material beneath the embroidery had shadows in it — shadows that seemed to move of their own accord. Although the value of the shirt weighed heavily on my mind, prompting me to make a mental promise I wouldn't go near anything that could be spilled on it, wearing the shirt made me feel different somehow, as if I was more than what I was normally.

"This is my mate, May Northcott," Gabriel said suddenly in English, turning to present me to three dragons. They wore cloth bright with black and silver African designs, the man in a loose-fitting tunic and pants, the women in garments resembling caftans, with head ties made of the same material. All three murmured a greeting, their silver eyes oddly startling against dark mahogany skin.

"It's a pleasure to meet you," I said politely, knowing better than to offer my hand. Citizens of the Otherworld did not touch one another unless invited to do so, either overtly or indirectly. Too much could be sensed by skin-to-skin contact, and although I wasn't sure the dragons followed such etiquette, I didn't want to start off on the wrong foot with members of Gabriel's sept.

"This is Eniiyi and Nkese," Gabriel introduced the women. "They are from Nigeria. Eniiyi is a close friend of my mother's."

The older woman studied me for a moment, a curious look in her eyes; then without warning she enveloped me in a hug that threatened to squeeze the breath right out of me. "Kaawa will be pleased with this one," she said as she released me.

I assumed Kaawa was Gabriel's mother, wondering about the "this one" comment — had Gabriel brought other women home for parental approval?

Gabriel said nothing, just nodded and introduced me to the male dragon. "Cibo is from Botswana. He had business in England and stopped in Paris for the *sárkány.*"

"I cannot express just how pleased we all

are to know that a mate has been found for Gabriel," Cibo said in a clipped English accent. He didn't hug me, but he did take one of my hands in both of his as he spoke. "Not only is he worthy of such an honor, it brings hope to those of us who have yearned for mates of our own."

"Thank you. I will do my best to live up to the job."

He released my hand, bowed to Gabriel, and returned to his seat. We continued down the aisle toward the long conference table, but before we got to it I asked Gabriel in a low whisper, "Is that all the silver dragons who are here?"

"Yes. We did not know until yesterday when you would be released, so there has not been time for other members of the sept to travel to Paris. Most of them live outside of Europe. Eniiyi and Nkese were here awaiting your arrival. My mother wished to be here to greet you, but her work kept her from coming. We will make a trip to Australia to see her soon."

I glanced around, trying to estimate the number of people present. "There have to be at least two hundred people here. Are you saying all these dragons live in Paris?"

"No. Most are blue dragons, who live all over Europe. That group over there are green dragons, summoned by Drake. The ones at the back of the room are red dragons."

"But our sept is really underrepresented," I said, worrying about the imbalance of at least fifty percent more blue dragons to the other three septs. "Is that going to affect anything? And how did they all get here so quickly?"

"The numbers of members mean nothing in this situation; only a wyvern and his or her mate can speak at a *sárkány.* The other members are here just to see history being made. They assembled quickly once word was received about your release."

"History? What sort of history?"

The doors at the back were flung open with a reverberation that echoed down the long room. We all turned to look. Kostya stood for a moment in a dramatic pose as he eyed everyone; then he strode down the aisle toward us, flanked by five men who I assumed were also black dragons. I touched the chain around my neck to make sure the phylactery was there, hidden away, relieved for a few seconds that Kostya was not accompanied by a blue-eyed brunette who just happened to have created me.

That relief was short-lived, as Cyrene bounded through the door next.

"I have come!" Kostya yelled in a dramatic manner, tossing his head so the sweep of dark auburn hair that had come down over his forehead was flipped back.

"Hello, everyone! Mayling! Isn't this exciting?" Cyrene called, ruining Kostya's big moment.

He glared at her.

"Oh, I'm so sorry. Go right ahead, punkanoodle. I know you want to make a good impression on everyone."

Even the sigh that Kostya heaved was filled with drama. "I told you not to call me that! It's not fitting."

"Sorry," Cyrene said, looking remorseful. "Forgot. Go ahead, Kostie."

Even at the distance we were from the door, I could see Kostya cast a glance upward as he obviously sought patience. Gabriel made an odd snorting noise, as if he was trying to hold back laughter. Normally I would have had a hard time keeping my own face straight, but I was more concerned about what Cyrene was doing here than the fact that her personality and Kostya's were so obviously unsuited to each other.

"I have come," the latter repeated in a loud voice. "The black dragons —"

"Greetings, fellow members of the weyr,"

another voice bellowed, the doors at the far end once again being slammed open. A blond man who was so handsome it almost hurt to look at him marched in, two incredibly handsome men behind him. "The blue wyvern has arrived. Let the *sárkány* begin!"

Kostya spun around to glare at the man who had interrupted his grand entrance. "Sfiatatoio del Fuoco Blu," he hissed, lifting his chin and glaring at the slightly shorter man as he approached.

"So *that's* Fiat Blu," I mused under my breath as I slid a glance toward Gabriel. All amusement had drained out of his eyes, leaving his face impassive as he watched Kostya and Fiat meet, but I knew he was not terribly happy to see Fiat. "Are you sure the phylactery —"

"I am sure. No one will sense it on you."

"Konstantin Fekete," Fiat said with a sneer, stopping in front of the man in question. "Come to beg the weyr for a few crumbs?"

"The black dragons do not beg!" Kostya said, and obviously would have gone off on one of the diatribes to which he was prone, dealing with the grand and glorious (if tragic) history of his doomed dragons, but Fiat caught sight of Cyrene at that moment and gave her a dazzling smile.

127

"And who do we have here? A water sprite?"

"Naiad," Cyrene said with a startled glance at Kostya as she allowed Fiat to kiss her hand.

"Most charming," Fiat cooed.

"I'm Cyrene. I'm with him," she added, taking Kostya's arm.

"Ah, but I can make amends for such a terrible tragedy," Fiat answered, kissing the knuckles of her free hand again. "I have not had a naiad in my entourage. Why don't you cast off the barbaric Kostya and allow me to show you how a dragon should treat a lady?"

"You dare?" Kostya asked, bristling with indignation.

"He's just trying to rile you up," Cyrene told him, retrieving her hand in order to pat him on the arm. "Just ignore it. You know full well I'm your mate and I'm not going to let any other dragon woo me away."

Kostya's frown cleared slightly.

"No matter how good-looking he is," Cy added with a smile at Fiat.

The look Kostya shot her should have dropped her dead on the spot, but Cy is oblivious to that sort of thing.

"Mate?" Fiat asked, narrowing his gaze at her.

"Oh, no," I murmured.

Gabriel leaned close to me. "She thinks she is a mate? Did we not disprove that point when we first met?"

"Yes, and yes. She swears she's Kostya's mate, and that the only reason she hasn't exhibited any signs therein is because he's not yet a wyvern."

Gabriel shook his head. "It doesn't work that way."

"I assumed not, but you know how she is — once she gets an idea, she runs with it."

Cyrene had been explaining her theory of mateness to Fiat while I was talking to Gabriel. Fiat shot Kostya a speculative glance, but neither said anything to burst her bubble. I had a horrible feeling that job would fall to me.

"If you should change your mind, *cara,* I will be happy to oblige you," he murmured. I think he would have gone into full seduction mode, but at that moment he caught sight of us.

"Gabriel, my old *friend,*" Fiat said, the emphasis unmistakable as he approached us. "I have not heard from you these long months."

Gabriel made a little bow. "I have been busy, as I assume you have."

Fiat's cold sapphire gaze slid over me, appearing startled for a brief instant. "Either my eyes deceive me, or this lovely lady is identical to the one I just left."

I didn't flinch at his close examination, although I badly wanted to shadow to escape his penetrating scrutiny. To my surprise, I felt his mind brush against mine. I quickly erected my mental defenses, glancing at Gabriel to see whether he had noticed.

The muscle in his jaw twitched once. He'd noticed.

"Identical and yet not identical," Fiat continued in a soft voice. "A mate? Can this be?"

"Yes, and she's claimed," Gabriel said with much less suavity than was the norm for him.

Fiat blinked; then a slow smile crept over his handsome face. He embraced me with great care, pressing a cold kiss to each of my cheeks. I stiffened, bracing myself for the moment when he realized that I wore the phylactery, but Gabriel's assurances were not false. Fiat didn't so much as sniff in the region of my chest.

"A mate at long last! I am so pleased for you, my old friend. And for you too . . . er . . ." He paused.

"May," I said, scooting over an inch or

two until I was pressed against Gabriel. "Cyrene is my twin."

"Indeed."

I prided myself on my ability to retain an unbiased mind when it came to people, and despite hearing much from Aisling about Fiat, I was determined to give him the benefit of the doubt. Something about him rankled, however. Oh, he stood chatting politely enough with Gabriel, but there was a tension about him, an awareness of his surroundings and everything in them that made me wary. A sense of expectation emanated from him, leaving me feeling restless and itchy with the need to get away. I glanced around, wondering whether I was influenced enough by Aisling to attribute false motives to Fiat, or whether my senses were accurate, and he really was planning something.

The dragons around us didn't seem to notice anything. Gabriel spoke in a low tone to Fiat, Maata and Tipene hovering with an unworried air behind us. Kostya had moved over to stand with his brother, Cyrene chatting brightly to Drake's men while the two brothers watched us with unreadable expressions. A small group of dragons entered the ballroom, all Asian, one woman and three men. They stood in the back assessing the situation, not approaching anyone.

I watched them, listening with half an ear until Fiat flashed a smile that was nearly identical to the one he'd turned upon Cyrene. "A doppelganger. How unique. I never doubted that you would find a mate, Gabriel, although I always assumed you would simply take Ysolde."

Gabriel looked surprised for a moment. "Ysolde de Bouchier?"

"Yes. She was the mate of your wyvern Constantine, was she not? Ah, what am I saying?" Fiat made a wordless noise of chastisement. "She was the mate of Baltic first. Perhaps you did not wish to taint yourself with her."

"The question is a moot one since Ysolde disappeared before Constantine was killed," Gabriel answered, the muscles in his arm tensing a smidgen.

"Just so, just so." Fiat turned back to me with a little bow. "You have my felicitations, *cara*. I can only hope that someday I, too, will find such a mate as my dear friend Gabriel has done."

Gabriel's expression was serene, but his arm slid around my waist, and Maata and Tipene moved a step closer behind us.

"Thank you," I said politely, my lips closing on any further comment I might be tempted to make. I waited before he moved off to greet a waiting clutch of blue dragons before addressing Gabriel. "I think he's responsible for the kidnapping of Maata and Tipene."

Gabriel clearly wasn't expecting me to say that, for he stepped back in surprise. "Why do you think that?"

"There's something about him, something expectant, as if he's been putting things in motion and is sitting back like a giant spider just waiting to pounce on an unsuspecting victim. And I have the feeling we're the flies."

"It's a big leap in judgment to go from someone who has an expectant air to someone who is responsible for kidnapping my guards. I've talked to both Maata and Tipene about their experience with the kidnapping. They maintain that the dragons who captured them were ouroboros — unconnected with any sept."

Maata nodded. "I'm sure I would have recognized a dragon belonging to a sept, and the ones who held us were completely unfamiliar. They were not blue dragons, May."

"There is also the fact that Fiat would have no reason to kidnap any silver dragon," Gabriel added. "We have not come down formally on Bastian's side, and there are no bad feelings between Fiat's blues and our sept. In fact, we've had . . ."

Gabriel's voice trailed away as the small group of dragons in the back of the room moved forward en masse, the woman in the lead.

"You are Tauhou, silver wyvern," she said, stopping in front of Gabriel. She spoke with a clipped Chinese accent, the words shooting out of her as if they were bullets. As someone rather lacking in the height department, I seldom see women much smaller than me, but this dragon was a good couple inches shorter, something that was not reflected in her personality — there was an aura of power about her that made the air feel full of static.

He made her a bow. "I have that pleasure. This is my mate, May."

The woman's dark-eyed glance brushed over me with an indifference that relieved me. As a rule I disliked being the center of anyone's attention — anyone but Gabriel — but especially so when I was wearing a valuable treasure in a room full of dragons. "I am Bao. I am wyvern of the red dragons. You will recognize me as such."

CHAPTER EIGHT

I stared with everyone else as the small woman made her surprising statement.

"Indeed. Chuan Ren is dead, then?" Gabriel asked politely.

"No." Bao tossed her head. She had short, spiky hair, and an attitude to match. "She remains in Abaddon. I have taken over the sept. This is Jian, her son. He will tell you that she wished for me to be wyvern should anything happen to her."

A tall, lanky man next to her placed his hand on his chest, giving both Gabriel and me a little bow, but he said nothing. I wondered how he felt about someone stepping into his mother's shoes.

"You must come and meet the others," Gabriel said after acknowledging Jian. "They will be very interested to hear of Chuan Ren. How does she fare in Abaddon?"

Bao gave another head toss and proceeded

in front of Gabriel. "That is immaterial. I rule the sept now, not Chuan Ren. She is gone, and I wish to meet the others."

I took the hand Gabriel offered, glancing to the side at Jian as he followed his new wyvern over to where Drake and Kostya stood. Fiat moved to join them, making little coos of pleasure as he spoke to her.

"Shouldn't her son take over as wyvern?" I asked Gabriel in a whisper a few moments later, as Bao was meeting the other wyverns.

"Not necessarily," he said, a speculative gaze on Jian. His fingers tightened around mine. "Wyverns are picked by right of tanistry, not primogeniture, although the latter isn't completely unknown. What I find interesting is that Chuan Ren has a child yet living. The others were killed in the Endless War."

Jian, a tall figure, his head meekly inclined, stood behind the tiny Bao. He was a handsome man, I mused to myself, with high cheekbones and a sculpted look to his face that hinted he might be a model if he had been born mortal. He looked to be in his thirties, but that meant nothing — most beings in the Otherworld could control their appearance, settling on an age at which they felt comfortable. "He doesn't look overly sad about the loss of his mother. Were they not close?"

Gabriel smiled for a moment. "I am not privy to the workings of the red dragons, but I sincerely doubt if anyone could be said to be close to Chuan Ren. Still, it is interesting, is it not?"

"Very."

"The *sárkány* will start now," Bao suddenly announced, plopping herself down in the chair at the head of the table.

Drake gave her a level look. "The weyr is not yet complete. We cannot start the *sárkány* until all wyverns are present."

She narrowed her eyes at him. "You are here. The silver wyvern is here. So are the blue and black wyverns. How is it not complete?"

"How indeed," Fiat said smoothly, taking the chair on the side of the table. "I have no doubt Drake is referring to that tiresome relative of mine who persists in delusions of controlling my sept. But as my dear uncle Bastian is not present to face the decision of the weyr, I believe we can proceed without him. And speaking of troublesome relatives . . ." He turned to Drake. "Where is your mate? Does she have so little respect for the laws governing the weyr that she refused to attend?"

"She is heavy with child," Drake said, moving to stand behind the chair at the foot of the table. His two redheaded bodyguards accompanied him. "Although she wished to attend the *sárkány,* her condition is too delicate for her to travel. As you know, there is precedence for female mates to be excused from attendance at weyr functions in such a situation."

Fiat smiled at him. "Naturally, we would not wish Aisling to risk herself or your child. Please be sure to tell her I'm thinking of her."

If Drake interpreted that as a threat, he didn't indicate it. Gabriel heaved a silent sigh, gave my fingers one last squeeze, and moved to the last remaining chair, but like Drake, he did not sit. "Since this *sárkány* has been called by Bastian to address the issues of your claim to the blue sept, I believe it will be in the best interests of all to wait for him to arrive, rather than begin without him."

"He did not conduct a challenge in the proper manner," Fiat said, an edge of anger to his voice despite his placid appearance. "It is not valid. I am wyvern of my sept, and you may trust me to deal with the situation he poses."

"If I did not conduct it as weyr laws

demand, it is because I had no need to," a man called from the other end of the room. Everyone turned to look, many of the dragons who had not risen to greet Fiat now doing so as the man walked alone down the aisle. When he reached the end, two men joined him, clearly his personal guard.

I blinked a couple of times as the man strolled up to us, glancing between him and Fiat. I gathered this was the missing Bastian, uncle to Fiat. The two were almost identical, and for a few seconds I wondered if there was a doppelganger I'd never heard of. That thought was dismissed as I realized that what I was seeing was simply two men who bore a close resemblance to each other. Both had the same blond Adonis good looks, although Bastian's hair was a few shades darker, the slightly curly locks brushing his shoulders. Where Fiat was dressed in an expensive-looking navy suit, Bastian wore a mandarin-collared sapphire shirt and black leather pants.

"Lies!" Fiat snarled, leaping to his feet as he slammed his fist down on the table. "You would face the weyr with your lies, but I will not allow it! I demand the weyr name this dragon ouroboros and remove him from our presence."

"You had me kept prisoner rather than

face me in a true challenge," Bastian said in a voice filled with scorn. "I do not have to challenge you, because you have not legally held the position of wyvern. I was named wyvern by Pierozzo Blu, not you. It was me the sept accepted, until you spread your poison and convinced those in power that I was mad. And rather than have them see the truth in a real challenge, you shut me away and claimed my position. But I will remain silent and hidden no longer, Fiat. I was named wyvern long centuries ago, and I have come to claim my heritage."

Drake gestured to one of his men. István took an empty chair that lined the wall and set it on Gabriel's side of the table. "This weyr has been called to settle the question of who is wyvern. Until such time as a decision is made, you will both have a place at the table."

Fiat spat out something rude but sat back down, his eyes glittering dangerously at the other blue dragon. Bastian hesitated for a moment but nodded and took his seat. Gabriel cocked an eyebrow at Tipene, who fetched another chair, which he placed a few inches from Gabriel's other side. He waited until I was seated before taking his own place, Tipene and Maata taking up positions immediately behind us.

"We are now all present," Gabriel said in his beautiful voice as he eyed the other wyverns. "As I have been asked to lead this *sárkány,* I believe we are ready to proceed."

"Not yet," Kostya said, snatching up a chair and setting it down next to Fiat with a good deal more force than was necessary. His men lined up behind him as he threw himself into the chair, spreading antagonistic looks among everyone. "Now all are present."

"Hello!" Cyrene smacked him on the shoulder none too gently. "I'm standing!"

"You have appeared to have forgotten your *mate,*" Fiat said with a hint of real amusement in his eyes.

"I have not forgotten her," Kostya said calmly. "Not that she is technically my mate, but I have not forgotten her. It is impossible to do so."

Cyrene gasped and whomped him again on the shoulder. "I am so your mate! You said I was!"

Kostya stood up with a heavy sigh. "No, I said you could be my mate based on the fact that your twin is Gabriel's, but I never said you actually were. I just . . . er . . . implied the possibility existed."

"So am I or aren't I?" she asked, her hands on her hips. I noted the dangerous

141

look in her eye and wondered whether she had been with Kostya long enough for him to recognize it.

Evidently he had. He took her hands in his and said something in her ear that evidently placated her.

"This is wrong," I murmured to Gabriel. "He's leading her on."

"Yes, but that is his own affair. It has nothing to do with weyr business."

"No, but it is important to me." I took a deep breath and stood up. "And I'm not going to let him continue with a charade that is only going to end badly. Cyrene, I'm sorry, but the truth is that you're not Kostya's mate. You're not any dragon's mate."

"Oh!" she said, outrage dripping from every pore. "How dare you say that about me! If you didn't have a dragon of your own, I'd say you were jealous."

"Well, I do, and I'm not. Cy, I've never lied to you, and I'm not lying now when I tell you that you are not a dragon's mate. Gabriel tested you last month."

"I'm sorry," he told her, his voice rich with sincerity. "But May is right."

"But . . . but . . ." She cast a sorrowful glance at Kostya.

"You cannot handle dragon fire," Gabriel said gently. "You cannot even tolerate it.

Any dragon mate can do so, especially a wyvern's mate. There is also the fact that none of us sense in you any other attributes of a mate." He cast a glance toward the other wyverns. They all shook their respective heads.

A curious parade of emotions passed across Cyrene's face. Anger, dismay, and sorrow were followed by a look of determination that had me slumping back into my chair.

I turned to Kostya. "Will you please tell her the truth?"

He cleared his throat, opened his mouth to say something, but just made unhappy noises.

I shook my head. "Why on earth do you let her go on thinking she's your mate when she's not?"

He looked embarrassed and made a vague gesture. "It's . . . er . . . complicated. She's . . . she's . . ."

"It's because I'm good in bed," Cyrene suddenly announced, the determined look settling firmly upon her face. "Which you well know. Well, not from firsthand experience, but because you're my twin, and if I'm good, then you must be good at it, too. At least I assume you are." She turned to Gabriel. "Is May —"

"Don't you dare ask!" I interrupted with a look that, by rights, should have scorched the hair right off her head.

She ignored it as she always does, clearly too involved in convincing herself of the suitability of a relationship with Kostya. "Physical compatibility is very important. Never underestimate that, Mayling. That, and Kostya obviously is head over heels in love with me. That's why he wants me for his mate when it may possibly be that I'm not technically able to fill that position." She hugged his arm and gave him a look that made me want to shake her. "It's so romantic, I could just melt. Oh, Kostya! I knew we were good together, but I never knew I meant that much to you!"

Kostya sat down with a comical look of disbelief tinged with resignation. Cyrene, not seeing a chair forthcoming, simply plopped herself down on his lap and spread a smile around at everyone.

I sat down as well, sighing to myself. This day had all the signs of being one I suspected I could do without.

CHAPTER NINE

"I'd say Kostya deserves every little bit of discomfort Cyrene causes him, but I'm going to end up the one she comes to when he breaks her heart," I whispered to Gabriel.

He nodded but was obviously focused on what he felt were more important things.

Drake, rightly interpreting Gabriel's meaningful glance, said with reluctance, "Kostya, you know the laws of the weyr as well as I do. You have not been named wyvern, nor has your sept been recognized and accepted. You do not have a place at the *sárkány* table."

"I am willing to recognize both the sept and the wyvern," Fiat said suddenly, smiling at Kostya. It wasn't a nice smile in the least, but at least he wasn't ranting or baiting the ever-volatile Kostya.

"I knew I liked you," Cyrene told Fiat, beaming at him. "Not enough to leave Kostya for you, you understand. I'm not fickle at all, despite May saying the opposite, but that is very kind of you to show such support for Kostya after you were so snarky to him earlier."

There was silence for a moment while everyone stared at Cyrene.

"You see?" Kostya finally said. "Fiat is ready to recognize my right to be here. A simple vote will end the matter once and for all."

"The issue of recognition of a black dragon sept is not why the meeting was called," Gabriel countered, a frown darkening his expression. "This *sárkány* is to establish which of the two blue dragons who claim they are wyvern should be acknowledged as such, nothing more. You have not petitioned the weyr in the proper manner, Kostya."

"You break the rules when it suits you to do so," he answered with a pointed look at me. "Why should I not do the same?"

"Damn straight!" Cyrene said.

I tried to catch her eye, but she was clearly enjoying herself too much to allow me to rain on her parade by appealing to her reason . . . what remained of it.

"Gabriel is correct," Drake said slowly. "A *sárkány* is called for a specific matter of business, and was done so in the correct fashion by Bastian in order to receive official recognition of his right to the title of wyvern. If you wish for the weyr to consider the matter of the black dragons, you must proceed via proper channels, Kostya."

"This is a foolish waste of time. He was named by Baltic to be his successor; thus, he is wyvern. I move for the recognition of Kostya, and reinstatement of the black dragon sept into the weyr," Bao said, snapping off each word.

"I concur," Fiat said quickly. "The blue dragons are officially prepared to recognize Kostya and his sept."

"You have no right to speak for my sept," Bastian said quickly, a little wisp of smoke escaping him.

"And you have no right to address an issue that did not call the *sárkány*," Gabriel told Bao.

She bared her teeth at him in what I assumed was meant to be a smile. Covertly, I reached for the dagger I keep strapped to my ankle, my fingers curling around the reassuringly solid length of its handle.

"These rules are antiquated. Why should we not deal with all weyr business at once?" she countered.

"It is not the way of the *sárkány*," said Gabriel, turning a fearsome glare upon the two blue dragons. "The sooner we attend to the matter at hand, the sooner we can all leave. Shall we get started?"

"It was *your* mate we were all forced to wait upon," Fiat snapped. "Clearly, you fear the arrival of Kostya and his sept and are doing your best to keep them from the weyr, but the rest of us have no such problem. Let us deal with the matter here and now, once and for all while we are all gathered."

"I vote yes on Kostya," Cyrene said, making herself more comfortable on his lap.

Kostya looked like he was thinking about dropping her onto the floor, but at a raised eyebrow from me, he stopped fidgeting.

Gabriel, however, was as tense as a snake about to strike. I gave his knee a little squeeze to remind him that fighting with Fiat would serve no good purpose, no matter how much he deserved to be punched in the face.

"He is too afraid of what might happen should the black dragons be recognized," Kostya sneered, his expression as dark as night. "He knows the silver dragons should never have been recognized in their own right."

"You know, I think I have to agree with Kostya on this," Cyrene started to say, but I had had enough.

"I realize that I'm new to the position of wyvern's mate, and I'm probably speaking out of turn," I said, standing to gain a slight height advantage over everyone sitting, "but I've just about had enough of this crap. What part of no do you not understand, Kostya?"

Kostya looked startled, both at the fact that I was addressing him in such a discourteous manner, and at the fact that I held a wickedly sharp dagger.

"Mayling!" Cyrene said, outraged. "How dare you threaten my boyfriend!"

"For the love of the twelve gods, will you stop it," I ground out through my teeth. "You are here merely as a courtesy — both of you — and I for one would appreciate it if you'd let Gabriel and the others get to the business they came to deal with."

Kostya puffed up like he was going to snap out a reply but said nothing, contenting himself with a glare that could have cut steel.

I sat down, sliding Gabriel a worried glance. I had a feeling that I'd greatly overstepped the bounds of what was proper behavior in a mate, but I didn't care. We'd be here all day if Kostya and Fiat were allowed to carry on.

Gabriel's face was impassive, but I saw amusement in his eyes, and he took my hand for a moment to give my fingers a reassuring squeeze.

"It would seem your mate is going to act as referee for this *sárkány*," Drake said dryly.

"Such behavior is not proper —" Fiat started to say, but Gabriel cut him off with a sharp, "Shut the hell up, Fiat. Let's get this done. Bastian, you called the *sárkány;* present your case."

Behind us, I heard Maata muffle a snicker. I straightened my shoulders and prepared to keep my mouth shut while Gabriel dealt with the weyr business. Four hours later, I was sagging in my chair, wanting nothing more than to sink into a hot tub and soak away the tedium. Bastian evidently had used his time well while I had been in Abaddon, for he presented a thoroughly documented case against Fiat, bringing forth not only sept documents and affidavits, but witness after witness who attested to the fact that it was he and not his nephew who was to have been made wyvern.

Fiat shouted, swore, argued, and threatened the entire time, but in the end, justice was upheld.

"The weyr recognizes Bastiano Giardini Blu as rightful wyvern of the blue dragon sept," Gabriel pronounced. He, too, looked a bit worse for the wear, the strain of having to keep everyone in line starting to show in grim lines around his mouth and eyes.

Bastian smiled and thanked the wyverns present. I was a bit surprised that Bao didn't fight the decision since she had seemed to favor Fiat, but after only a token protest, she agreed to go along with the majority and declared that the red dragons would recognize Bastian.

"It is not important," she had shrugged, and voted with the rest of the wyverns.

"This is not ended," Fiat shouted, jumping to his feet just as I knew he would. Half the room rose with him, his supporters glaring across the aisle at the blue dragons who were under Bastian's banner. "I do not accept this ruling! Bastian is incapable of ruling the blue dragons! You will rue the day you allowed him to take power!"

"Clearly the concept of gracious defeat has escaped him," Cyrene told Kostya in a whisper loud enough for everyone to hear.

Fiat certainly heard, for he snarled something rude at her before he leaped onto the table and glared at Bastian. "Do not believe you have won, old man. You may hold the day, but I will win the battle!"

"I name you ouroboros," Bastian said,

slowly getting to his feet, his eyes narrowed as he turned to look at the standing dragons. "As I will so name all who follow you. What say you? Will you remain in the sept with your friends and families? Or will you turn your back on it all and be cast out? Will you follow one who has brought the noble blue sept close to disaster with his treacherous dealings of other septs? Will you stand by while he strives to ruin all that we stand for, all that we worked to rebuild? Or will you return to sanity and reclaim that which Fiat has tried to destroy?"

A couple of the blue dragons glanced hesitantly across to what were assumedly their relations, but none of them moved. They were almost all male, each of them silent as Fiat postured and Bastian pleaded.

"They have no stomach to serve under you," Fiat said, jumping off the table to stroll with studied nonchalance to his uncle. "It is you who will destroy the sept, you who will alienate everyone, but by then it will be too late. You think naming me ouroboros will harm me?" He laughed, the sound harsh and grating as his gaze slipped to Gabriel. "We will prosper. For we will not be alone. Have you never thought to wonder who was behind the actions of two months past, old friend?"

"I knew it," I whispered, reaching for my dagger. "I told you he kidnapped them."

Gabriel stayed my hand with a look, facing Fiat with a placid expression that I knew he didn't feel. I could feel the dragon fire building in him, threatening to burst free. "What are you implying, Fiat?"

Fiat laughed again, tossing his head back in an affected manner. "Just what I said — I will not be alone. Nor will I forget what has happened here today. I have a very long memory, Gabriel. And my friends, my *old* friends, have even longer memories than me."

Bastian made an abbreviated gesture, as if he wanted to punch Fiat but knew he shouldn't. I gripped my dagger, wondering whether I could slip into the shadow world and follow Fiat without Gabriel noticing.

"No," Gabriel said under his breath, having read my mind. "He is posturing, nothing more, little bird."

"Very well. You have made your choice. What's done cannot be undone." Bastian gave each of the standing dragons a long, steady look. "Your families will not suffer for your actions, but know that as of this day, you will be dead to the sept."

Fiat rolled his eyes in an obnoxious display, stopping only to looked past us, directly at Kostya. "I'll give my friend *your* kind regards, shall I?"

Kostya pushed Cyrene off his lap, standing slowly, his head lowered, his eyes mere slits as he stared at the ex-wyvern. "You lie."

"Do I?" Fiat smiled, looked as if he was going to say something else, but changed his mind. "We leave," he told his followers, and they did just that. With their exodus, the air seemed to warm up several degrees, but whether it was due to the tension lightening or the actual physical removal of them, I had no idea.

I looked from Kostya to Drake and back to Gabriel. "Did he just say what I think he said?" I asked.

"What did he mean? Who is his friend? And why was he looking at you?" Cyrene asked Kostya.

"He lies," the latter repeated, exchanging a look with his brother.

Drake didn't look too convinced.

"What is he lying about?" Cyrene asked, tugging at Kostya's shirt. "Who was he talking about?"

"His name seems to crop up with increased frequency," I pointed out. "Are you guys really sure he's dead?"

"Oh!" Cy gasped, her eyes widening as she understood. "You're talking about that

154

Baltic person, aren't you? The one who tried to kill Kostya? But I thought he chopped his head off or something."

"I did," Kostya said, turning to Gabriel. "I wish to formally petition the weyr to call a *sárkány* in order to grant recognition to the black —"

The lights suddenly went out. Instantly I shadowed, but before I could grab Gabriel, the double doors at the far end of the ballroom were thrown open, and a shower of automatic gunfire from four silhouetted figures who appeared in the doorway immediately followed.

There was instant uproar as everyone in the room threw themselves out of the spray of bullets. We might all be immortal, but being shot still hurt. Gabriel called my name, his hand closing tight on my arm as he yanked me to the side of the room, shoving me to the floor as he moved to shield me.

The people at the door lobbed in a couple of smallish objects. I had time only to wonder if they were bombs when loud explosions rocked the room, the noise deafening as smoke began billowing forth.

"Smoke bombs?" I whispered to Gabriel, keeping a tight hold on his shirt so as not to lose him in the darkness and confusion.

"Stay here," he ordered. "Protect the phylactery."

I'd forgotten about that. I released his shirt in order to grope at my neck, pulling the large locket out to verify it was still safe.

"Don't use it unless —"

Another explosion filled the room, this one lighting the darkness with an intricate pattern of fire. Gabriel and Tipene moved off, leaving Maata to scoot over into Gabriel's spot.

"I don't need protecting," I told her in a whisper, coughing as the smoke filling the room began to choke me. "Go help Gabriel."

"Stop fussing. Can you see anything?" she asked, coughing between words.

The room was utter chaos — it was impossible to see what was going on, impossible to breathe without choking. Four men remained at the doorway, sweeping the room with bullets. Nearest the door, I could see outlines of overturned chairs, and now and again movement as someone crawled past. There were occasional cries and some swearing that indicated bullets, raking the room in a steady stream, were finding marks, but otherwise, it was beyond my means to see what was happening.

"I'm going into the shadow world," I

whispered, leaning toward a dark shape that was Maata. "Go help Gabriel. I'll keep the phylactery safe that way."

She didn't say anything as I slipped into the safety of the shadow world, that slightly altered version of our reality. Things always looked a bit different in the shadow world, and the instant I stood up, I saw what it was that had been hidden from my eyes in our world — behind the four men who continued to pump the room full of bullets, another man paced, a tall man in a long black duster, with a blue aura of power around him the likes of which I'd never seen.

Smoke still obscured my view, although it was lessened greatly in the shadow world. I walked toward the man, intent on getting a closer look at him. I was safe from bullets or other physical attacks, facts that drove my curiosity as I made my way around the struggle that was going on in the room. I passed Gabriel, Drake, and Kostya as they huddled together, Drake giving the other two orders. They split up, a group of dragons going with each wyvern as they skirted around the edges of the room, clearly intent on ambushing the men at the door. Bao and Bastian were on the other side of the room, obviously following a similar plan.

I walked down the middle of the room, trying to get a better look at the man who continued to pace back and forth behind the gunmen. Two dragons hauled another one to the side of the room, the injured member groaning piteously. I hesitated, wondering whether I should help, but a shout from another group of dragons as they ran for the door distracted me. The pacing man stopped, spinning around to peer into the room, but it wasn't the distracting rush that held his eyes. I took a step forward and was suddenly flung a good three yards back as his gaze locked onto me. He turned toward me, and I saw his face in the light: high cheekbones and deep-set black eyes lending him a faintly Slavic look. His hair was dark as well, pulled back from a pronounced widow's peak into a long ponytail.

I stumbled, shocked that he could see me in the shadow world. He was a dragon, of that I was sure, and dragons as a rule couldn't enter the shadow world. Gabriel was an exception due to his shaman mother, but I'd never heard of another dragon who could see someone in it, let alone enter. And yet as he strode forward toward me, he slipped as easily into my world as if he had been born to it.

I scrambled backwards at the same time I reached for my dagger. Dimly, I heard Gabriel shout my name. A spike of fear ripped through me as the man continued to approach. I glanced around quickly for an avenue of escape, not wanting to engage him in a battle until I was sure of who he was. He stopped suddenly, the quick intake of breath a hiss as his gaze narrowed on the object hanging outside my blouse.

"Lindorm Phylactery," he said, and slowly reached out a hand as if he was going to take it. I scrambled backwards, falling over a table and a dragon who lay on the floor groaning, clutching the platinum case so hard it cut into the flesh of my palm.

To my horror, it didn't seem to want to be held. It slipped out of my hand and rose straight off my chest, the chain cutting sharply into the back of my neck as if it was answering his call. I grabbed at it again, using both hands to pull it back to me.

The man snarled something,

"Mayling!" Gabriel yelled, his voice coming through to the shadow world faint, as if he was a great distance away. It was hard to hear over the dull noise of everything going on around us, but I could pick out a few words. ". . . use it!" he shouted. Behind the mysterious man, the wyverns had commenced their attack on the gunmen, Drake's people swarming the one nearest them, a full-fledged battle going on as the other three gunmen were simultaneously attacked. I caught sight briefly of Gabriel as he and Tipene fought one of the shooters, Gabriel ripping the automatic weapon from the latter's grip, slamming the butt of it down onto his attacker's head. He turned back to me and yelled something, but it was impossible to make out the words. Three more men appeared in the doorway, throwing themselves on Gabriel as he called out again.

"Use it!"

The phylactery — he wanted me to use the phylactery. He must have seen the mysterious man as well, and he wanted me to use it in order to protect it from capture.

The man in front of me snarled again, making a sharp gesture. The platinum casing that held the phylactery exploded, small bits of metal piercing my hands and stomach.

I bit back an oath at the sudden pain, clutching the vaguely dragon-shaped lump of gold that was revealed. I studied it for a fraction of a second, unsure of how I was to use it. I wasn't a dragon; such things were not instinctual to me.

The man took a step toward me, lifting his head slightly as if he was scenting the air.

"Mate," he said, the word holding equal measures of disbelief and anger. "Silver mate?"

"Who are you?" I asked, unable to keep from speaking.

He shook his head, and for a moment I thought he was going to turn and leave. But he launched himself at me, knocking me painfully backwards onto overturned chairs.

Gabriel shouted again, and time seemed for a few seconds to telescope. The doorway was black with bodies as reinforcements streamed in, attacking the dragons, who had managed to take three of the four gunmen down. There was no way we were going to be able to stand against those sorts of numbers, not when we had been taken by surprise.

Light was blotted out as the man rose above me, his eyes glittering with a bluish black light that scared me to death. Electricity gathered in the air around him, giving him a blue corona that made the air crackle.

The phylactery began to shake in my hand as it struggled to free itself from me. I had a momentary vision of me telling Gabriel I'd lost the phylactery, the horror that it instilled within me giving me the strength I needed.

"I may not be a dragon, but I am a dragon's mate," I yelled, and gathered to myself not only the shadows that were so much a part of me, but Gabriel's fire. I let both build within me, clutching the phylactery tightly with both hands as I started to channel the shadows and fire through it.

The man hesitated for a moment, a curious expression passing over his face. "No," he simply said, as if he couldn't believe what he was seeing.

"Oh, yes," I said, then released the phylactery.

It hung in the air in front of me for a moment, suspended in time and space, then exploded in a nova of fire that made the very earth tremble. The explosion knocked me back several feet, the room filling with a giant fireball that, in my last few seconds of consciousness, seemed to consume everything in it. I sank down into the conflagration, giving myself up to it, becoming one with the dragon fire.

CHAPTER TEN

"Is this going to become a habit, Mayling?"

I struggled up from where I was floating mindlessly, wrapped in an onyx cushion that blotted out all thought. I frowned. The voice that spoke was familiar, all too familiar. I was mildly annoyed that Cyrene would pull me out of such a lovely dream, for such I assumed it was.

"Is what going to become a habit?" I heard another voice ask, and was surprised to find it belonged to me.

"Burning down hotels."

I opened my eyes at that, my memory returning with her words. "The phylactery," I gasped, immediately reaching for the chain that hung around my neck.

There was no chain. I stared in stark horror at Cyrene as she sat in a chair next to me, my mind madly twirling as it tried to piece together the last confused moments before I'd lost consciousness.

"It's gone," Cyrene said placidly, setting down a magazine as I immediately began to search the bed upon which I was lying. "Evidently it just — *poof!* — blew up. Along with the entire top floor of the hotel, I might add. Honestly, Mayling, I don't think you had to go to quite such dramatic lengths to clear out those bastard dragons who were attacking us."

I pulled myself up to lean against the headboard of the bed. I was back in Aisling and Drake's Parisian house, but how I got there was a blank. "I blew up the hotel? I don't think so, Cy. I never do anything that would draw attention to me."

"Well, you blew up the phylactery, which was the same thing. It blew out a couple of walls with a huge fireball, blasted a huge hole in the center of the floor, and set fire to pretty much the top floor of the hotel. You're just lucky that it contained only the conference center, and that everyone there was immortal, or you'd be talking to the watch about killing innocent people."

Fear twisted my gut. As someone born of the shadows, I always avoided any action that might force me into the limelight, but more importantly, I made it a policy to never kill another being.

"As it is, most of the dragons escaped

164

harm, except for those bastards with the guns, and they fell through the hole in the floor, so that's no problem. I had a burn on my arm, but Gabriel fixed it for me," she said, holding out one unmarked arm.

"That was nice of him," I murmured, my thoughts black with unhappiness.

"I had to wait until he was done fixing you first, but I suppose that was to be expected. You were pretty hurt."

"Me?" I moved my legs, then arms, not even a slight twinge answering the movements. "I'm not hurt."

"You're not now, not after Gabriel spent the last twenty hours working on you, but I saw you when they hauled you in here, and you were in pretty bad shape." Remorse filled her eyes as she placed her hand on mine and gave it a little squeeze. "I was worried."

"Silly twin," I answered, returning the gesture. "You know I can't be killed."

"No, but you can be damaged in ways that would leave you a mental vegetable, and you had lost so much blood, I wasn't sure if you were going to come back to us. But Gabriel never lost hope."

"Where is he?" I said, surprised he wasn't there.

"Oh, he went downstairs when Kostya

challenged for you. I said I'd watch you while he did that." Her face and voice were as serene as ever.

Swinging my legs out of bed and getting to my feet, I shook my head at that fact that she could still surprise me. I felt a moment of lightheadedness, but my legs seemed as solid as ever. "I swear if I live a thousand mortal lifetimes, I'll never understand you, Cy. You don't mind that Kostya is challenging Gabriel for me?"

"Don't be silly," she said, her airy laugh brightening the residual wispy dark cobwebs in my mind. "He doesn't really want *you*, you know. He wants what you are. And besides, I don't think he's going to get you. Gabriel can be awful obstinate when he wants."

"What I am?" I shook my head again, moving over to the wardrobe to gather some clothing. Why would Kostya suddenly care that I was a wyvern's mate? He wasn't even recognized as a wyvern. Perhaps this was just one more way he had struck upon to cause Gabriel grief. "You know, I think I'm just going to talk to Gabriel and find out what's been going on." I stopped at the door to the bathroom and looked back at her. "Did you say I'd been out of it for a day?"

"Yes. Gabriel worked all night on you."

She hesitated for a moment, a faint shadow passing over her face. "I think he loves you, Mayling."

I didn't say anything, just nodded and went into the bathroom.

"Did you hear what I said?" she asked a few minutes later when I emerged, clothed and freshened up as best as I could manage in a short time.

"Yes." I grabbed my dagger from where it sat on the nightstand and strapped it to my ankle, hurrying out of the room and down the hall to the stairs.

"Well?" Cyrene demanded, following me. "Don't you have anything to say to that? Like how you feel about him?"

"My feelings aren't important at this point. What is important is what bull Kostya is trying to pull now. Where are they?"

I paused at the foot of the stairs. Cyrene pointed to the door to the right, which I remembered from past visits had led to a large sitting room.

"Mayling," she said slowly as I was about to open the door.

I cocked an inquisitive eyebrow at her.

"You do love him, too, don't you?" She took a couple of steps forward, her gaze searching mine. "I mean, you wouldn't want to trade him in for another dragon, would you?"

A little smile curled up the edges of my mouth. "I can assure you that I have no designs on, desires for, or even patience with Kostya."

"Good," she said, her chin lifting. "Because he's mine, and although I understand him challenging Gabriel and all, I wouldn't want to have to do something serious if you were willing to switch allegiances."

"Serious? Serious like what?" I asked against my better judgment. "Cy, are you saying you'd take me down if I messed with your boyfriend? You've never been like that."

"This is different," she said firmly. "And no, I wouldn't take you down, as you put it. I'd just . . . well, I'd make things miserable for you."

I bit back both a comment and a smile, contenting myself with a brisk nod before I opened the door.

"I refuse to discuss this any further," Gabriel was saying as we entered the room.

"I refuse to let you refuse my challenge! I, Konstantin Fekete —"

"No!" Gabriel said in a louder voice. "You may not challenge for her!"

Kostya stormed over to him (he was always storming places), his nostrils flaring as he stopped. "I challenge you for —"

"May is a wyvern's mate," Gabriel interrupted. "Only a wyvern may challenge for her, and when last I looked, you were not included in the weyr."

"I would be if you hadn't stopped me!"

A voice spoke from the far side of the room. "Oh, blow it out your —"

"Jim!" Aisling squawked from where she sat on the couch. "Out!"

"Man, I never —"

"Out!"

"That baby is making you really mean. Can I just say Rosemary's baby, here? Because . . . All right, all right, I'm getting! Sheesh! Hiya, Cy. How they hangin,' May? Boy, some people really take the term 'demon lord' to heart."

"Are we interrupting?" I said, taking in the scene as Jim shambled out of the room, muttering to itself.

The conversation came to an abrupt halt. Instantly, Gabriel was at my side, his eyes filled with concern. "Your twin was supposed to tell me when you'd woken," he said, taking my hands in his.

I curled my fingers around his, unable to keep from smiling up at him when Cyrene said abruptly, "Gabriel, May is awake. Pookie! Has he been mean to you?"

The expressions that crossed Kostya's face as Cyrene hurried over to him were comical, but I had better things to do than watch him be embarrassed by love talk.

"Would it shock you to the tips of your dragon toes if I kissed you in front of everyone?" I asked, leaning into Gabriel.

"No. It would, however, violate the strictest dragon etiquette," he answered, his eyes lit with passion and laughter.

I grabbed two handfuls of the soft brown dreadlocks that hung to his shoulders, and pulled his head down for a kiss that was guaranteed to raise the temperature of the room at least five degrees.

"I like her," Aisling said with approval.

I gave Gabriel's lower lip a little nibble. "Perhaps this should wait until there is less of an audience?" I whispered.

"She knows what she wants, and she goes after it. I like that," Aisling said again. "Drake, you'll notice Gabriel isn't lecturing her about what's proper and what isn't proper."

"You tempt me beyond reason," Gabriel responded, pulling me to him so that we fit together as if my curves were specifically designed for his hard lines.

Drake raised his eyebrows at his wife. "Are you implying you actually listen to those lectures?"

"No. Arm." Drake rose and bent over her, obviously about to lift her off the couch. She pushed him back and grabbed his arm, using it as leverage to pull herself to her feet.

"I thought not. If I offered to not lecture you for the next six weeks, would you allow me to lift you when you wish to rise?" he asked, opening the door for her.

"I'll think about it. Now, stop hovering and pay attention to just how nicely Gabriel is allowing May to kiss him. You don't see him complaining."

Drake frowned. "*Kincsem,* I have yet to complain about the methods you use to show your affection; it is the times you choose to indulge in them that I —"

The door shut briskly in his face.

I giggled into Gabriel's mouth, teasing his lips, nibbling and licking and tasting him, just enough to stir the dragon fire between us, but not enough to ignite it fully.

"That must wait until later," he said, agreeing with what I was thinking.

"Someday I'm going to be able to read your mind, too, and then you're going to be in trouble," I said, sucking on his lower lip one last time. Regretfully, I released it and stepped back, warmed to the depths of my being by the look in his eyes.

"If you are done with that wholly inappropriate show of affection, perhaps we could get on with the challenge?" Kostya said, and he probably would have stormed over to us while he said it, but Cyrene was clinging to his arm like a naiad-sized leech, cooing little love words and tucking long strands of his auburn hair behind his ear.

Gabriel said something in Zilant, the now archaic language of the dragon weyr.

Kostya looked shocked for a moment. Drake's lips quivered.

I nudged Gabriel. "Was that the equivalent of 'get stuffed'?"

"Not quite so polite, but yes," he answered, one dimple flashing momentarily. "The issue is moot, Kostya. May is mine, and you may not have her."

"Now, don't let him get you all riled up, pookums," Cyrene told him as she dragged him to a love seat. "You said yourself that if you kept your so-adorable nose clean for a bit, no one would have any right to refuse recognizing us as black dragons."

Kostya looked like he wanted to roll his eyes, but he managed to stop himself in time. "You don't know of what you speak, woman. Stop tugging on me. I don't want to sit there!"

"Well, fine!" Cyrene said, dropping his arm with an exasperated noise. "Where do you want to sit?"

Kostya's face was mutinous. "I will stand. Until the glorious black dragons retake their rightful place in the weyr —"

Identical long-suffering expressions appeared on Gabriel's and Drake's faces, as one no doubt did on mine. Once Kostya got going on his tirade about what the black dragons had suffered, it was difficult to stop him.

"Oh, shut up," I said, exasperation overriding my better judgment.

Kostya opened his mouth to reply but instead burst into flames.

The other two men eyed him with surprise, all three turning their gazes on me.

"Er . . . did I do that?"

Kostya crossed his arms and shot me an outraged glare.

"I don't think that was me. Was it?"

Gabriel nodded. Drake sighed.

"Would you mind putting him out?" the latter asked me. "Aisling will be annoyed if the heat builds up enough to set off the sprinklers."

"Sorry," I said, focusing my attention on extinguishing the flames that continued to consume Kostya. "I didn't realize I had pulled Gabriel's fire."

"Indeed." Drake cleared his throat. "I am pleased to see you well, May. I take it you are feeling no aftereffects of the explosion?"

My happiness dimmed at the reminder of what I had to do.

"Yes, thank you, I feel fine. I'm sorry about losing control of Gabriel's fire, Kostya. That hasn't happened before."

Kostya snapped something and plopped himself down in a chair. Cyrene perched on the arm of it, patting out a few leftover tendrils of fire that were licking at his ears.

"Gabriel." I brushed his hand with mine, needing the reassurance his touch brought me, but hesitant to ask for it in the face of what I had to confess. "I don't know how to tell you this, but the phylactery . . . er . . ."

"It was destroyed when you used it," Gabriel finished for me. The amusement in his eyes that had been spawned by the sight of Kostya in flames fizzled away until they were left shiny and flat, just like polished silver plates.

"I'm very sorry," I said, uncomfortable with his placid expression. That was the face he used with others, not me. "You should have warned me that it had that much power. Cyrene said no one mortal was hurt, thank the gods, but still, I wish you had

174

warned me what to expect."

"I did warn you," he said, his eyes still flat and hard. "I warned you to protect it."

"No, I'm talking about after that, when you told me to use it —"

"Use it? You told her to use the phylactery?" Drake's voice cut across my explanation.

"No." Gabriel frowned slightly as he examined my face.

I frowned right back at him. "Yes, you did. When that man came into the shadow world, you yelled at me to use it."

"Man? What man?" he asked.

"The dark-haired one who was pacing behind the gunmen."

The three dragons exchanged glances.

The door opened behind me, Aisling returning from her trip to the bathroom.

"You're not going to tell me you didn't see him?" I asked them all.

"See who? What did I miss? Why do I smell smoke?"

She settled next to Drake, who spoke quietly in her ear, obviously explaining to her what had been happening while she was gone. She giggled as she looked at the still slightly smoking Kostya.

"Describe this man you saw," Gabriel said.

"He was about your height, with long dark

brown hair that was pulled back into a ponytail. He had dark eyes and a widow's peak. Oh, and he was a dragon."

Gabriel looked confused. "Are you certain? A dragon followed you into the Dreaming?"

"What's a dreaming?" I heard Aisling ask Drake.

"It's another term for the beyond," he answered at the same time I nodded.

"Yes, quite certain. He even knew I was your mate. He said that, as a matter of fact, kind of like he couldn't believe it. Then he saw the phylactery, and he named it, so when you said to use it in order to protect it from him —"

"I gave you no such order," Gabriel said, his face unreadable.

"I heard you. You told me to use it."

"I told you that under no circumstances should you use it," he corrected, pity suddenly filling his eyes. I wanted to turn away, sick at the sight of it.

"I didn't hear that. It was hard to hear anything," I mumbled. "Then, I destroyed the phylactery for nothing. Which means I destroyed that dragon-heart shard inside it. I'm so sorry, Gabriel. I thought I was doing what you wanted me to do. I thought I was protecting it."

He watched me for a moment, then pulled me into his arms. I melted against him, wanting to cry out my horror and sorrow, but I've never been the sort of person who gets relief from weeping, so I contented myself with simply drawing comfort from his embrace.

"Is there any way it can be repaired?" I asked his chest, my face being pressed firmly into it.

"The phylactery? No."

I pulled back, sick at my own stupidity. How could I think Gabriel would want me to use something he gave into my safekeeping? "I don't know what to say. I'm more sorry than I can possibly express that I inadvertently destroyed that precious bit of dragon history. I know the dragon-heart shard was irreplaceable — you told me that enough times — but I honestly thought you told me to use it when that dragon came after it. I would never have done so if I thought that using it would mean its complete annihilation. *Agathos daimon!* I wouldn't blame you if you demated me for this."

His expression was partly disbelief, partly something I had a hard time putting a name to.

"She doesn't know?" Kostya asked, his

voice sullen.

"It would appear not," Drake answered, considering me.

"And no wonder; you guys never tell anyone anything unless we come right out and ask you," Aisling said, punching Drake in the arm. "Tell her!"

"It's her wyvern's job," he said, capturing her fist and kissing her fingers.

"Tell me what?" I asked, lifting my gaze to Gabriel's.

"Mayling . . ." He hesitated for a second, an interesting parade of emotions passing over his face. "You didn't annihilate the dragon-heart shard. You simply changed its form."

"It's not gone?" Relief filled me as he shook his head. "Oh, thank the twelve gods and all their little acolytes. Where is it? Did the phylactery get melted into a gold blob? Can we have it reforged, or whatever it is you do to make the phylactery, so we can put the shard back into it?"

"Tell her!" Aisling said.

"Yes, please do," Cyrene said. "The suspense is killing me!"

I looked at Gabriel and waited.

He took my hands, his thumb rubbing over my knuckles. "The phylactery was merely a vessel, May. The dragon-heart shards cannot be destroyed, not by means within your abilities."

"I'm delighted and relieved to hear that," I said, confused by the looks I was getting from everyone. "So what's the big secret that everyone but me knows?"

"The shard must have a vessel. It cannot exist on its own — it must either be a part of the whole, which would provide a weapon of infinite power, and thus cannot be allowed, or it must be safeguarded in a vessel. That is law."

"So you have it tucked away in another amulet, but you don't want me to guard it?" I asked, taking a stab in the dark. "I don't blame you at all for that. I have certainly proven unworthy of the responsibility of guarding it."

The silence that followed was thick with unspoken comments.

"No, little bird. We did not need to make another phylactery." Gabriel's thumb swept over my fingers in a featherlight touch. "We did not need to because when the phylactery was destroyed, the shard found a vessel of its own."

A chill skittered up my spine.

His eyes bore down into mine, piercing my soul, silver brilliance that filled me with light. "You are the vessel, mate. The fifth shard of the dragon heart chose you to safeguard it. *You* are the phylactery now."

CHAPTER ELEVEN

"I can't believe I've become the dragon heart." I don't often wail, but I admit that at that exact moment, I found the idea seriously attractive.

"You haven't. You're simply the vessel that holds one-fifth of the heart."

"You say that like that's an everyday occurrence, as if it was something unimportant, and yet, here we are — ow — bouncing our way across a dry riverbed in order to consult the most learned source of dragon lore you could think of, in hopes of fixing the situation." I bit my tongue as the jeep jounced over yet another huge bump in the track, sucking it briefly while I squinted through the dusty window. "Are those wild horses?"

Gabriel glanced at the small herd of horses that raced across the scrubby landscape, moving effortlessly through the beige spinifex grass, their elongated shadows rippling across earth as red as the sun that was sinking below the horizon. There wasn't a lot to see in this area, mostly tall grass, small dry-looking shrubs, and acacia trees, but I found it oddly appealing.

"Brumbies," he said.

"Pardon?"

"Wild horses here are called brumbies."

"Ah."

"I intended to bring you here eventually," he said, jerking the wheel to avoid hitting a small brown animal. "Bilby."

"Bilby to you, too," I said brightly, feeling out of my depth.

Gabriel laughed and turned on the Land Rover's lights. "That was a bilby, little bird. They're endangered, and nocturnal by nature, so it's rare to see one out in the open like this. They're part of the reason why we're out here."

"Out in the boonies?" I peered through the grime-specked window, watching the collection of small buildings fade into the distance. The sky glowed reddish orange as the sun slipped downward, casting a lovely amber glow over everything. "There don't seem to be a lot of people around. Is it because it's so arid?"

"Partially. Lajamanu is a relatively new settlement. The white powers that be relocated the Warlpiri people here, my mother's family included. There was some trouble, but eventually the people settled. It may not seem like a thriving community, but they're holding their own."

"I see." We'd flown into a tiny airport on a plane that appeared to be held together by nothing but duct tape and hope. The town itself was very small, but I didn't have time to do much but admire a local artist who was painting a vibrant canvas before Gabriel sent Maata and Tipene off in one direction, the two of us taking charge of a beat-up old Land Rover that had clearly seen better years.

"The Wulaign rangers in this area stay out in the bush and monitor wildlife, including those that are endangered or threatened." We jounced over a couple of deep ruts and chugged our way up the side of the dried riverbed, avoiding a mammoth spiky rock formation as we headed for an area rich with trees. One last ray from the dying sun burst with glorious color at a spot between the trees. "That's the river up there. We'll likely have to spend the night." He slid me a curious glance. "I never asked whether you liked roughing it. I suppose now would be a good time, eh?"

"Cyrene wouldn't be caught dead camping, not for the largest lake in the world, but I have nothing against nature." A large cicada flew in through the window and smacked me on the face. Startled, I instantly shadowed and batted frantically at my face. It buzzed upward, into my hair. I shrieked and tried to cram my upper half out of the window in an attempt to dislodge the beastly thing.

Gabriel drove with one hand while plucking the large bug off the top of my head. He held it in front of me, one eyebrow raised as I deshadowed.

"All right, perhaps I would have never made it as a Girl Scout, but you can't judge me by my reaction to being assaulted by a large, hairy bug. I like animals. On the whole. And they like me. I just don't like them flying into my face intent on making me look bad in front of you."

The cicada made an odd little chirping sound, just as if it was agreeing with me. Gabriel laughed and tossed it out of the window. "You're not nervous, are you?"

"Oh, goodness, no. What do I have to be nervous about?" I looked out of the window again. Dusk was falling quickly, the horizon still streaked with orange and red, but above it, deeper colors were starting to claim the sky, indigo and navy and a velvety blackness that felt to me just like a warm blanket of safety. "The man to whom I have sworn my eternal devotion has just informed me that I now hold one of five priceless dragon artifacts, which means I'm fair game to every unattached wyvern who would like to get his — or her — hands on it. My temporarily absent employer is doing who-knows-what out in the mortal world. My twin is tangled up in all sorts of messes that evidently only I can unravel, and, oh, yes, I'm going to meet the mother of the aforementioned mate, a woman so knowledgeable about dragon lore that she attracts visitors from the world over. Nervous? Don't make me laugh."

There was a definite grim note in my voice that I regretted but was unable to eliminate. Gabriel cast another sidelong glance toward me, his eyes bright even in the dimming light.

Suddenly the most overwhelming emotion filled me. I looked at him and saw not just an incredibly handsome man, but *my* man, my mate, silver eyed, velvet throated, and as sexy as hell. He was mine, and I was filled with the most incredible cocktail of need, lust, desire, want — it all swirled around in a blaze within me, building until I thought my skin would burst into flame.

"Stop the car," I said in a low voice that I barely recognized as mine. "Stop now."

He shot me a startled look as I lunged for him. Luckily, he got the car stopped before I got my hand down the side of the seat, finding the lever that moved the seat back. "Mayling? What —"

I jerked the lever upward. The seat back crashed downward, Gabriel falling with it. I was over him in a flash, writhing with the sensation of his body between my legs. "So hot," I murmured, ripping off the thin cotton shirt I wore. "Your fire burns me, Gabriel. It makes me want to do things to you. Wicked things. With my tongue."

"I can see that," he said, his gaze molten, but not nearly as hot as the fire that raged within me. "I have no objection to putting out your fire, little bird, but I'm not sure this is the best place for such an act."

"Too much talking," I said, leaning down over him and licking his lips with fire. "Too many clothes, as well."

"Definitely too many clothes," he agreed as I rose off him, doing an intricate dance to extricate myself from the khaki pants I'd donned just a few hours before, when we'd landed in Australia.

The fire and need continued to build within me as I struggled to contort myself in a way that would allow me to remove my clothing. It was impossible to do so while remaining in a position that straddled him, a fact that made me whimper in frustration, until I simply started shredding my clothing off my body.

Gabriel's eyes widened at the sight. I followed his gaze to my hands, which had changed shape somehow, covered in the same iridescent silver scales that I'd seen on him, my fingertips now bloodred claws.

A fresh wave of desire swept over me. I shivered, but not with cold. I tore the last of my clothing off and looked upward, panting as if I'd been running a race. "I need you, Gabriel. Right now. Sooner."

He burst into flames as I yanked the shirt off of his marvelous chest, dipping my head to lick one pert little brown nipple. The taste of him almost pushed me over the edge into an orgasm, driving the strange, overwhelming need even higher.

"Please," I said on a half whisper, my mouth finding his. I poured the fire that roared within me into him, taking back his own in return. He didn't answer me with words, simply managed to free himself from his pants, his hands urging me onward. The skin of my belly rubbed against his, my breasts, aching and heavy, brushing against the soft hair of his chest. The touch of his flesh against mine caused the most incredible sensations to roil around inside me. I stared down at him in surprise, unable to sort out what was happening to me. "It's as if I'm one big erogenous zone," I murmured, closing my eyes in bliss as I rubbed against his chest again, my back arching as flames burst up around us.

"It's the shard," he said, his voice rubbing against me in an orgasmic rush matched only by the sensation of his hands on my breasts, teasing and tormenting me until I wanted to scream with both pleasure and frustration. "It's part of the dragon heart, the essence of all dragonkin. You're sharing some of the sensations we feel."

"Then the gods be thanked that I'm a doppelganger, because I don't think I could survive this," I gasped as he took one of my nipples in his mouth, bathing it with a heat hotter than the sun. I saw stars — I literally saw stars as I slid my hands up his sides, my scarlet claws leaving little trails of fire on his skin.

"You will survive this and much more," he said into my breast before turning his attention to its mate. I groaned as he bit gently on the nipple, my body tightening as he pulled me downward again, claiming my mouth once more.

The fire burned around us, but it was nothing to what was consuming me from within. I writhed against his body, my tongue dancing around his as it swept into my mouth, tension mounting deep inside me until I knew I was going to climax.

A burning brand bit into my hip as he dug his fingers . . . claws . . . into my flesh before trailing even lower, down over my hips and behind, parting sensitive flesh. I suckled his tongue hard as his finger dipped inside me, a thousand little muscles tightening, the intrusion as hot as molten steel. It pushed me over the edge, and I went flying in a way I'd never done before, time holding its breath for a moment as I changed, shifted into a form that was different, yet familiar. I was bathed in fire and light, and I threw back my head to roar my rapture to the heavens, but the voice crying aloud was not my own.

"Do not fear the change, little bird," Gabriel said as I returned to myself. His eyes shone like lights in the gathering darkness, and despite an instinct of self-preservation that told me to get away from him, get away from what was happening to me, I was comforted. "I will not let harm come to you."

"I never thought you would," I said, bending over him to brush his lips with my own, but the second my breasts touched his chest, the need rooted deep inside returned, and my hands changed to claws, and my senses went back into overdrive, and I suddenly wanted him, all of him, inside me and around me. I wanted to submerge myself in him until he blotted out everything in life that wasn't the two of us.

I screamed when he shifted my hips and plunged me down onto his penis, a high, reedy sound, startling me when I realized that it came from me, but that concern was short-lived when he moved within me, and I was once again sent spinning into a state of being that went far, far beyond mere sexual climax.

Time held no meaning for me as we made love out there in the bush, enveloped in darkness, filled with fire, surrounded by nothing but sky and earth. I suspect that little time passed, simply because Gabriel's fuse was notoriously short — as was my own — but it seemed to me, as I lay gasping back on my own seat, that eons had passed. I lifted a hand, relieved to see in the dim light of the car that the hand held familiar fingers, somewhat stubby, but my own.

"If you say a single word about not having foreplay, I swear I'm going to deck you," I said, turning my head to look at the man who still lay prone on his seat. I mused again how beautiful he was, his body taut and lean, but not gaunt, not sparse in any way.

Gabriel chuckled, a rich, sensual sound that made me shiver as the cooling air pricked at the tiny drops of perspiration that still clung to me.

"I wasn't going to, but now that you mention it . . ."

I curled up one fist and waved it in the direction of his face. He laughed again, pulling his seat upright, grimacing briefly as he looked down at his side.

The stripes left by my claws were still visible.

"*Agathos daimon.* Tell me I didn't do that to you," I said, leaning over to examine the wounds. They were red and raised, but not bleeding.

"It's all right, little bird. You don't have to look so stricken. They don't hurt. Much."

"Oh, Gabriel, I'm so sorry. I don't know what came over me. It was just . . . it was just . . . suddenly you looked so good to me. Not that you don't always look good, but this was different. This was very different. And those claws . . . I had no idea that I would hurt you, though. What can I do to heal them?"

Gabriel took my hands, which were fluttering around the stripes on his ribs, pulling them to his mouth. "They are mating marks, little bird. They are common with mating pairs of dragons, and I assure you, I would much prefer to bear the slight discomfort they bring than have you forgo making them."

"But why aren't they healing?" I frowned at the marks. "They should be healed by now. Enough time has passed."

"Mating marks heal slower than other injuries. Don't worry about them, May," he said with a smile. "You gave me much pleasure when you embraced the shard."

I looked back at my hands, my emotions conflicted. I couldn't deny that the experience we'd just shared had been beyond anything I'd ever imagined, but I didn't like the strange feelings that possessed me. "It was the shard that changed my hands? It wasn't just something that happens to wyvern mates?"

He watched me for a moment, kissing the tips of my fingers before releasing them. "I'm sorry you were frightened, May. I would like to assure you that being the vessel to the shard will change nothing about you, but I can't. It is part of you now, and until such time as it is removed, you will experience some of the sensations of what it is to be a dragon."

I shivered, cold despite the relative balminess of the night air. I suddenly realized that I was naked, my clothing in shreds around us. A little noise of distress slipped out of me as I sorted through the torn fabric, trying to find something wearable.

"Take this," Gabriel said as I clutched the wad of useless clothing.

I took the shirt he had pulled off, fortunately still whole since Gabriel had had the presence of mind earlier to unbutton it while I was struggling to get out of my clothing.

"It's lucky you are so small," he said after a quick search in the backseat of the car. "There's nothing else here. I'm sorry I can't offer you my pants, but they would not fit. I had not expected that we would need a change of clothing, or I would not have sent Maata and Tipene off with our things."

"This'll do," I said, buttoning the shirt all the way down. The tails reached to my knees, and I had to roll the sleeves up several inches, but at least it was a covering. "I hate to think what we're going to tell your mother, though. She's going to know just exactly what we were doing."

"I think everyone within a hundred-mile radius knew what we were doing," he answered, amusement in his beautiful eyes. "You yelled your pleasure loud enough to wake the sleeping animals."

I made a face at him.

He pulled me to him, kissing the tip of my nose. "It pleased me to know you were so affected."

I rubbed my cheek against his chest, saying nothing, troubled by the remembered feelings that had possessed me. I didn't want to be slowly taken over by a dragon essence so potent it could change me into something alien. I was happy being myself, troubles and all.

The question was, did I have a choice in the matter?

Chapter Twelve

"We should get moving. My mother will no doubt know we are near and come looking for us if we do not arrive in a reasonable time."

"Does she know you're here because she's your mother, a dragon expert, or a shaman?" I asked a few minutes later as we were once again bouncing our way across the arid near desert of the region.

"The answer is probably all of them. As a shaman, she knows who enters the area. She senses their beings and keeps track of those who belong to her. But she's also my mother, and I have no doubt that word reached her of our arrival in Lajamanu."

I thought about that for a few minutes, arguing with myself about whether or not I should ask the question that was uppermost. I decided that it was better to ask now, before I met Gabriel's mother. "You mentioned your father to me once but haven't said anything about him since. He's not dead, is he?"

"Dead?" Gabriel looked surprised. "What gave you that idea?"

"Well, you've talked a lot about your mother, but not so much about your father. I just figured they wouldn't be separated unless one of them was . . . well, dead."

"He's not dead."

"Oh. Good. He's here with your mother, then?"

"No." Gabriel kept his eyes on the nonexistent road, avoiding breaking the axle on rocks and bits of dead vegetation, driving carefully through the deepening light, occasional flashes of animals in the headlights making me jump. "You know of the curse, Mayling. You know that no mate is born to a silver dragon. That includes my parents."

"I know about it. I just thought . . ." I made a vague gesture. "I just assumed they must be mated in everything but name."

"They aren't. My father lives in Tanzania. The only thing he shares with my mother, my sisters and me excluded, is a passion for animals. That's how they met. My father came to Australia a few centuries before the white settlers, wanting to see for himself the wildlife that was so abundant here. My mother was shaman for one of the aboriginal tribes and healed him when he got himself into trouble with a tiger snake. He stayed for about ten years, but eventually they went their separate ways."

"That's rather sad." I mused on how I'd feel if one of the other wyverns attempted to steal my shard-infested self from Gabriel. "I take it your mother is immortal, then? How can she be that if she's not his mate?"

"She's a shaman."

"And shamans are immortal?" That puzzled me. I'd never heard of shamans being anything but mortal.

"Not technically. Shamans can walk in the Dreaming, though. My mother simply sends her spirit there when her mortal body wears out, and returns to the mortal world when she's reborn."

"Ahhh. Very smart. How many times has she come back?"

"Too many to count. That should be her camp up there." His eyes glittered in the darkness of the car as the headlights picked out a small cluster of ratty tents. As the noise of the car reached it, a couple of people stood up from where they'd been sitting around a large campfire.

A little spike of nervousness gripped my stomach.

"You have nothing to be nervous about,

little bird. My mother will love you," Gabriel said, reading either my mind or the wary expression that no doubt planted itself on my face.

A tall, elegant-looking woman with skin the color of espresso beans strode forward, her smile when she saw Gabriel as warm as the waves of heat that still rose off the cooling dirt of the desert.

She called out a greeting and enveloped him in a huge bear hug, kissing him on both cheeks and examining his face for a moment before she allowed him to introduce me.

"You look well, child. You look . . . happy."

"For that, you have May to thank," he said, holding out his hand for me.

"I am Kaawa Mani. I have heard of you from my friends, child," she said as she eyed me from the top of my head down to my dusty walking shoes.

"I'm very sorry about my appearance. We had a little accident with my clothing," I said as she paused to note the fact that I was clad in only Gabriel's shirt. "But it's a great pleasure to meet you."

She looked for a second at the hand I held out, then examined my face closely. I had to steel myself to keep from shadowing, so piercing was her gaze. I felt naked before her, as if she'd immediately stripped away all the outer layers of my being and was looking directly into my soul. "You share a dreaming with wintiki, the night bird," she said, suddenly hugging me.

I was surrounded in the warmth of her being and felt immediately welcomed into something that seemed to encompass both her and the earth itself. "I do? I hope that's good."

Kaawa laughed. "It is rare for a nonindigenous person to share a dreaming. It is a good sign."

"Then I'm very pleased," I said, glancing at Gabriel. He stood watching us with a rather somber expression. "Although I'm not quite sure I understand what exactly a dreaming is. I thought it was the same as the shadow world."

"Dreaming can be many things," she said, putting her arm around me and escorting me to the fire, where three other people stood waiting. "Generally it is the story of origins, of how things came to be. But in your world, it can also mean an existence beyond the mortal plain. It is all that, and more. Do not attempt to understand it all; just simply accept that it is."

"That sounds like very wise advice."

"This is Adobi, Maka, and Pari," she said,

introducing the three men who greeted me with big smiles and firm handshakes. "They are fellow rangers from the local area. Before them, I name you daughter, and so shall you be known to all. Gabriel, I think you remember Pari from — what on earth?"

She had turned to face him and obviously just noticed the red stripes he bore on his sides. I felt my face flush and had to fight to keep from shadowing as she marched over to examine the markings.

"These are mating marks," she said, straightening up. "*Dragon* mating marks. I thought you said your wintiki was a shadow walker?"

A small fire broke out at my feet. The three men, dressed in identical dusty khaki shirts and shorts, looked askance and stepped back a few paces as I stomped it out.

"There was a situation with the Lindorm Phylactery," Gabriel said slowly, glancing briefly at the three others.

"You may speak in front of them. They will not carry tales," his mother said, pulling him toward the fire.

He took my hand and pulled me with him. One of the rangers, the oldest, a man with gray hair and wise brown eyes, waved his hand toward a camp stool.

"Thank you, I'm fine," I murmured, and carefully perched myself on a beat-up plastic cooler that was evidently also used as a seat.

"I think you'd better tell me about it," Kaawa said, and offered us both coffee.

Gabriel quickly recounted the events of the last day. I shifted uncomfortably when her gaze slipped to me as he told how I had misheard him, resulting in the phylactery being broken, and I had to resort to sitting on my hands when my fingers repeatedly ignited.

"That is all very interesting," she said slowly, her gaze searching his face. "But you have not yet mentioned the most interesting part of all."

Gabriel's lips thinned. His knees burst into flame.

"Sorry," I said, and focused hard on damping down the fire. It fizzled out to nothing.

"May is feeling the effects of the dragon shard," he said as an explanation. "Hence the mating marks. As you can see, she is still learning to control the fire."

"Yes, yes, I understand that — it was such with Ysolde, when she became the Avignon Phylactery — but that is not what I mean, and you know it. Tell me about this dragon who could walk in the Dreaming."

Gabriel was silent for a moment. "I believe it is as you think. I do not understand how he could survive, and yet the proof is before us."

"Bah," she said, making a dismissive gesture as she poured herself a cup of thick black coffee and took one of the canvas chairs. "Resurrection is not difficult. It can be done. But for a dragon to walk in the Dreaming, to be able to interact in there . . ." She shook her head. "That is truly a feat I had not thought possible. You are certain he started to take the phylactery from you, wintiki?"

I nodded.

"Then Baltic must have been resurrected by someone very special indeed," she said thoughtfully, her gaze on the fire.

"But that's unlikely, isn't it?" I asked.

Gabriel's nod was slow in coming. "The signs point to it, and yet it seems to me impossible."

"I agree it fits with everything that's happened lately," I said, pausing to pick my way through my conflicting thoughts. "Or does it? I could swear that the man who was in the shadow world with me was genuinely surprised to see the phylactery, and he tried to take it from me. If you suppose it was Baltic back from the dead, as I assume you must from everything that's happened, why would he have given Kostya the phylactery if he wanted it for himself?"

"I don't know," Gabriel admitted. "It doesn't seem to make sense, and yet, I have felt for the last few decades that something was not right in the weyr. There was a disturbance, a faint ripple of something that should not have been there."

"He gets that from me," Kaawa told me with obvious pride. "His good looks come from his father — have you met him? Horrible personality, but such a good lover, it made you forget about the former for a while. But it gives me great pleasure to know that Gabriel's finer points come from me."

"I can see that they do," I agreed politely.

"You don't yet, but you will," she said complacently before returning to the subject at hand. "I know that you wish to consult me about May becoming the phylactery — what are you going to call yourself, child?"

I was a bit surprised. "What am I going to *call* myself?"

"Yes. All of the phylactery are named. That is to identify the shards within. You must bear an official name since you are now the vessel."

"I don't know," I said, looking in openmouthed surprise at Gabriel. "I have to change my name?"

"Not change your name, but it is tradition to name each phylactery." He thought for a moment. "You could use your surname, unless you think your twin would object."

"I don't see why she would. So now I'm May Northcott, doppelganger, wyvern's mate, consort to Magoth, and also the Northcott Phylactery?" I blew out a breath. "Why am I suddenly feeling overwhelmed?"

Gabriel's dimples flashed. "The wyvern's mate is the most important part, and you handle that extremely well."

The look in his eyes brought the fire within me to roaring life, sudden pinpricks of pain causing me to leap to my feet as I pulled my hands out from where I had them tucked under my thighs to keep the flames from sprouting.

My fingers were back to being silver scaled, and scarlet tipped.

"Fascinating, simply fascinating," Kaawa said, taking one of my hands to examine it closely. "I've read of Ysolde de Bouchier, of course. She detailed her experiences in becoming the Avignon Phylactery quite well, but it's not the same thing as seeing it in person. My dear, I hate to be a nagging mother, but would you put out the fire in

204

my tent? It's the only one I have, and I don't have plans to go back to town for another fortnight."

Two of the rangers had risen at the same time I twirled around to see one of the tents on fire. I closed my eyes, instinctively shadowing as I concentrated on putting out the fire. By the time it was out and I had deshadowed, the two younger rangers were backing away from the camp. Pari, the older man, simply examined me with interested eyes.

"You have made a good choice," Kaawa told Gabriel, giving him a smile. "She will keep you from being bored."

He laughed. "Boredom was never an issue, but I disagree that May is a good choice — she is the *only* choice."

A little stab of pain pierced my heart. He was right — I was the only one who could be his mate, whether or not he wanted me to be so.

"Stop that, little bird. You know I did not mean it in that way," he said.

"Stop reading my mind," I parried.

"I was reading your charming face, if you must know," he said, brushing his thumb across my chin. "You don't hide your thoughts very well."

I let my gaze drop, not wanting to discuss

the issue in front of others.

Kaawa gazed from Gabriel to me with a startled expression. "You can read her mind? Then truly you must be fated to be together. It is very rare for dragons to do that. You must be special indeed, wintiki."

"She is, which is why I do not wish to spend the rest of our lives fighting off challengers," Gabriel said. "I am prepared to deal with anyone who thinks he can take my mate away, but now that she bears the fifth shard, she will be prey to anyone who wishes to use her. I do not want to subject her to that."

"No, of course not," Kaawa agreed.

"Is it possible to get rid of the shard?" I asked her. "In some way that it won't be harmed, that is?"

"And will not harm May," Gabriel added.

"Hmm." Kaawa studied the fire again, clearly lost in thought. "The dragon heart is the essence of dragonkin, that which formed with the first dragon. It was he who recognized that its power would be too much for any one dragon to wield, and so he separated it into five pieces, the shards you know now. One was given to the green wyvern, one each to red and black, and two to the blue dragons."

"Two? Why two?"

"The first dragon formed the blue sept. He kept a shard for himself, and one for his sept, given to the wyvern he chose."

"Is he still around? The first dragon, I mean?" I asked, wondering if there was some connection between him and the mysterious Baltic, who may or may not be pulling the strings for everything going on.

"No," Gabriel said. "No one is certain he ever truly existed. He is more myth than reality."

"He existed. He still exists, in all dragonkin," Kaawa said with calm assurance.

"So the shards were divided up. How did this Ysolde person end up having one?" I asked.

"Ysolde was mated to the black dragon Baltic but was claimed by Constantine Norka as his mate. There is some confusion as to which wyvern she accepted — her diaries for that time are missing. But we do know that she was torn up by the Endless War, and determined to bring about its end before more dragons died at the hands of the two men who fought over her. She somehow acquired the shard of the first dragon, and used it along with the shards of Baltic and Constantine in an attempt to bind together the other shards. It didn't work, of course — the dragon heart has a mind of its own, and it did not wish to be used in such a manner — and in the process, the phylactery which held the first dragon's shard was destroyed, and it claimed her as its vessel."

"What happened to Ysolde?" I asked. "I've heard her name mentioned before. Is she still alive?"

Kaawa was silent for a moment, absently stirring the fire with a long stick. "She disappeared when Baltic was killed by his heir. Some said that was proof she was truly his mate, but there is some evidence that she survived his death, remaining hidden. Nothing was heard from her after Constantine Norka was killed by an avalanche, however, so it could be that she was really his mate. It's likely we'll never know."

"And was the shard destroyed with her?"

"No. She successfully decanted it into another vessel." She raised her eyebrows as she looked over at Gabriel. "You will have to find the other shards, child."

He nodded. "I know where they are."

"Why do we have to find the other shards?" I asked, confused.

"The shard that resides within each vessel cannot be separated from it unless the vessel itself is destroyed."

"Urgh," I said, not liking the sound of that.

"Exactly," she said, nodding. "It can be formed into the dragon heart, however, and then resharded into appropriate vessels. That is how Ysolde eventually decanted her shard — she brought together the shards, re-formed the heart, then separated the pieces again into their current phylacteries. Current with the obvious exception of you."

"I thought you said that when she tried to bring the pieces together the heart objected and the phylactery was destroyed," I said, more confused than ever.

"That was the first time, when she tried to use the heart for her own purposes. The dragon heart is immensely powerful," she answered, her dark eyes serious as she considered me. "It has the ability to destroy entire septs, child, possibly the entire weyr itself. The shards themselves contain much power, but they are nothing compared to the sum total. To wield such a thing is beyond most beings, dragon or otherwise. Ysolde meant well, but she did not have the ability to control the heart, and it recognized that fact, causing the first failure. But when she sought to re-form it for the purpose of ensuring the safety of all the shards — for by that time, the weyr was in disarray, with many septs close to complete annihilation — it allowed her to do so."

"So you're saying we need to repeat that? To bring together all the shards, re-form the dragon heart, then break it back up again into the individual shards and put them in nonhuman vessels?"

"It is the only way to separate the shard from your being," she said, nodding.

I glanced at Gabriel, filled with hopeless dismay. "How am I supposed to do that? Ysolde was a dragon, wasn't she? Is this dragon heart going to allow me to re-form it when I'm only your mate?"

"We have to try, Mayling," he answered, his jaw tightening.

I nodded but said nothing. There was nothing else to say — either we succeeded in re-forming the dragon heart and separating it back into shards, or I'd be stuck being a vessel for the remainder of my days. There was Magoth to think about — he hadn't been able to access any of my abilities thus far, but who knew whether the dragon shard would be accessible by him? I couldn't risk giving him any more power than he had.

Given Magoth and the number of dragons out there who would literally kill to gain power over others, there was simply no other option.

CHAPTER THIRTEEN

"Gabriel is nervous," Maata said out of the blue the following day.

I stopped pacing back and forth across the small room to which we'd been shown. Outside the room, thousands of people passed through the Auckland airport, but inside it, noise was muffled to the point of being almost inaudible, as was the conversation I could see Gabriel holding with a couple of customs officials, one of whom had reservations about my (admittedly hastily forged) passport.

"I don't blame him. I wish he'd just let me shadow to get through customs. There's going to be hell to pay if they discover the passport isn't genuine."

She smiled. Maata didn't often smile, and it made me wonder how she came about being one of Gabriel's elite guards. She was a pretty woman, her appearance reflecting more Polynesian influence than Aboriginal, and that stirred up even more curiosity about the woman who would literally give her life for her wyvern. "You think he's worried about mortals? He's dealt with much worse, I can tell you. He's worried you won't like his home."

I gave her a puzzled look. "Why on earth would he think I wouldn't like it?"

"He's worried you'll compare it to Drake's homes and find it lacking . . . find him lacking."

"Oh, for the love of the twelve gods. I've told him before I don't care about that. I know he doesn't have a lot of money like Drake. I am completely fine with living a modest lifestyle. My flat in London is really nothing but a room with a sink. I'm totally fine with staying within a budget, although I wish now I hadn't let him buy me all those expensive clothes."

"Gabriel isn't one to hold on to money for long," she said matter-of-factly. "He has never accrued wealth, as most dragons do. He has a lair, but it is filled with things that are precious to him and wouldn't necessarily be viewed by others as overly valuable."

"Sounds like my kind of man. I'm not heavily into possessions, either. I've never had the resources to develop that taste, and if I did, I had Magoth to consider. He'd never allow me to keep anything with any true value. So, honestly, Gabriel has nothing to be nervous about."

She gave a little half shrug, watching along with me as Gabriel, Tipene at his side, argued some point or other with a growing circle of customs officials. "He has not had enough time to be sure of you."

"He's not sure of me?" I asked, pain biting into my gut. Gabriel had doubts about us? About me?

"It's not surprising given how little time you have spent together," she said, and I saw the truth in that. "How many days have you spent in each other's company?"

I cast my mind over the last couple of months. "Just a few," I admitted, feeling like a fool. How could I have allowed my common sense, the common sense that Cyrene had given up to create me, to be so completely overlooked? Of course Gabriel wasn't sure of me — we'd known each other for only a few months, ninety percent of which I'd spent in Abaddon. But my heart had managed to ignore the obvious and fall madly in love with him, building all sorts of wonderful rosy images of a future together, images that suddenly turned to dust and wafted away.

"He is in no doubt that you are his mate,"

she continued, watching as suddenly the bulk of customs people turned and walked away, leaving Gabriel and Tipene alone with one important-looking official. "No one can be in doubt of that. But it is your feelings he is unsure of."

I said nothing, just rubbed my fingers, suddenly cold.

"He does not see as I have that you have given him your heart," she said, turning back to me with yet another smile. "But he is male. We will cut him some slack for that handicap, yes?"

"Is it so obvious?" I asked, horrified that I'd been caught wearing my heart on my sleeve. Gabriel had not once mentioned the moment when I'd blurted out that I loved him. I figured he hadn't heard me, or had chosen not to acknowledge it. "Does everyone know?"

Her smile turned wry. "I did not get to see you with Kaawa, so I do not know if she saw the truth, but it is very hard to hide anything from her. She sees beyond this realm."

I remembered the odd look Kaawa had given me as we'd left her camp that morning. She hadn't said anything other than to bid us farewell, and to come back for a longer stay, but there was something in her manner that had me thinking she was holding things back.

I shook off the premonition and returned my mind to the present. I might have had a lapse in judgment in falling so quickly in love with Gabriel, but I wasn't Cyrene with her many love affairs. I wasn't ready to tell the world of my feelings, especially if Gabriel was so unsure of me that he had doubts about our relationship.

"I do not tell you this to upset you, May," Maata added, suddenly looking worried herself. "I wanted you to be prepared, so you would not upset Gabriel by a lack of enthusiasm for his home."

A note in her voice pulled me out of my dark introspection. "You love him, don't you?" I asked.

"Yes," she answered promptly, surprising me. "Not as a lover or a mate, as you do, but as a leader. He is truly an exceptional wyvern. He would die to protect the sept, and has given himself selflessly his entire lifetime to bettering our lives, to keeping the peace within the weyr. His actions may not be viewed by all in that light, but I know the truth. He was born to be wyvern, and his strength comes not from vast wealth as it does for some dragons, but from the true depths of his character. I hope you can see that and value him for what he truly possesses."

"I do," I said, watching as he shook the official's hand. It was a loaded handshake, one I hoped did not contain too many folded New Zealand dollars.

"Come along, little bird," he said as he opened the door and waited for us to file out. "We have the passport issues sorted out and can go to the cottage now. It's outside of Auckland, on the water. I think you'll like it."

"I'm sure I'll love it," I said, allowing him to take my hand, tightening my fingers around his as a sudden spurt of emotion filled me.

"Don't be so certain." He gave me a little peek at his dimples. "It's not up to Drake's standards, not even up to those of the house in London I took for the winter. It's just a modest little cottage on the beach, but it's mine. I designed it myself."

"Sounds like heaven to me."

The ride out to Manukua City didn't take long. Gabriel and his two bodyguards chatted about sept business, plans for a meeting at which I would be formally presented, and updates on various members. I listened with only part of my attention, watching as the busy Auckland streets changed to those of suburbia, which in turn morphed into a beach community. I kept a pleasant expression on my face, determined to love Gabriel's house, no matter what it was.

"Here we are," Gabriel said as the car suddenly turned into a private drive guarded by a gate. Tipene, who was driving, punched a couple of buttons on a remote, and the gate slid silently open. "My little cottage."

The car pulled up outside a pair of double doors. I looked at the expanse of sixteen-foot-tall glass doors, pale melon-colored stone, and tall fluted marble columns, and promptly socked Gabriel in the arm.

He laughed as I got out, staring with openmouthed amazement. "What do you think, little bird?"

"I think I'm going to hit you again. Little cottage, Gabriel? How many rooms are in your *little cottage?*"

"Bedrooms?" he asked, taking my hand in order to smooth out my fist. "Ten. But ours is the best. It has an unobstructed view of the water. Come in and see the house. Cyrene will love the room with the indoor pool — it's directly below our room and also has a fine view."

The interior of the house was all light, with fresh white walls, huge floor-to-ceiling windows that must take weeks to clean fully, glass skylights allowing the room to fill with sunlight, and a gorgeous curved white stone staircase that emerged from the profuse plant life that was everywhere. I remembered the dark house in London that Gabriel had rented for a short while, the one that felt so empty to me, and reflected that this house was the reason for that. This house had heart — Gabriel's heart — and I fell just as much in love with it as I did with its creator.

"What do you think?" he asked after taking me on the grand tour. Tipene and Maata had disappeared into rooms Gabriel indicated as their private domain. We left his bedroom for last, with its gigantic, mosquito-netted bed, array of electronics that would dazzle any computer geek's eyes, and breathtaking view of the water.

"I think it's heaven on earth," I said truthfully, turning to him, noting that Maata was right; he had been worried. At my words, he visibly relaxed, pulling me into a loose embrace.

"It wasn't before you came here, but I agree that now it approaches perfection."

"I'm just sorry we can't stay here long," I said, leaning into him and allowing the wonderful woodsy scent of him to sink into my bones. "Maybe Cyrene can put off

219

Neptune for a bit."

"Unfortunately, there is too much to be taken care of elsewhere to stay here," he said, rubbing his chin on the top of my head. "We must talk to the other wyverns about reforging the dragon heart."

"I know. It just seems like everything is so far away from here; it's tempting to just let it all go."

"What you need," he said, scooping me up in his arms and marching me out to the balcony that opened off the room, "is some incredibly satisfying sex with an even more incredible dragon, and I know just the man to do the job."

"Really?" I asked, getting into his suddenly playful mood. I tugged gently on one of his dreadlocks, twining it around my finger. "Would he happen to have the most amazing silver eyes that melt me with the merest look?"

"He might. He might also have every intention of giving you more pleasure than you've ever had before he takes his own," he said, setting me down on a wide chaise longue. "Stay there. Don't move."

He disappeared back into the room, and I took a moment to look around the balcony. Tall plants bordered either side of the deck, providing privacy from neighboring houses.

Only the front facing the vast sapphire ocean was unobstructed. A few sailboats dotted the coastline, but they were too far off to see what we were doing. I started to take off my shirt, but Gabriel called from inside the bedroom, "Do not undress yet, Mayling. I plan on disrobing you slowly. Just sit there and mull over the many ways I'm going to pleasure you."

"You're not going to insist that we try to do foreplay, are you?"

His head popped around the opened French door. "I promised you foreplay, and I fully intend to fulfill that promise. I am a wyvern. I have immense self-control. Just not around you, but that will change, mate; just you wait and see. I will control my seemingly insatiable desire for you and pleasure you as you deserve."

He disappeared before I could answer. "I think you're beating yourself up unnecessarily," I called to him, relaxing against the sun-warmed chaise, closing my eyes to better enjoy the thought of Gabriel, naked, and allowing me to frolic all over his delectable body.

A small fire broke out next to me. I beat it out as Gabriel answered, "That is not the point. As your mate, I am honor bound to show you certain respect. That includes giving you foreplay."

"Somehow I doubt that 'Must provide reasonable amount of foreplay' made it into the wyverns' handbook."

He leaned out of the door to grin at me. "You'd be surprised what makes it into the handbook."

"Are you naked yet?" I asked, noting that what I could see of his chest was bare. I held out my arms. "Come foreplay me, you handsome dragon, you."

"Not just yet." He withdrew back into the room. I began to wonder just exactly what it was that he was doing — not to mention why it was more important than making love to me. "Well, so far as I'm concerned, foreplay is overrated. The way you do things is perfectly all right by me."

"It's not all right by me," he answered, a loud thump punctuating the sentence, followed by a muffled oath. "Would you mind saying something lengthy?"

"Something lengthy?" I sat up and leaned over to peer into the door, astonished by the site of Gabriel blindly groping his way out of the bedroom. *Agathos daimon.* What on earth are you doing?"

"Pleasuring you," he said, waving a hand around in the air. "Say something. If I can follow your voice, I'll find you."

"Pleasuring me?"

"Well, I will be once I find you." His hand waved around in the air as he took another couple of steps forward. "Speak, mate."

"How about this: I highly approve of the fact that you are naked. No, more than highly approve, am sincerely grateful and completely enjoying the fact that you're naked. But the bowl, the eyeshade, and the peacock feather have me more than a little concerned. You haven't been hiding some deviant dragon-sex secrets from me, have you?"

He grinned again, grabbing the hand I had held out for him, edging forward until he found the small round glass table next to me. Carefully, he set down the covered bowl and the feather. "Not deviant, Mayling. Well, perhaps a little. Now I shall undress you, and then we will be able to proceed."

I watched with amusement as he groped his way over to my chest, unbuttoning my shirt. "I wouldn't be female if I didn't attribute the fact that you've had to blind yourself before touching me to a sudden, overwhelming disgust at my appearance, but knowing you, I suspect it has something to do with some perverted sense of determination to provide me with foreplay. Or are you just suddenly indulging your tactile senses?"

"The sun will never rise on the day in which I do not look at you and am overwhelmed with my incredible luck in having such a breathtaking mate, Mayling."

My toes curled at his words. "Thank you," I said, attempting to accept the compliment with more grace than I normally possessed. "But if that's the case, then why —"

"I am a visual person. If I see you sitting there, all naked and silky skinned, I will not be able to control myself. I have tried, and failed, but at least I know why I have failed. By limiting my ability to see, I will eliminate the worst part of the temptation. It will still be a struggle to exhibit control over my other senses —" His hand froze for a moment when I shifted so that my breast brushed his palm. His Adam's apple bobbed up and down for a moment. He cleared his throat and moved his hand away from my breast to pull my now-unbuttoned shirt off. "— but I think it will help."

"You are a strange man," I told him, watching as he tossed my shirt onto the floor of the balcony. Before he could reach for me again, I divested myself of my pants, shoes, and underwear.

"I am a dragon, Mayling. As the shard has shown you, we feel things differently than humans. Now for your jeans." His hand descended upon my bare belly. His fingers flexed for a moment.

"Already off," I said, leaning forward to press a kiss crookedly on his mouth. "What do you have in the bowl? Is it something sticky? Honey?"

"Better than honey," he said, clearing his throat again. I smiled to myself. Gabriel normally had an incredibly sexy voice, made up of tones that stroked my skin like velvet, but whenever he struggled to control himself, it deepened, becoming huskier, which in turned aroused me all that much more. "It's gold."

"Jewelry?" I asked, remembering how gold affects dragons. It seemed to act as both an aphrodisiac and a sort of dragonish catnip, driving them wild.

"No." He smiled and reached for the bowl, pulling off the cloth covering it. Inside was a small fan brush and a pool of goldish powder. "Gold dust. I'm going to paint you with it and lick it off. I believe that will qualify as — *oof!*"

I had a momentary image of what Gabriel was proposing when the scent of the dust reached my nose. A tidal wave of desire crashed over me, sending me forward as I shoved him backwards onto the floor, one hand grabbing the bowl, sprinkling the gold all over him. My fingers elongated, turning silver, the crimson tips biting into his sides as I gave in to the unbridled emotions that churned within me.

"Take me," I said, rubbing my body against his in a sinuous, gold-flecked dance. His entire body stiffened for a second; then I bit his shoulder and squirmed against him again, overwhelmed with the need to be joined together. "Now."

Luckily, his control wasn't as great as he thought it was, because all it took was one little bite, and in a flash, I was on my back, Gabriel looming over me, his head blotting out the sun, the eyeshade askew, leaving one silver eye uncovered. I knew the moment the scent of the gold hit him. His body tightened as if he was going to spring, and then he was there inside of me, our bodies and souls joined in a wild frenzied dance that was more beautiful than anything I'd ever beheld.

Deep, primal urges drove me on, visions flickering in my head of things I couldn't begin to understand. I moved, and he moved with me, our bodies moving in a manner that was unlike anything I'd experienced. We rushed toward a climax, driven too mad by the scent and taste of the gold to do anything else, and at the moment when I gave myself up to it, up to him, the world changed. It shifted even as I shifted, my body elongating at the same time Gabriel's did, arms and legs and tails and necks entwined with a glittering silver brilliance, a nova of passion that exploded even as a star explodes, filling the sky with its radiant light.

We fell back to the earth one silver-scaled microscopic piece at a time, our beings gently twirling around each other, as if someone had sprinkled the air with glitter. I lay strewn upon the surface, content just to be, content to know that whatever else would happen to or in my life, I could never be separated from Gabriel.

A loud knocking at the door, accompanied by muted voices, disrupted my philosophical meanderings. I was brought back to reality with a sudden jerk as Gabriel lifted me off of the floor of the balcony and carried me into his room.

"What is it?" he called, setting me down next to my bags. I grabbed the nearest one and made a run for the bathroom even as he jerked on a pair of jeans to answer the door.

My legs were weak, my hands shaking as I dug through the bag, then stepped back to rub the sudden crop of goose bumps that rose on my arms. The experience I'd just shared with Gabriel was still strong in my mind, too strong. "It wasn't me," I told the mirror that did not contain my reflection. "I'm not a dragon; I'm not."

I looked down at my gold-dusted torso and shuddered. I was being consumed by the dragon shard. I was changing, turning into a dragon, and that scared me to the tips of my toenails.

What if Gabriel preferred me as a dragon? What if he'd prefer to have a dragon mate, someone who understood his emotions, his needs, the things that drove him? How could I possibly begin to explain to him the fear that I was losing myself?

The door opened. I clutched at a piece of clothing in an attempt to cover myself, but it was just Gabriel. He marched over to a large shower and yanked the faucet so that the three showerheads burst to life. "I wish I had time to wash the gold off you in a manner that would please us both, but we do not have time, little bird."

He held open the shower door for me, following me as I entered. "What's wrong? Who was that at the door?"

"Jian." He gave me an earthy-smelling soap and a loofah, taking another for himself.

I dutifully scrubbed the gold dust off myself, my feelings conflicted — part of me wanted to shove away the sea sponge he was using and lather him up with my hands, stroking the entire length of his wet, soapy body, the other part of me shying away from the thought of another lovemaking session that would end with me losing yet another piece of myself to the dragon shard. I dragged my mind back from that subject to more important matters. "The red wyvern's bodyguard? What's he doing here?"

He tossed his sponge to the side, stepping out of the shower, grabbing a towel to briskly dry himself. "He wants our help."

"Our help with what?" I asked, hurriedly rinsing off, following Gabriel out of the shower. I accepted the towel he tossed my way, going to the door as he strode out into his bedroom, heading for a bank of closets that lined one wall.

"He wants us to rescue his mother."

A chill swept over me that had nothing to do with the balmy ocean air striking my wet flesh.

Gabriel's mouth was grim as he grabbed a shirt. "He wants us to bring Chuan Ren back from Abaddon."

Chapter Fourteen

"Are you sure this is the right road?"

Cyrene consulted the map we'd purchased in Faro before setting off west along the coastline to the small town of Sagres. "It's the only road, so it has to be the correct one."

"I just hope we don't end up lost. I don't have a lot of time to deal with this situation of yours." I slowed the car as the road shot around a hairpin curve, perched high on a rocky cliff overlooking the pounding surf. Judging by the intensity of the waves crashing into the cliff side, I wasn't surprised people came to Portugal for surfing.

Cyrene slid me a coy glance. "Are you going to tell me about that?"

"About what?" I asked, knowing perfectly well what she was talking about. I still hadn't decided what to tell her about the conversation Gabriel and I had had with Jian the previous day.

"You know perfectly well that you're hiding something from me. It's written all over your face."

"Nonsense," I said, wishing for something like the five thousandth time that I could see my reflection. "I have a perfect poker face."

"If that's the case, then you've got a full house and you're trying to make me think you've only got a pair, so spill."

I drove silently for a few minutes, trying to decide if I could trust her with the details. I'd never kept secrets from Cyrene, not big ones, and I was fairly uncomfortable with holding back information that I knew would interest her . . . and likely impact her, if she continued her fling with a certain black dragon. But I had promised to protect Gabriel and his dragons, and if that meant keeping things from my twin, then that's what I must do.

It was just all so confusing.

"It's something to do with Kostya, isn't it?" she asked, watching me avidly.

I schooled my face to the same blank expression I wore around Magoth. "Not really, no. It has to do with another dragon sept."

"Oh? Which one?"

"Red," I said reluctantly, torn with conflicting desires.

"Mayling, I'm your twin, your creator," she said, patting me on the arm. "You can trust me."

I slid her a quick glance, shifting the car into a lower gear as we tackled a long incline. "What about Kostya?"

"What about him?"

"You were pretty insistent at the *sárkány* that you were his mate. That implies you'd feel honor bound to tell him about anything related to dragon politics."

She examined a perfectly buffed and polished fingernail. "He was just as insistent that I was not his mate."

I pulled the car off the road into a narrow overlook intended for tourists, turning to face her in the small rental car. "What are you going to do about that?"

"About Kostya, you mean?"

I nodded.

She made a little face. "Nothing. He's just in denial right now, Mayling. I told you he was suffering from some emotional issues that had to do with him being held prisoner. He's confused about our relationship; that's all. Once he gets his feet back under him, he'll see that we were meant to be together."

Her words struck a sore spot. Gabriel and I belonged together — even without the

232

dragon shard prompting me to exhibit dragonish tendencies, I knew that we were fated to be together, to share our lives. Perhaps Cyrene felt the same thing about Kostya? Stranger things had happened.

"All right, then; let's say you are Kostya's mate. That doesn't give me a lot of confidence about revealing things that I'd rather not have him know right now."

The look she gave me was filled with injured dignity. "If you told me something in confidence, I would never repeat it!"

"Cy, you've blabbed just about every secret I've ever told you, including a few that weren't even true."

"Those were your own fault," she said, ruffling up just a little. "Telling me you were a lesbian just so I'd stop trying to fix you up . . . Honestly, May!"

"We've moved past that misunderstanding," I said, not wanting to open up that particular can of worms again. "What I want to know is whether or not you'll go running to Kostya with everything I tell you."

Her nose wrinkled up as she thought about that for a moment. "Probably I will."

I sighed and took the steering wheel again.

"Unless you tell me specifically not to, that is. Despite what you think, I *can* keep a secret. But I don't want to be in a position where I have to make a choice between you and Kostya. I love you, Mayling. You're my twin! But I love Kostya, too, and I don't want to have to pick one of you over the other."

"Fair enough," I said, pulling the car back onto the road, noting a sign that indicated that the small town where a local surfing competition was being held was only a few kilometers away. "What I have to say doesn't concern Kostya directly. However, I don't want you to repeat any of this to him."

"Grace of the naiads," she swore, drawing a symbol representative of water elementals over her heart.

I took a deep breath, relieved that we'd come to an understanding. Cyrene may not be the wisest or most savvy person on the earth, but I knew her heart was good, and if she swore by the grace of her kind not to tell, then she wouldn't. "You remember the red dragon named Jian?"

"The good-looking one?" She nodded. "Kostya said he was the son of the previous wyvern."

"That's him. Well, he came to see us yesterday, asking for our help."

"To overthrow that witchy wyvern? I don't blame him one bit. I didn't like her at all. But what do the silver dragons have to do with the red ones? I thought all of the septs were fairly insular."

"It's a bit more complicated than that. It concerns me being the phylactery for the dragon shard."

"Oh! Speaking of that, where is it?"

The road was particularly twisty as it followed the ragged coastline, but I chanced taking my eyes off the road for a moment to shoot a surprised look her way. "Where is the shard?"

"Yes. Is it inside you, like a tumor or something? Can you feel it? Does it hurt?"

"I believe it's inside me, yes. There's a small mark below my rib cage that wasn't there before the Lindorm Phylactery exploded. But it doesn't hurt."

"So you don't even know it's there?" She blew out a relieved breath. "That's good."

I didn't correct her. The fact that I was slowly losing myself to the dragon-heart shard would become apparent in time; until then, I wouldn't mention it.

"What do Jian and his mother have to do with the shard inside you?"

"A few months ago Aisling banished his mother, Chuan Ren, to Abaddon."

She nodded. "I heard that. That's some kind of awesome, huh?"

"Impressive, yes. Jian wants us to get her

back. Specifically, he wants me to get her back."

"You?" Her forehead wrinkled. "But you didn't cast Chuan Ren into Abaddon, Aisling did. Why isn't he asking Aisling to bring her back?"

"That's where the complicated part comes in. I guess he tried, and Drake wouldn't consider the request. It's understandable given how delicate Aisling is right now."

"I suppose, although she doesn't strike me as particularly delicate."

I grinned at her. "To be honest, I agree, but I do understand Drake not wanting her to get involved. Chuan Ren must be absolutely furious with her."

"So that's where you come in? Gabriel is doing this as a favor to Drake?"

I hesitated for a moment, using a tricky turn as cover for my silence. "Jian asked me if I could use my connection to Abaddon to locate and free his mother. In exchange, he offered us the use of the dragon-heart shard that the red wyvern holds."

"Why do you need that?" she asked, still wearing a puzzled expression.

I explained briefly about the dragon heart.

"So, the red dragons will hand over their piece, and that will give you two of the five?"

"Temporarily hand over, yes. It'll be

returned to them."

"Two isn't going to do you much good," she pointed out. "Not if you need all five shards."

"Gabriel has that worked out. Drake will loan us his piece in exchange for helping Jian."

"Why would he want to help Jian . . . ? Oh. To end the war?"

"Yes. That'll be part of the deal Chuan Ren is going to have to agree to in order to be freed. Assuming I can free her, that is."

"You're going to need Magoth for that, I bet," Cyrene said with surprising prescience. "Do you know where he is now?"

"Oddly enough, he's been keeping a low profile. Gabriel has had people watching for him, but as far as we know, Magoth and Sally are holed up in his house in Paris."

"Hmm. I'd have thought Magoth would have been raising hell by now. Ha. Hell."

I couldn't help but smile. "I'm sure he would if he could, but I think he's finding out just how limited he is without any powers."

"Is he going to be able to help you with Jian, then?" Cy asked.

"He should be able to, but whether or not he will remains to be seen." I skimmed over the horror that thought brought me. I truly did not want to think of what I'd have to do in order to get Chuan Ren released.

"That still leaves you two shards short of a complete dragon heart."

"One. The blue wyvern has a shard, as well."

"Oh. So who has the fifth one? Gabriel?"

"No." I was silent for a moment. "We think the dragon I saw in the shadow world has the fifth shard."

Her eyes widened. "Baltic, you mean?"

"Yes."

She whistled. "That's going to be a hard one to get."

"It will indeed. The hope is that the other four shards together will give us the ability to get the fifth."

"Hmm." Cyrene thought for a few minutes. "I bet that Bao is going to have a thing or two to say about all of this."

"I'm sure she will, but that's no affair of ours. Jian insists that Bao is not what she seems, and she has no right to bear the title of wyvern. We really have no reason not to believe him."

"You don't really have a reason to believe him, either, but I guess that point is moot. Oh! That's it, over there," Cyrene said, pointing to a stretch of beach and sapphire water that was glimpsed between starkly white stone buildings.

It took a few minutes to find a spot to park, so popular was the surfing event, but at last we tucked the car away in the shade of a church and walked the length of the town to the beach, where a large crowd was gathered around a couple of rickety tables. Surfboards lay glistening in the sun up and down the beach, their owners standing negligently beside them, or bent over them waxing the colorful boards with gentle caresses.

"Which one is Neptune?" I asked, allowing myself a moment to admire all the eye candy. Most of the surfers were shirtless, wearing standard knee-length cargo shorts, or brightly colored wet suits, all of them showing off physiques honed by years of swimming and surfing. There were surprisingly few women included, although the ones who were there were as buff as the men.

"I think that's him, down there," Cyrene answered after scanning the people. She pointed to the far end of the beach, where two men were emerging from the foaming surf, water glistening on their wet suits, their boards slung to their sides. A third man stood with his board balanced on his head, clearly about to go into the water.

"Which one?" I asked as we set off toward them.

"The one who looks like Neptune, of course," she said with an exasperated roll of her eyes.

The two men stopped in front of the third, shaking water from their hair as they set their boards down.

"Brah!" the dry man said to one of the two guys. "That was sick air! Epic, totally epic! It's just too bad that frickin' Grom snaked you and knocked your stick. You'd have that tail slide otherwise."

"Snakes suck," the taller and blonder of the two surfers agreed. "It was a perfect barrel, too. The big mama is fully macking some sick grinders. For a couple of groats I'd shove a tin of surf wax up that snake's . . . whoa, femmes."

"Er . . . hello," I said as the taller man noticed us. The other two men turned to look at us. "I'm sorry, this is completely random, but snakes? In the ocean?"

All three men looked at me as if I was the crazy one.

"You didn't actually mean *snake* snakes, did you?" I asked the largest of the men. He had an air of relaxed command that I took to mean he was the head of all the water elementals.

"Dude, a snake is someone who drops in out of turn."

"Not epic," the dry man said, shaking his head. "Totally."

"No, of course not," I agreed, not having the slightest clue what they were talking about, but deciding to leave the surfer lingo alone. I turned back to the large man. "Are you by any chance Neptune?"

"Name's Ned when I'm on the circuit, but you two femmes aren't heavies, are you?" the man said, flashing me a very white-toothed smile before his gaze slid over to Cyrene. His eyebrows rose a smidgen. "Dude! You must be the naiad with the dirty doppel! Tasty! But weren't you like totally owned last week?"

"I don't suppose any of you speaks actual English?" I asked.

Cyrene gripped my arm and made a half bow, half curtsy, hissing at me as she did, "May! You don't speak to Lord Neptune like that!"

"Groms," the dry man said with a little shake of his head as he headed out into the surf.

"I meant no disrespect, I assure you," I told Neptune as he hoisted up his board and started up the beach. "Maybe we'd better start all over. I'm May Northcott, and this is my twin, Cyrene. What exactly is a Grom?"

"Grommit," Neptune said, setting his board down on a blanket. "Wallace and Grommit, you know? Groms are noobs, kinda clueless. What are you two beach bunnies doing here? Yo, dude, I'm starving. Go find us some grindage?"

"On it," the other man said, and headed off to where some food vendors had set up.

Neptune cocked an eyebrow at us, clearly waiting.

"Lord Neptune," Cyrene said, making another of her odd little curtsies. "My twin and I have come to explain about the recent unpleasantness with my spring. You see, May is a wvyern's mate, and also, through a very complicated series of circumstances, bound to Magoth, the demon lord."

"Totally gnarl," Neptune said, nodding. He leaned a hip up against a wooden table that held the surfboard. "But nothing to do with your puddle."

"I can see why you would think that, but . . ." Cyrene shot me a pleading glance.

I took pity on her. "Cyrene helped me avoid banishment to the Akasha. In the process of doing that, she devoted a great deal of time to my welfare and couldn't attend to her spring as she wished."

"That so?" Neptune looked thoughtful as he eyed first me, then Cyrene. "Brah, word on the street is that you're shackled to a dragon, and that's why your puddle got barreled."

"Er . . ." Cyrene looked as confused as I felt.

I picked out the words that made sense and drew a few conclusions. "Because of my involvement with the dragons, Cyrene has been drawn into their society as well. But I can assure you that she takes her position very seriously and is totally devoted to the welfare of her spring. If you could see your way clear to reinstating her as a naiad, I'm sure you would have no reason to regret it."

"No reason," Cyrene said hastily. "No reason at all! I'm so into my spring!"

Neptune pursed his lips and unzipped his wet suit to scratch a spot on his chest while he thought it over. Cyrene clutched my hand in a grip that was almost painful.

"Sorry, brah, can't do it," he said finally. "I hate to bowl you, but there's rules, you know?"

Cyrene's lower lip quivered as she turned large, liquid blue eyes on me. "May, please," she whispered.

My heart broke for her. Oh, Cyrene was

no end of trouble, but she was my twin, and I knew how much being a naiad meant to her. "What would it take for her to prove to you that she is worthy of the position?"

Neptune grabbed a couple of cloths and started wiping down his board. "Gonna take some work, dude. Lots of work."

"Wait a minute. What sort of work?" Cyrene asked in a suspicious tone.

I pinched her and said, "She's not afraid of work and is fully ready to prove herself to you. What exactly does she need to do?"

Neptune grabbed a can of surfboard wax. "You took from the big mama. That's not cool, not cool at all. You gotta give the big mama back her own, and then we'll see."

I toyed briefly with the idea of asking for a translation but figured we'd just end up with more snakes and Grommits, and decided the less time Cyrene had to put her foot in it, the better. "We'll do that. Thank you. And . . . er . . . break a leg, or whatever it is you do out there."

The sound of his laughter trailed after us as I hauled Cyrene down the beach. She was prone to argue with me, but I had neither the patience nor the time to tolerate it. That didn't stop her, however, from unloading her opinion of both Neptune and my high-handed (as she called it) treatment on the way back to Faro.

"Go get us tickets to Rome," I said after we turned in the car to the rental agency.

She glared at me. "That's all you're going to say? Just go get tickets? May, I shouldn't have to prove myself to Neptune —"

"You're the one who messed up," I interrupted her, pulling out my cell phone. "Now you have to pay the price. So stop complaining and go get us tickets so we can see just how badly damaged the spring is, and then make some plans to clear things up so I can get back to figuring out how I'm going to spring a wyvern from Abaddon."

"Bah," she snorted, but went off to find out how quickly we could get to Rome.

"Do you need help?" Gabriel asked after I explained the situation to him. His voice was as delicious as ever, even after getting beamed all around the place by assorted satellites. Just the sound of it nestled so close to my ear sent little goose bumps of pleasure up and down my arms.

"No, I think we'll be OK. If we can't get a flight, we'll get to Lisbon and use the portal place there, although I heard it's a bit dicey. But I expect we'll find a flight. It means, however, that I won't be back in Paris until tomorrow."

"One moment," he said, and I heard

muffled voices in the background. A minute later he was back. "Maata will meet you in Rome. She can take a portal from here."

I know how little dragons liked to portal — it had something to do with the tenuous quality of portals, since objects were frequently lost during transit — but it wasn't for that reason alone that I objected. "You're not pulling a Drake on me, are you?" I asked.

"A Drake?"

"Aisling says she can't step foot out of the house without one of Drake's bodyguards accompanying her. You haven't suddenly gone into overprotective mode, have you?" I asked, smiling despite myself. "Because if you have, let me disabuse you right now of the notion that I need protection. I'm quite capable of taking care of myself."

"I have no doubt of that whatsoever, little bird," he answered, amusement rich in his voice. "Although I do have to admit that I understand more now what drives Drake into protecting his mate. But it is not a question of you being able to protect yourself. Maata is fluent in Italian, and since you said that neither you nor your twin speaks it well, I thought she might be able to help."

I bit back the response that it wouldn't

take much linguistic power to eyeball a spring, saying simply, "That seems like a lot of trouble to go to on Maata's part, but if she wants a little break from her regular bodyguard duties to hang out with us in Italy, we'd be delighted to have her. Oh, hang on, here's Cy with the tickets."

"I just hope you know what you're doing," she said, a little pout ruining her normally sunny expression. "This is the best I could get."

I glanced at the flight information and passed it along to Gabriel.

"I would come to help you myself, but I have a meeting with Bastian scheduled. Drake believes he will be wholly agreeable to giving us access to the blue shard, but I don't wish to take anything for granted."

"And you thought it was for your handsome looks and that satin voice I agreed to be your mate," I said, "when all along it was your brains."

"Indeed," he said, and I frowned. It wasn't like him not to respond to a flirtatious comment.

"Is everything all right there?" I asked. "Is there something you're not telling me?"

"I would not keep things from you, mate," he said with more formality than was the norm. "I hope your trip goes well, and that you'll be able to return soon to your guest."

"My guest?" I asked, worry starting to build inside me. "What guest?"

"She wishes to have a word with you. Maata will meet you at the airport. Be careful, May. The sea is not necessarily calm in that area of the world."

His metaphor didn't escape me any more than did the true reason he wanted a bodyguard along while we visited land that was traditionally held by the now-ousted Fiat. But the identity of my so-called guest was a mystery to me . . . at least until a familiar happy voice chirped in my ear.

"Sugar! You didn't tell me what a delicious hunk of burning love you had hidden away. He's just too, too yummy, even if he is a dragon. Since you have Magoth as well, I don't suppose you'd mind sharing, hmm?"

CHAPTER FIFTEEN

It took the full length of the train ride from Rome to Onano, the town in the north of Italy that was closest to Cyrene's spring, to get the details out of Maata as to what Sally was doing at the suite Gabriel had taken for us all in a Paris hotel.

"Before I tell you that, you have to answer me a question," she said, laughing as we claimed our seats. Cy and I sat on one side of a table between two banks of seats, with Maata across from us.

"Ooh, food! I'm famished. I'll get us some lunch," Cyrene said, catching sight of a sandwich vendor outside the train who was doing a brisk business.

"You miss the train, and you won't hear the last of it for decades," I promised her.

She rolled her eyes and hurried down the aisle to the exit.

"What was it you wanted to know?" I asked Maata, one eye on my errant twin as she pounced on the sandwich seller.

"Did you threaten Sally on the phone?"

"Threaten?" I cleared my throat and put on the face I used with Magoth. "Why would I threaten her?"

Maata's smile changed into a knowing grin. "Because she ran to Gabriel and told him he was making a big mistake, that you were definitely meant to be a demon lord's consort."

I relaxed back into my seat as Cyrene re-boarded the train, her arms full of small sandwich packages and bottles of water. "Was that before or after she propositioned him?" I joked.

"After, as a matter of fact," she said, then laughed again at the look on my face. "Oh, don't worry; you're Gabriel's mate good and proper. Dragons mate for life, you know. He couldn't leave you if he wanted to, and believe me, dalliances are the last thing on his mind."

"I don't doubt Gabriel's fidelity," I said, looking at the people as they started to blur when the train rolled out of the busy station. I had the worst urge to spill my worries out to Maata. I desperately needed reassurance that I wasn't losing myself to the dragon heart, that Gabriel wasn't bound so firmly to me not because I was meant to be his mate, but because of what was carried inside me. Passions faded; the gods knew I'd seen that often enough with Cyrene's love affairs. Who was to say that the sexual attraction that Gabriel first felt for me was now replaced by his response to the dragon-heart shard?

"Here we are. Mayling, you can stop scowling; I got you a chicken one since I know you don't eat mammals. Now, what did I miss? Did you tell Maata about threatening to cut off all of that junior demon lord's hair and glue it on backwards?"

Maata choked on the mouthful of water she'd just taken. "Is that what you threatened Sally with?" she asked me.

"Disregard anything Cyrene says about me," I said calmly, taking a chicken sandwich. "She's peeved because she's going to have to earn back her wings. So to speak."

"If you had just thrown your weight around with Neptune, he would have reinstated me instantly!" she grumbled. "Honestly, what is the point of having a twin who is consort to a demon lord and mate to a powerful wyvern if she won't help out with a few little problems?"

"A list of the little problems I've helped you with could fill a few books," I answered, giving Maata an encouraging nod. "You were going to tell us what Sally was doing there."

"She claimed Magoth told her to go bother you for a bit, saying that you and he could split her apprenticeship. Since she's done a week with him, it's evidently now your turn. Once she heard Gabriel tell me to meet you, I had a devil of a time getting out without her following."

"Did she say what Magoth was doing?" I asked, chewing slowly on my sandwich as I mulled the situation over. Sally didn't worry me much — she had little to no powers as an apprentice — but I had been concerned about the lack of information regarding Magoth during the last few days.

"Not really, no; just that he was still in Paris, working on a dozen or more different plans."

"What sort of plans?" I asked, wondering if I should worry or if Magoth's apparent quiet was a sign he was frustrated by lack of powers.

She shrugged. "She didn't say, but Gabriel wasn't worried, and I don't think you need to be concerned. Magoth is being watched and hasn't done anything to merit concern."

"Yet," I said, tapping my fingers on the water bottle.

"I agree with Maata. I think you're worrying about nothing. You said yourself he was powerless here," Cyrene pointed out.

"He may not be able to wreak the havoc and destruction that he'd like, but that doesn't mean he's completely harmless. And he's inventive. I just hope he doesn't find some source of power we haven't thought of."

Cyrene happily chatted with Maata about Sally, Magoth, and pretty much any other thought that happened to occur to her. I spent the couple of hours it took to get to Onano alternating between worry about the dragon shard and how I was going to convince Magoth to help me win Chuan Ren's release from Abaddon.

We spent the remainder of the daylight examining Cyrene's spring to evaluate just how tainted it was and what steps she'd have to take in order to give back to the "big mama," or Mother Earth in plain English.

By the time we'd helped Cyrene create a plan of action that we hoped would impress Neptune, the sun was setting, and we headed wearily into town to find a hotel and a hot meal.

"They only had two rooms," Maata reported, plopping down at the table we'd taken at an outdoor café located on the fringe of a busy town square. "I figured you'd probably want to share a room, but if you'd prefer one to yourself, May —"

"Not necessary," I interrupted, gratefully receiving the tall gin and tonic from a handsome waiter with flashing black eyes. "Cyrene and I have roomed together before. Besides, she snores. You'd never get any sleep with her."

"*I* snore!" Cyrene said, mustering an indignant look. "I like that! You could bring down a roof."

"Don't be ridiculous. Doppelgangers can't snore. Everyone knows that . . ." My voice trailed to a stop as I watched a man walk across the square. It was fully dark now, and although lights from the various shops and cafés lit up the square, the very center of it had a puddle of shadow that seemed to ripple. Couples strolled around the edges, younger people laughed and joked as they darted in and out of the shops, and dogs barked as they romped after playing children. It was a typical Italian scene, with nothing out of the ordinary, nothing to make my inner warning bells sit up and take notice, and yet, that's just what they did.

The man with dark hair pulled back in a long ponytail strode across the square, pausing in the center, where the shadows were the darkest. A woman with hair the color of a shiny penny emerged from an alley to meet him. They spoke for a few seconds; then the two proceeded on to where a small, sleek sports car was parked on a side street.

"Do you have the car keys?" I asked Maata, my eyes narrowed on the figure of the man as he got into the car.

"Yes. Do you want them?" She started to rummage in her pockets for them.

"Stay here," I ordered Cyrene, snatching up my bag. I dug out a few coins and tossed them on the table, grabbing the keys that Maata had produced.

"Where are you going?" Cyrene asked, frowning.

"I don't know. I see someone who looks familiar, and I really would like to know where he's going. Stay here. I'll call you and let you know where I am."

"Not on your life!" She grabbed her jacket and purse and followed me, Maata on her heels.

I gave them both an exasperated look. "This might be dangerous —"

"Do you have any idea what Gabriel would do if he found out I let you go off on your own?" Maata asked, giving me a stern look.

I didn't have time to argue my ability to handle myself. The car was already driving away from us, out into the darkness. I simply bolted for the rental car, calling back, "I'll drive; you two watch for the blue Alfa Romeo."

"You're a doppelganger — you probably have better night vision than me," Maata answered as we reached the car. "I'll drive; you act as navigator."

"Smart thinking." I tossed her the keys and got into the passenger seat.

"I'll help!" Cyrene said, and threw herself into the backseat just as Maata gunned the engine and shot off after our target.

It took my fullest concentration to follow the car as it wound in and out of the twisty streets of town, but at last we left the city behind and headed southeast on a highway.

"Who is this man you want so badly to follow?" Maata asked in a quiet voice as Cyrene answered a call from one of her concerned sister naiads.

I glanced over my shoulder. Cyrene was busy retelling our meeting with Neptune and probably wasn't paying much attention. "I think it's the same man who followed me into the shadow world at the hotel in Paris."

"What?" Maata shrieked.

The car spun around as she jammed on

the brakes, jerking the steering wheel to keep us from going into oncoming traffic. Cyrene cried out as she was bounced around the backseat, ending up on the floor. Thankfully, the cars behind us were at a distance enough to allow them to swerve around us, horns blaring as they made gestures that left us in little doubt as to their opinion of Maata's driving.

"What in the name of the seven seas is wrong with you?" Cyrene asked, climbing off the floor. "You could have broken my cell phone! As it is, I probably hung up on Thalassa, and she's the head of the naiads!"

Maata's eyes were not nearly as bright as Gabriel's, but they glittered dangerously at me now. "No," she said.

"We have to," I said, gesturing toward the distant taillights as they disappeared into the night.

"We are *not* going after Baltic."

"You don't know it's him," I argued, frustrated at her refusal.

"Baltic!" Cyrene gasped. "The dead guy?"

Maata's eyes glowed in the darkness. "Gabriel would kill me if he knew I helped you confront Baltic."

"No, he wouldn't," I said, letting her see the resolution in my eyes. "He wouldn't be happy, but he wouldn't *kill* you. He's not that sort of man."

Her lips thinned for a moment. "He wouldn't physically harm me, no. But his disappointment in me would shame me to death. I cannot do this, May. Do not ask me to."

"Fine," I said, getting out of the car and hurrying over to her side, ignoring the wrath of the car occupants coming up behind us. "Move over. I'll drive. Gabriel can be as pissed at me as he likes — I'm not letting this guy get away from me again."

Maata was going to refuse, but I didn't give her a chance. She might be several inches taller and several pounds heavier than me, but I simply dropped my shoulder and shoved her over into the passenger seat, quickly getting the car back onto the highway.

"Cyrene, check the map," I said, flipping on the overhead light and clamping my foot down on the accelerator in order to catch up. "See if there are any major towns coming up."

"Not immediately, but Santa Cristina is about seven kilometers from here." She looked up, a happy smile on her face. "That's on a lake that's fed by my spring. I can pop over and detoxify it quickly, and take care of that item on my list. Oh! I should call Thalassa back."

Maata made an almost inaudible intake of breath at Cyrene's words, but all my senses were on red alert as I wove in and out of traffic, my eyes searching the blackness ahead for a pair of familiar taillights.

I shot her a quick look, but her face was impassive. "What's in Santa Cristina?" I asked.

She hesitated for the count of ten. "That is where Fiat Blu has his home."

"Oh, really? How *very* interesting." My mind sorted through the pertinent facts as the car raced through the night. I hoped the police weren't overly vigilant, since there was no way I was going to stop for anything short of nuclear war. What was Baltic — assuming the mysterious dragon really was him — doing in Fiat's territory? And if it was him, how on earth had he come back from the dead?

Before I had long to mull over those questions, the exit to Santa Cristina was upon us . . . with no sign of the sports car.

"What do we think — should we chance it that he got off at this exit, or keep on the highway and try to catch up with him?" I asked as I swerved onto the shoulder to go around a slow car that insisted on straddling two lanes.

"Get off, get off!" Cyrene cried as she pulled herself up from where she'd been once again flung onto the floor. "I'm going to be one big bruise at this rate!"

"I think it's a coincidence that's hard to overlook," Maata said.

I agreed, and jerked the car off the exit at the last minute, scattering apologies as Cyrene squawked.

CHAPTER SIXTEEN

"Do you know the way to Fiat's house?" I asked Maata as we careened around a corner, zipping around the outskirts of the town.

"I've never been there, no. But I know it looks over the lake and has an extensive underground structure."

"Where there's a lake and underground structures, there are tunnels and grottoes," my twin said, straightening her clothing.

"I'm inclined to think the back way is easier to get into," I agreed, pulling up to a stop at a gas station. "Let's see if we can get an address for Fiat; then we'll tackle him from the lake side."

Fifty euros later, we were on our way around to the far side of the lake, where the man Maata had bribed into talking had said the very wealthy Signor Blu lived. We stopped before we got to the house, leaving the car pulled off into a nearby cul-de-sac, then carefully picked our way through a large house's exquisitely manicured lawn to reach the lakeside.

"See anything that says 'secret entrance to subterranean passage'?" I asked Cyrene as she stood at the water's edge. My voice was hushed, since it was early evening and conceivably residents might pop outside for a breath of fresh air. And since the area around the lake was populated with very expensive homes, security systems were sure to be bountiful.

"Not a thing." Cyrene frowned down at the water. "I can feel an underground stream, though. Not the feed that comes from my spring — that's up north. This is something different, running deeper. And it's tainted, too. Oh, goddess, what have I done to this poor lake?"

"Now is not the time to suffer regrets; now is the time to find the tunnel or whatever it is to get us into the bowels of Fiat's house," I murmured, tugging her along the shoreline.

"Before we go any farther, why don't I slip up to the house and see if the sports car is there?" Maata asked in a soft voice. "If it's not, there's no sense in spending time trying to get in."

"Smart thinking," Cyrene said, giving me

a quelling look. "Why didn't you think of that, Mayling?"

"I did. I just figured it would be worthwhile to get a peek at Fiat's house regardless of whether the supposed Baltic is there or not."

"Really? Why?" Cy asked as Maata melted into the night.

I clutched Cy's arm and carefully skirted around a lit dock. "Because Aisling said that someone who had Baltic's books was living in Fiat's basement. Kind of makes you wonder, hmm?"

"Very suspicious," she agreed.

It took us about twenty-five minutes to find what we were looking for. Maata had returned to report that she could see no cars whatsoever outside of Fiat's house, which could mean anything, or nothing.

"Here," Cyrene said, pointing down at the earth. "It's here. There's an input to a cavern directly below us. I can feel the flow of the stream."

"I don't see anything," I said, looking around. We were at the edge of Fiat's property, right up against a tall hedge that marked the boundary between his yard and that of his neighbor. "Where is it?"

"Right here, below us." Cyrene made an impatient noise as Maata and I peered into the hedge. "No, in the water below us."

"An underground entrance? Gotcha," I said, slipping off my leather jacket and tucking it away in the hedge. "Very clever of Fiat. The water's bound to be cold, but we should be able to handle a quick dip. You lead, Cy, and we'll follow."

Cyrene shed her coat and hat, wading into the water with a sharp exclamation. "Chilly!"

"We'll warm up as soon as we're out of the water," I told her, about to follow when Maata grasped my arm.

"May . . ."

"Hmm?" I turned back to look at her. Her face was troubled as she watched Cyrene dive into the cold water of the lake.

"I . . . there's something you should know about silver dragons."

"You can't swim?" I asked, making a wild guess.

"No. We don't like water. It's not our element."

"Cy!" I called out softly.

Cyrene's head popped up out of the water, making her look like a blue-eyed seal. "What's the holdup?"

"How far under is the entrance?"

"About fifteen feet. You can hold your breath easily."

"If you held on to me, do you think you'd be able to hold your breath long enough for us to make it through?" I asked Maata, not sure at all how long dragons could go without oxygen. Cyrene was practically a water breather, she could go so long without it, and I had inherited some of that ability.

"It's not a matter of holding my breath," Maata answered, looking worried. "It's the fact that it's water."

"I know you don't like to play in water because your element is earth, but does that mean you can't get near it at all?" Gabriel didn't seem to mind the shower we'd taken together, although I noticed he didn't linger at all in it as I might have done.

"No," she admitted, but she watched the water warily as if she expected it to reach up and strike her. "We bathe and such."

"Then you can do this," I said, turning my back to her. "Grab hold of my belt with one hand, and follow as close as you can. If you get into trouble, give me a yank and I'll help you out."

"May —" she said, resisting as I started for the lake.

"Either you come with us, or you stay here," I said, not really wanting to leave her behind. I didn't doubt that I could handle any situation I came up against, but there was definitely strength in numbers, and only a fool would go charging into an unknown situation alone.

She muttered something that looked like a prayer and touched the silver necklace bearing the sept emblem that she always wore.

"I won't let anything happen to you," I said, pulling her into the lake. "I promise."

She grimaced, fighting me every step. "I'm the one who's supposed to be protecting you."

Cyrene watched silently, treading water about ten feet offshore, as I alternately coaxed, pulled, and ultimately threatened Maata into the water. I thought she was going to come unglued when I had to force her head under the water so we could dive. She started struggling with me and probably would have done a good job of drowning me if Cyrene hadn't come up from behind and grabbed her neck, putting enough pressure on Maata's carotid artery to effectively knock her out. I slapped my hand over Maata's mouth and grabbed the back of her shirt, while Cyrene did the same to her nose. We took deep breaths and dived down into the murky darkness of the lake, hauling Maata with us.

She started coming to just before we

surfaced, damned near climbing my body in order to escape the water. By the time I hauled myself and her out onto a rocky outcropping, I was exhausted and bruised from the struggle with her.

"Sorry," Maata gasped, crawling backwards to get her legs out of the water. "I tried; I really tried."

"Not your fault," I said, catching my breath. "I'm just glad I took Cyrene with me to a martial arts class a couple of decades ago."

"I was top in the class at the sleeper hold," she said proudly, flipping on a small flashlight, the light from it flickering around our little cave.

And it was a little cave, with a low ceiling that was supported by wooden struts that looked like they'd seen better days. A little twinge of claustrophobia gripped me as I got to my feet and did my best to wring out my clothes. The air was cold enough to make me shiver, but I put my discomfort out of my mind as I looked around.

"There's the stream," Cyrene said, flashing the light on a small stream that had cut into the earth to empty out into the lake. A narrow ledge ran alongside it, providing a passageway that dissolved into blackness.

Maata lifted her head and smelled the air.

It was musty and smelled of damp earth. "Dragons have been here."

"Recently?" I asked, looking for footprints in the damp earth next to the stream. There were none.

"No. But I feel it. They are nearby."

Cyrene pointed the light up the passageway. It didn't penetrate the darkness very far. "Er . . . you go first," she said, shoving the flashlight into my hands.

"Chicken," I murmured, scooting past her to take the lead.

"You're the one with all the deadly skills," she pointed out, taking up the tail as Maata marched behind me.

We saw nothing more disturbing than rats and a few scattered animal bones before we came to a sharp corner. The stream disappeared into a culvert, the narrow ledge broadening to a more walkable pathway. I stopped, examining something that flashed overhead. "Someone has strung electric lights here. Should we chance turning them on?"

"Oh, yes, please," Cyrene said, rubbing her arms against the chill air. "Anything is better than walking in the dark."

"Better not," Maata said. "Just in case someone is down here."

"She has a point," I said, and continued

up the path until we came to a point where the passage divided. "Great. Left or right?"

Maata smelled the air in both passages and shrugged. "No idea."

"Cy?" I asked.

She shook her head. "The water is deep in the earth here. That's all I can tell you."

I tossed a mental coin and headed up the right path. "We can always turn around and come back if we have to."

"Assuming we can find our way back," Cyrene said in a morbid voice.

"Stop being so pessimistic. It hasn't been bad so far, and there are lights we can turn on if the batteries die . . . oh." Our passageway came to an abrupt end in the form of a pile of debris. "I guess we go back the other way."

I had turned around and taken a step back the way we came when Maata stopped me. "We should go this way."

"Why?"

She stood stock still for a few seconds. "I sense anger. Intense anger."

"You think someone is near us?" I asked in a whisper, unable to keep from glancing around. There was nothing to see but rocks, dirt, and broken wood from where the supporting struts had splintered.

"Yes."

I flashed the meager light on the obstruction. "That's all well and fine, but we'll have to take the other passage. We can't get through this mess."

Maata's teeth flashed in the dim light. She patted a bit of rock emerging from the debris. "I may not be good in underwater adventuring, but this is the earth. It knows me and will heed my wishes. Stand back, the pair of you. I'll ask the earth to allow us to pass."

To my amazement, she did as she promised. Cyrene and I watched as she managed to clear a hole at the top of the debris pile seemingly effortlessly, just as if the earth was obliging her.

"It's too bad you're a dragon," Cyrene said admiringly as Maata stepped back and dusted off her hands. "You'd have made a great elemental being."

"Some say the first dragon sprang from an elemental being, which is why all dragons have an affinity for one element. I think we can get through that opening if we're careful."

I eyed the hole she'd made at the top of the debris, feeling more than a little bit claustrophobic, but told myself if I could subject Maata to the horrors of water, I could survive skinnying through a small hole deep in the earth.

We made it through unscathed, and continued our careful ascent up the passageway when it became obvious that we were approaching a lit area. I shadowed and crept ahead of Maata and Cyrene, pausing as the passageway made a sharp turn.

Before me was a door, partially opened, and a large collection of crates. I made my silent way around them and peered through the door into a bedroom.

Voices, indistinguishable in gender and identity, were audible through the closed door opposite.

"What is it?" Cyrene asked in a whisper, trying to see around me. "Is that a bed?"

"Yes. Stay here. I'm going to see who's in the room beyond," I answered, gesturing the two of them back.

Maata made a noise of distress.

"No one will see me," I reassured her and, being careful not to disturb a couple more crates placed in front of the opened door, tiptoed my way across the bedroom. Carefully I cracked the door open just enough to see out.

All I could see was the edge of a wall, and the entrance to a larger room that evidently served as a living room. A man leaned negligently against the wall, his back toward me, but the long brown ponytail stirred memories.

Blue flashed as another man crossed the room, his hands gesturing as he spoke. "—be so unrealistic? What you ask is not possible at all. I will not put my sept in jeopardy by allowing it."

A woman's voice answered. "Your sept, such as it is, is in ruins. The situation has changed, and we must change with it. With the silver dragons possessing a shard — and surely they will be given access to the green sept's shard — we must gather together the remainder."

"Who is it?" Cyrene asked in an almost silent whisper. Both she and Maata had crept up behind me, Cyrene kneeling in order to peer through the crack in the door, while Maata, a good foot taller than me, simply looked over my head.

"Fiat, the man who may or may not be Baltic, and some woman, I don't know . . . *agathos daimon,*" I swore as the woman marched over to stand toe to toe with Fiat. "It's Bao."

"You are allowing your greed for the dragon heart to override the reality of the situation," Fiat answered, his eyes glittering wickedly. "That is a mistake your predecessor did not make."

"Chuan Ren is not pertinent to this discussion," Bao said dismissively, turning away from Fiat and moving out of my range of vision. "*I* rule the red dragons now, and they will follow *my* commands. If you wish for our aid in restoring your sept to you, then you will release the Marcella Phylactery and cease wasting my time."

"And place myself in a weaker position than I currently occupy?" Fiat shook his head. "I see little sense in that."

"You see little because you are short-sighted and ignorant," Bao snapped at him.

Fiat jerked as if he was holding himself back from striking her, forcibly relaxing his hands as he tried for a lazy smile. He raised an eyebrow at the mysterious man who still leaned casually against the wall, calmly observing the scene. "And what of you, my old friend? What do you say to this change in plans the red wyvern demands of us?"

"I have never sought the dragon heart, not even when it was within my grasp," the man answered slowly, his voice deep and slightly roughened, as if he wasn't used to speaking. "So long as my own plans are not affected, then I have no opinion on the subject."

Annoyance flashed in Fiat's eyes. "Such an attitude is admirable, but lacking in foresight. Your plans may well be affected should the red wyvern achieve her goal and reassemble the heart."

The dark-haired man shrugged. "It remains to be seen whether or not the heart wishes to be used."

"Bah," Fiat snorted. "The heart is there to be used. It has no will of its own. You have lived too long in the past, my friend. Times have changed, and with them, so have the dragonkin. We no longer cling to superstitious beliefs."

"Yes," the man agreed in a mild voice, but there was an undertone that sent a little skitter of fear down my back. "Time has changed."

"But you remain steadfast, eh?" Fiat asked, his voice and posture aggressive. "That will not do. You must make a stand, right here and now. Will you support the red wyvern's plan or our original one?"

"It matters not to me," he answered, waving a languid hand at Fiat as he straightened up. "Give her the shard, or do not. But think twice about summoning me again without due cause. I may be antiquated in your eyes, but I do not suffer fools gladly."

At that moment the same copper-haired woman who had been in the square appeared at the far doorway. She glanced around the room quickly, causing Maata,

Cyrene, and me to freeze, but apparently she did not notice our door was ever so slightly ajar. Her gaze settled on the mysterious man, and it was to him that she spoke.

"I have made the arrangements. We should leave soon, though."

"This is finished; we leave now," he answered, strolling past a silently fuming Fiat, pausing to eye the blue wyvern for a moment. "You aided me when I sought succor, and it is for that reason I will offer you a piece of advice: the natural flow of power should always be to a wyvern, never away."

Fiat said nothing but watched as the man and woman left the room, leaving him alone with the red wyvern.

"He is an old one, too old," Bao said with a curl of her lip. "He does not understand the power there is to be had in adapting."

"He is steadfast in all things," Fiat agreed, wandering over to stand just barely in view, in front of a marble fireplace. Over the mantelpiece a pair of authentic-looking swords hung, crossed in the traditional manner of weapon enthusiasts. Fiat touched one of the swords, adding in a thoughtful tone, "But much of that comes from experience, and if there's one thing I've learned over time, it's to never underestimate experience."

"It is not advice that will regain your position in the weyr," she responded with acid frankness.

"Perhaps not, but I have found a nugget of gold in that advice."

"Power flows to the wyvern, not away," she said in a mocking voice. "How . . . mundane."

"Oh, it's not what he said that I find valuable," Fiat answered, his lips curled in a friendly smile as he tidied a small vase on the mantelpiece. "It's the memory of when I first heard it that has provided me with a resolution to the current problem."

"Enough talk," Bao said, boredom evident in her voice. "I grow weary of this."

"Then let me tell you a little story, something that will relieve the tedium of your mind," Fiat said, turning to face her. "Once upon a time, as the mortals so dearly love to say, there lived a wyvern by the name of Baltic. He was a peaceful man, but forced into war by the stupidity and greed of others, dragons who wanted to see his sept disbanded. One day he found his friends departed, his sept all but eliminated, and his very own heir determined to see him dead."

"I have no time for this," Bao said, but was interrupted before she could continue.

"With death and the destruction of every-thing he worked so hard for staring him in the face, Baltic did the only thing he could do."

"Die," Bao said. "At the hands of his heir. Baltic was not a brilliant wyvern any more than this is a brilliant anecdote, although perhaps, given your situation, it is apropos."

"More so than you can possibly imagine," Fiat said with a smile that chilled my blood.

Bao snorted again and started to say something, but her words were cut short when Fiat, moving so fast he was just a blur, snatched the sword from behind him and leaped out of view, toward Bao.

There was a horrible sucking noise, fol-lowed by a wet gurgle, and a thump as something heavy hit the floor.

Fiat backed into view again, wiping a now bloodied blade on a piece of cloth. "As my good friend says, power flows to the wy-vern, not away from him."

He smiled contentedly as he replaced the sword on the wall.

CHAPTER SEVENTEEN

I clapped a hand over Cyrene's mouth even before she could draw breath to scream.

"Don't make a sound," I whispered, my mouth close to her ear.

Her eyes widened, and she struggled as if she was going to pull away from me and scream her lungs out.

"There is a madman with a very lethal sword just a few feet away," I pointed out.

She stopped struggling and nodded. I released her and reapplied my eye to the narrow space in the doorway.

Fiat stood at the opened door opposite, calling to someone. A couple of his bodyguards and two others trooped into the room.

"Remove that," he said nonchalantly, waving toward the area where Bao had stood.

The stark expressions of disbelief on his men's faces had to match the one I wore; they certainly mirrored Cyrene's.

"What are you waiting for?" Fiat demanded, raising his voice as his dragons just stood there, clearly too astounded to do anything. "I want that removed, and this place cleaned up. There is much I must attend to, and little time in which to ensure there will be no trouble from the red dragons."

One of the bodyguards grabbed a blanket that was draped over a chair and moved out of view. He returned hauling what I could only assume was Bao's body, thankfully covered with the blanket. Another man followed with another object, also wrapped.

"Clean up the blood," Fiat barked, waving an authoritative hand. "And remove all signs that she was here. Stephano, go upstairs and take care of her guards."

A handsome blond man lifted his eyebrows in silent question.

Fiat growled, "Just get rid of them. I won't have them interfering."

Stephano hesitated for a moment, but eventually nodded and left. I closed the door carefully, my heart beating wildly as I turned to look at a shaken Cyrene. Maata stood with an impassive look on her face, but her eyes were bright with emotion.

"We have to get out of here," I told them softly. "I really do not want Fiat to know we're here, or what we've seen."

"We will go out the way we came in," Maata agreed.

She waited until Cyrene and I hurried through the door to the tunnel before following us.

"That means we'll have to go back out through the lake," I pointed out, flipping on the tiny flashlight.

She grimaced. "It can't be helped. We must report this news to Gabriel."

Our trip out of the depths of Fiat's tunnels was fraught with tension, but no real danger. It was a bit of a battle to get Maata out, since she refused when Cyrene offered to deck her, but in the end we managed by dint of yet another sleeper hold.

Maata and I both ended up swallowing water in the struggle to get her out, however, and I swore, as I crawled onto the banks of the lake and collapsed, hacking and wheezing as I tried to replace the water in my lungs with air, that I heard her mutter something about never again accepting watchdog duty.

I had to admit I didn't blame her.

Gabriel, however, had another opinion, one that was made all too clear when, several hours later, we straggled into the Paris suite.

"You did *what?*" he asked Maata as she stood before him, his lovely smooth voice going a bit gravelly around the edges. His fingers flexed, a sign that I was coming to know also meant he was upset.

"You can yell all you want. I'm going to find Kostya," Cyrene said, dark smudges beneath her eyes. She didn't even say good-bye, just turned around and walked out of the room.

"May wished to follow the man she thought was Baltic, so we did. I did not leave her side at any time, and we were in no actual danger —" I heard Maata say as I went to the bedroom to drop off my over-night bag, but she was interrupted when Gabriel growled out a word I didn't recognize.

Maata's face, when I emerged from the bedroom, had adopted a stony look that spoke volumes. "I'm sorry, Gabriel. I thought —"

"Well, I'm not sorry, not one little bit," I said, stopping her before she could apologize further.

Tipene sat at a table beyond, silently tapping away at a laptop, but glancing between his wyvern and fellow bodyguard.

"Little bird," Gabriel started to say, but I held up a hand.

"Don't even think of telling me this is none of my business. Maata didn't want me to go after the mysterious dragon, but I weighed the options and decided that the chance to find out who he was made it worth the risk. So if you want to vent your spleen on someone, do it on me and not her."

Gabriel looked for a moment like he was going to explode, but suddenly relaxed and managed a wry smile. "Drake told me you were going to drive me insane. I thought he was basing his opinion on the fact that Aisling often puts him in that state of mind, but now I begin to see the true wisdom of his words."

"Except you are much more flexible and not nearly so stodgy as Drake is." I answered him with a smile of my own, drawn as if by magnetism across the room until I stood in front of him. I put my hands on his chest, stroking the soft material of his shirt, my fingers leaving little trails of fire. "Which means that once you realize that we were in no danger at all, you will stop feeling the need to do the protective male thing, and will sit down and listen to what we have to say. Am I right?"

"Grrr," he said, his fingers still flexing.

"Am I right?" I cooed, rubbing my nose

against his and biting his lower lip.

"If you're going to attempt to seduce me into a good mood, it'll take quite a bit more effort than that," he answered, his eyes lighting with renewed interest.

Inside me, love, lust, desire, need . . . a whole swirling mass of emotion flared to immediate life, powered by the dragon shard.

I stepped back, dropping my hands, not wanting to lose any more of myself. "Perhaps later. We have some important news to tell you, and I really don't think it can wait."

A curious look passed over his face but was gone before I could try to figure it out. "I have news for you as well, but by all means, tell me about the dragon you followed."

Maata murmured a few words and slipped out to change her clothes.

"She's been through a lot, you know," I told Gabriel as he led me over to a couch. "The only way we could get into Fiat's underground area was via the lake."

He refrained from shuddering, but I suspected it was a close thing.

"We'll skip over the part detailing how we got her through to the tunnel's entrance," I said, smiling as she emerged from her room, pulling on a dark sweater.

She made a face and took up a second laptop, sitting next to Tipene at the table.

I went over our actions that led us to the underground chambers, reporting most of the conversation between Fiat and the other dragons.

"You saw the man fully this time?" Gabriel asked.

"The dark-haired one? Not his face. He had his back to me in the room underground, and when we saw him earlier, in the square, he was partially in shadows."

"Interesting. Describe him to me," Gabriel said, one hand resting on my knee as he closed his eyes in thought.

I went over a description of the man, pausing as something occurred to me. "Something doesn't mesh. I think I'm wrong. He can't be Baltic."

One of Gabriel's eyes opened to consider me. "Why not?"

I sorted over the conversation again, picking out pertinent points. "Fiat made the comment to Bao about hearing the power-flowing-to-wyverns advice before, from Baltic. If the man was Baltic, then why would he say that?"

Gabriel shrugged, his fingers gently stroking my knee. I fought hard to stifle the fire that wanted to burst into being within me.

"He also called him old friend, and the dragon made reference to Fiat providing him with succor. That fits with what Drake found a few months ago, when he and Aisling made an attack on Fiat's lair."

"That doesn't explain how Baltic could be, period, given that Kostya swears he killed him."

"No, it doesn't." Gabriel looked thoughtful for a few minutes. I was about to broach the most important bit of news when he said, "Tell me about the female who was with him."

"The redhead?" I frowned, trying to pull together my memories. "I don't know what there is to tell about her. She looked perfectly normal, a little on the tall side, with coppery red hair and a slightly German accent. And she was a dragon."

"No," Maata said, looking up from her laptop.

"No what?" Gabriel asked her.

"No, she was not a dragon."

I looked at her in surprise. "Are you sure? She felt to me like a dragon."

"She was not a dragon. She had dragon blood, yes, but she was not a dragon," Maata insisted.

"Mixed heritage, you mean?" I asked, looking back at Gabriel. "But isn't that the definition of a wyvern?"

"Not necessarily," he answered. "A wyvern must have one human parent and one dragon parent."

"I don't see the difference."

"The woman with the dark-haired one was not human," Maata said, looking rather cryptically at Gabriel.

"Oh, I understand now. You mean she might have a dragon father and a nonhuman mother, say like a sylph or something?"

Maata nodded.

"You seem really interested in her," I said, eyeing the man at my side. "Should I work up a jealous fit or just go invest in a case of copper hair dye?"

His dimples flashed for a moment. "Neither. If I am interested, it is simply because of what the woman is not."

"Meaning she wasn't a wyvern's mate named Ysolde?" I asked, wondering whether he'd been thinking about that, as I had.

He nodded. "This female, whoever she is, was not Ysolde. Which I admit makes your case for the dragon not being Baltic a bit stronger."

"Because Ysolde was his mate, and if she died, then he'd be dead, too? I agree." I twined my fingers through his, momentarily comforted by the contact before the dragon shard decided I needed more.

I stood up and went to the window to look out on a rainy Paris.

"Ysolde was believed to have been Constantine Norka's mate, not Baltic's," Gabriel said in a neutral tone.

I leaned against the window and cocked an eyebrow at him. "That sounds like you're not sure she was."

"I do not know for certain either way — I am simply stating the facts as they are known. Regardless of the female's identity, your description of the conversation increases my desire to meet this mysterious dragon."

I glanced at Maata. She watched me with close attention, clearly leaving it to me to tell Gabriel of the important happening.

"There's more," I said. "Right after whoever-he-is left, Fiat and Bao had a few words."

"That doesn't surprise me," Gabriel said. "Fiat has always been subject to volatile emotions, and he seems especially unstable now."

I took a deep breath. "More than you imagine. He beheaded Bao."

To my complete and utter surprise, he didn't leap up or exclaim in shock. Instead he nodded. "I expected something of that sort."

"You expected it?" I asked. "Why?"

"It relates to my news," he said, rising to take my hands in his. "Two hours before you landed in Paris, Fiat sent a message to the weyr announcing that he had challenged and defeated Bao for control of the red sept."

"He did no such thing. He murdered her, pure and simple," I said, outraged. "There was no challenge language whatsoever — he just snatched a sword from the wall and lopped off her head. Or at least we assume that's what he did; fortunately, his men covered up the two separate parts of her that they hauled off."

"He has clearly overstepped the bounds of weyr laws and must be dealt with immediately." Gabriel looked past me, sightlessly gazing out of the window. "The problem is —"

"May! You're back! Oh, I'm so happy to see you again!"

Gabriel froze at the bright, sickeningly chirpy voice, followed by the person of Sally.

She hurried into the room, clad in some sort of frilly pink and lavender capri pant set, her face beaming with joy as she stopped in front of me, kissing the air millimeters away from my cheeks.

"Hello, Sally," I said slowly. "I see you're still here."

"She says she can't leave," Gabriel said in a voice completely lacking in expression. I assumed it was his way of being polite.

She giggled, shooting him a flirtatious look. "May, there's so much we have to talk about! That silly Magoth needed some me time — you know how men are, always thinking the world revolves around them when it's clearly we women who run things — anyway, he sent me here to learn all the ins and outs of consorting, not that I really need to do so because as you well know, I'm destined for greater things than a lowly position like the one you have. Hello again, Gabriel. You are looking especially handsome."

The hair on the back of my neck rose at the way she positively purred his name.

"More handsome than half an hour ago, when you told him the same thing?" Tipene asked with studied nonchalance as he continued to tap away at his laptop.

Sally ignored him.

"Sally," I said, smiling as pleasantly as I could. "Do you remember what I told you on the phone?"

Her seductive little smile at Gabriel faded

as she eyed me instead. "I do, and sugar, we need to have a little talk about that. While I applaud the style of your threat — the gluing hair on backwards part was particularly inventive, and bows made of entrails are always suitable at a torture session — I do have to withdraw a few points for lack of follow-through. Everyone knows a threat is really only intimidating if the threatener has the ability to actually conduct the action upon the threatenee, and you are so clearly not the sort of person who carries a disemboweling knife upon herself . . . oh."

Sally made a little expression of unhappiness as I pulled the dagger out of its sheath at my ankle.

"I see I was mistaken," she said, taking a step away from Gabriel.

"Have I mentioned how adorable you are when you're jealous?" the latter asked me, his eyes dancing with laughter.

"It's a mistake I would urge you to not make again," I told Sally pleasantly. "Forgive me for being blunt, but it's been a long twenty-four hours. What exactly would it take to get you to leave?"

"Well!" she said, her nostrils flaring in offense. She slid a glance along to Gabriel. "You see? This is what I was speaking of. She's clearly much more suitable as dear

Magoth's consort, not that he has any idea of May's true character, the poor, misguided fool."

I blinked in surprise. While Sally might be an unconventional candidate for demon lord, she had thus far maintained an attitude of respect for Magoth. "Did you just call Magoth a fool?"

"Did I? I wouldn't know; I'm too busy being hurt by your extreme lack of any and all social graces. But it does not take a leviathan to hit me over the head." She lifted her chin and tried for a quelling glare down her nose at me. "It is clear to me that you do not wish for my company at this time. Naturally, I will not stay where I am not wanted, even though my removal will clearly put you in violation of your role as consort, and thus will mean your imminent demise. But that concerns me not. I will go pack my things and leave as soon as I can."

Gabriel stopped her, not that she was trying very hard to leave. "What do you mean it will mean May's imminent demise?"

"And how, exactly, would asking you to leave be violating my consorthood?" I asked.

She issued an injured sniff. "If you had taken the time to read the pertinent section of the Doctrine of Unending Conscious, you'd know that consorts to demon lords are bound to follow the laws set down in the doctrine exactly, and that any violations would leave you in contempt of the very legal and binding contract you agreed to when you became Magoth's consort."

"I've read the Doctrine, and I don't remember seeing anything about contempt," I said slowly, poking through the memories of all the important points of the set of laws that govern Abaddon.

"Then either you have an extremely poor memory, or you simply didn't take in the full meaning of the Doctrine, because it's all there: the laws that you agreed to, and the punishments that will be meted out should you be found in violation, which, in the matter of consorts, means immediate and unconditional loss of status." She smiled, a ghastly smile, one that reaffirmed my belief that she would be well suited to the role of demon lord. "Loss of status is bound to mean your utter and complete destruction, in this and all other plains of existence."

Gabriel frowned at me. "May, you did not tell me about this."

"That's because there's nothing at all about a consort being destroyed in the Doctrine," I objected, horror growing inside me. "I swear I read the Doctrine the whole way through, Gabriel, and there was nothing there about a consort risking the loss of her existence."

"It's not in the Doctrine per se," Sally said as she examined a pale pink fingernail.

"It's not? Then why —"

"It's in one of the codicils," she said, interrupting me. Although her expression was still one of haughty disdain, there was a marked sense of enjoyment that even I could feel. "Surely you read the volume of codicils?"

I looked at Gabriel. He looked back at me, his face passive. I was about to explain to him that I didn't know there was such a thing as codicils to the Doctrine when the dragon shard decided that if I was going to be this near Gabriel, I should stop wasting time and get on with the business of mating.

Desire crashed over me in a tidal wave that left me breathless, and filled only with a deep, desperate need for Gabriel. I wrapped my arms around myself to keep from flinging them around him, struggling to calm my suddenly wildly beating heart. I closed my eyes, focused on the inner war that raged between the dragon shard and myself, determined to beat it once and for all. I was not going to give in to it. I would have Gabriel on my terms, and no other.

"May?" I heard him ask. "Are you ill?"

His voice rubbed along my skin like silk, causing me to shiver with arousal. I opened my eyes, fully intending to tell him that I was just suffering from exhaustion, but Gabriel, drat his sensitive dragon self, instantly read the emotions that roiled around inside me.

"Little bird," he said softly, his nearness leaving me trembling with a desperate, overwhelming, unending wanting that consumed everything I was. He took a step toward me, his eyes flashing with silver fire as he answered the silent call my body made.

The wall behind me started smoking. I squelched the fire before it could burn it, still fighting to control the emotions that swamped me. Gabriel took another step forward, his head lowered so he could look deep into my eyes.

"Hello? Excuse me, it's very rude to just suddenly ignore someone like this. May, if you really don't care about whether or not you exist, that's fine by me. I'll just go get a room at the nearest Sheraton. But I really don't think you've thought the whole situation through, not that I particularly mind, although it is a shame that Gabriel will have to die, too. That's right, isn't it? If a dragon's mate dies, he dies as well? I read that somewhere, although it sounds incredibly inconvenient to me."

"Mate," Gabriel said, the word as much a caress as his breath touching my cheek.

I closed my eyes for a second, digging my fingers into the cloth of my shirt in order to keep from touching him. I would not give in to the shard. I would not lose any more of myself.

His breath was warm on my neck. I opened my eyes and turned my head slightly, my fingers aching as I refused to give in to my untoward desires. He breathed in deeply, and I knew he was inhaling my scent, refreshing the memory of it in his mind, pulling it deeply into his body.

"Go," he said, his lips bruising my jaw as he spoke.

I stood trembling, fighting with myself, my body racked with a terrible need that blotted everything else from my mind but him. His eyes were molten, pure silver, the pupils having elongated until they were the merest slivers of black. "Fly, little bird."

And suddenly, I was running, racing out of the room, my blood pounding as I tore down the stairs to the lower levels of the hotel. The chase was all that filled my mind, that and the images that Gabriel shared with me of a dragon mating dance as old as time.

I was possessed with a yearning to touch him, to run my hands along the warm lines of his body. My body continued to flee, but my mind was busy with the thought of stroking him, of the feel of the warm skin covering steely muscles. I imagined my fingers tracing out the lines of his chest, and heard the answering moan of pleasure from his mind. I remembered what it was like to taste him, how silky his skin was as I slid my hands lower, along his flanks.

He growled in my mind, a warning that I was pushing his arousal hard and fast, and that he would not hold back when he found me. I ran down the stairs, the mental seduction almost too much for me to bear.

His voice spoke in my mind, words that held no meaning for me, but I knew that it was a mating chant, binding one dragon to another, part of the intricate dance we were even now conducting.

I flung myself down a final set of stairs, bursting out into the hotel lobby, seeing nothing, feeling only Gabriel as he set off in pursuit of me. His emotions were mine, a shared whirlpool fueled by the most primitive part of dragons — the need to chase, to conquer, and most of all, to possess.

But I was not a dragon.

Chapter Eighteen

He came to me in the shadow world.

I felt his presence before I saw it, a warm glow of lightness filling me as I huddled in a dark corner of what was, in the mortal world, the hotel lobby. Faint, vague shadows passed in and around me, echoes of human reality, visible in my world, but not really tangible. Nothing was. Nothing touched me.

Until Gabriel found me.

He sat next to me, his image all that he could project into the shadow world, but even though his body remained in the mortal world, the dragon-heart shard was aware that he was close.

"Do you want to tell me about it?" he asked, his voice mild.

"The reason I ran from you, you mean?"

He shook his head. Even here, his eyes were brilliant, glittering with so much emotion, they seemed to glow. "I know why you ran. It is part of the mating ritual. Females lead; males follow. What I want to know is why you are filled with so much fear and loathing."

I rested my chin on my knees, my arms wrapped around my legs. I didn't need to look at him to know he was hurt by my apparent rejection. "I don't loathe anyone. Well, perhaps Magoth, but that's natural, given the situation."

He was silent for a moment. "No, it is there; I can still sense it. You are afraid, desperately afraid of something, but there is also a self-loathing that completely baffles me. It was not there before. What has happened that you don't like yourself, Mayling? What has frightened you? More importantly, why do you feel you cannot turn to me for help?"

The fabric of my jeans was rough under my cheek as I tipped my head slightly, not soft and warm, as I knew Gabriel was. I wished with every ounce of my being that it was his chest my head rested on, the soft hairs tickling me as I breathed in his wonderful scent, my lips seeking out the silken stretches of skin as I kissed a path to his ticklish ribs, smiling a little to myself as he squirmed beneath my caresses, knowing how his little intakes of breath as I kissed his belly would change to groans of arousal as I slid down his body, my hands and mouth intent on bringing him to the very edge of pleasure even as I burst into a nova of ecstasy — no!

I jerked to the side, horrified that even in the shadow world, *my* world, the dragon shard had such a grip on me, it could override my reason.

"You do not want me," Gabriel said, his voice cold and lifeless. "You recoil from me."

It took me a moment to get a grip on my rampant emotions, and in the space of that moment, Gabriel withdrew, not physically, but emotionally.

"Do you seriously believe that I can burn down an entire floor of a hotel while engaged in lovemaking with you, and not want you? Gabriel, it's taking every ounce of strength I possess to keep from flinging myself on you and licking every square inch of your really incredibly hot body."

Animation returned to his face as he considered that for a moment. "Why would you not wish to fling yourself upon me? Have I done something to offend you? Are you upset because I asked Maata to accompany you to Italy?"

"No, although I'd like to point out that we would have been just fine on our own. And you haven't done anything to offend me. It's not you at all . . . it's me." I took a deep breath, dreading what I had to say. "Gabriel, I can't have sex with you anymore."

"If you are worried about Magoth —" he started to say.

"No, I'm not worried about him. Well, that's not strictly true, I am a bit concerned about what he's up to that he feels he can't have Sally around to see. Not to mention why he suddenly gave your people the slip."

"I told you that I would find him again. You must have faith in the silver dragons — we might not have the innate tracking ability of the blue dragons, but we are not stupid. He cannot hide from us for long."

"I know you'll track him down again, and I'm not worried in the sense you mean. This doesn't have anything to do with keeping you safe from Magoth."

"Then what has caused this change in you?" he asked, a rough edge to his voice. "Yesterday, you could not get enough of me."

I was silent as I slowly straightened up. "That is the reason why, I'm afraid."

He frowned. "I admit to being completely confused. Your physical attraction to me is not a good thing?"

"My physical attraction to you is a very

good thing," I corrected. "But my inability to control myself around you isn't. Haven't you noticed anything different the last couple of times we made love?"

"Well . . ." He grinned. "You seem to have lost your ability to control my fire. And you seem a bit more . . . intense."

I brushed a tiny speck of dragon scale off my knee. "You had to have noticed the fact that I shifted into a dragon form."

"I did." His grin faded when I didn't answer it with a smile of my own. "Is that what is concerning you, little bird? The fact that you shifted? You bear a shard of the dragon heart. As I explained before, it is that which caused you to shift."

Something about his expression, some glint in his eyes, confirmed what I had suspected. "You liked it when I shifted, didn't you?"

"Very much so." He leaned toward me, and even though he had no physical presence in the shadow world, goose bumps rippled down my arms at his nearness. "Shall I tell you a secret? Before I met you, I had never had sex with a human."

I gazed at him in surprise. "No humans? Not even immortals?"

He shook his head. "Only dragon females. You were the first who was not. I found it a bit awkward to begin with, since you did not respond to any dragon signals, but now — yesterday morning will remain in my memory for a very long time."

My face froze in what I prayed was a blank expression; all the while my gut churned with misery.

"That is why it pleased me so much a little bit ago when you initiated a mating dance. But I see now that the intensity of the experience frightened you. I promise that in the future, we will go slower, little bird. There is much I look forward to you learning about dragon ways, but you have an eternity to learn them. Do not fear I will rush you."

I dragged my gaze up to his, sick as it was driven home just how much he preferred a dragon version of me to the original. The question that remained was whether I was willing to allow the dragon shard to consume me. Gabriel certainly would have no complaints. Was it really such a big sacrifice? And wasn't he worth it?

"What is it?" he said suddenly in an annoyed voice. Immediately, he looked contrite. "My apologies if I startled you, Mayling. Tipene seeks my attention. I will return."

He faded away into nothing as he returned

to his body.

I contemplated remaining where I was, but I've never been much for introspective moping, no matter how overwhelming my problems seemed. I reminded myself that I was not Cyrene and, mentally girding my loins, returned to Gabriel's suite.

He was hanging up the phone just as I entered the living room, his face a study in resignation.

"What's wrong now?" I asked, quelling the need to rub my body against his.

"It's Magoth. We've found him at last."

"Why do I suspect I should not break out the champagne and doves just yet?"

A wry little smile twisted his lips. "Perhaps because you know him too well. Magoth is in jail."

"Jail?" My eyebrows rose. "The watch nabbed Magoth? What on earth did he do to attract the attention of the L'au-dela?"

"He is not being held by the watch," Gabriel said, watching me carefully. "He was arrested in Paris by the *préfecture* and is being held at a station on the rue de la Montagne-Sainte-Geneviève."

"He's been arrested by the mortal police?" I asked, aghast.

"Yes. Apparently for indecent exposure."

I blinked a couple of times, unsure of what

303

to say about that.

Gabriel held my coat out for me. "And he's asking for you to get him released."

I took the coat and tossed it onto a chair. "Are you crazy? I'm not going to help him get out of jail. This might not be the ideal method of keeping tabs on him, but at least if he's being held by the mortals, he won't be able to stir up who knows what trouble."

Gabriel picked up the coat again and slung it over my shoulders. "Have you forgotten Jian?"

"Not in the least. Magoth probably won't help us with the problem of finding Chuan Ren and getting her released."

"You don't know that for certain," Gabriel argued.

He had a point, dammit.

"I don't like it," I said, allowing him to push me toward the door. "There must be a way we can keep him in custody and still get assistance in the matter of Chuan Ren."

"I doubt if he'd agree to lend any aid without some in return," Gabriel pointed out.

"Well, there you are!" Sally said, bustling into the room with a large carrying bag. "You picked a fine time to do a disappearing act! Did you hear? Magoth is in trouble, and the poor dear needs our help. We have to get out to him on the double. He's probably being tortured even as we speak!"

I thinned my lips as Gabriel escorted us out of the suite. "Let's take the scenic route to the rue de la Montagne-Sainte-Geneviève. Maybe a few thumbscrews and bamboo under the nails will make him more agreeable."

"May, for heaven's sake," Sally said, rolling her eyes as she hurried ahead of us to the elevator. "They don't use thumbscrews and bamboo anymore. Now it's all high-tech. They'll probably attach a taser to his genitals or something."

She paused, looking thoughtful.

"Somehow, I have a feeling Magoth wouldn't consider that torture so much as foreplay," I said, getting on the elevator, Gabriel and his two bodyguards following.

"I admit, it does sound rather . . . intriguing . . . ," she said, clearly lost in thought, only just managing to get into the elevator car before the doors closed.

Unfortunately, the ride to the fifth arrondissement didn't take that long, Tipene being familiar with the area. Twenty minutes hadn't passed before I found myself standing in the police station, reading with interest a notice about an attached crime museum. "It says they have a real guillotine blade," I told Gabriel. "I'd like to see that."

"A guillotine blade? Is there a torture section, as well?" Sally asked, pushing me aside to read the notice. "There's nothing I love more than a good torture exhibit, unless, of course, it's the actual practice itself."

"What say we have a quick tour before we have to see Magoth?" I suggested.

A corner of Gabriel's mouth quirked.

"Madame Northcott? This way, please," a pretty woman said, giving Gabriel a not-very-subtle eye before she turned and started down a hallway.

"This is going to get old very fast," I grumbled, taking his hand in a show of outright possession.

He grinned, and tickled my palm with his thumb.

"My darling wife!" Magoth said when the policewoman opened a door to a small interrogation room, standing aside for us to enter.

I stopped, glaring at him. "Do *not* call me that."

"Why not? You are my consort, my queen, my second in command . . . or at least fifth or sixth in command. I have a cadre of wrath demons who are above you, I'm afraid, but you're definitely in the top ten. Possibly twenty."

I slid a worried glance to the police-woman. "I think that's just enough about your cadre."

He rolled his eyes. "Why you insist we play these games when things could be so much easier . . ."

"Magoth! Are you all right? Have you been abused in any fashion?" Sally asked, slipping around me to hurry to his side. "I don't see any blood or even some bruising. Shouldn't there be some blood? I expected there to be blood!"

"I like how your mind works," Magoth told her.

She preened.

I felt it was time to break up their admiration society. "What in the name of the spirits of sanity were you doing to be arrested for indecent exposure?"

"Nothing at all," he said with a dismissive wave of his hands. Someone had found him some clothing, a T-shirt and pair of jeans that weren't his usual style, but he was incredibly handsome in them, regardless. "It is all a misunderstanding. I was visiting a quaint little fountain outside of a church, that's all. No different from any other tourist."

"A church?" Sally asked, startled.

I frowned. What was he doing near a

church? Demon lords tended to avoid those places that were respected as holy ground, no matter what the religion. All too frequently sites were chosen because the ground was founded, or seeped in that quality that enhanced abilities that could be used against those of dark origins.

"Monsieur was witnessed by a wedding party of two hundred, including three cardinals, and a papal legate, as he attempted indecent acts with a stone mermaid that sits on the top of the fountain," the policewoman said, turning her attention on him.

"Sins of the master," Sally swore, looking at Magoth with something that looked very much like respect.

"You were trying to have sex with a statue in a fountain?" I asked. Gabriel's lips twitched as if he was having a hard time keeping from laughing.

"It was a very *large* misunderstanding," Magoth told me before switching his attention to the policewoman. The look he sent her was positively lecherous. "If you get my drift."

The woman slid me a quick glance.

"Oh, don't mind her," he said quickly, leaning back in a wooden chair in a pose that was seductive despite the bleak surroundings. "We have an open marriage."

"Very open, to the point of being non-existent," I snapped. "And while we're on that subject, stop telling people we're married. I'm Gabriel's mate, not yours."

"Sweet May, it wounds me near unto death that you would deny the fact that you are my consort," he said, still making eyes at the policewoman, who was starting to look doubtful.

"That's true, you are, and in" — Sally's voice dropped to a whisper — "in this world, the equivalent would be a spouse."

"I don't care. I won't have you slighting Gabriel in order to pump up your own ego," I said, taking Gabriel's hand again.

The policewoman watched with growing suspicion. "You are monsieur's legal representative?" she asked Gabriel.

Gabriel smiled his usual charming smile. "That's right. And if you do not mind, madame and I would like to talk to my client. Privately."

She left us alone with Magoth, but only after insisting the others remain outside. Sally raised a bit of a fuss over being excluded.

"It's not like I don't have a right to be here," she told the policewoman. "I'm his apprentice! Well, at least I was until he sent me to May, but even if you consider that

309

binding — and I don't, not at all, because I didn't sign on to learn how to be a consort! — even if you consider that binding, then I should still get to stay because she does, and I'm her apprentice."

"Only family and legal representatives may remain with the prisoners," the police-woman said, politely but firmly herding Sally out the door.

"I'll be right outside if you need me!" the latter called as the door was closed.

The second it was closed, Magoth was on his feet, storming around the room waving his hands in the dramatic fashion he favored when irritated.

"Get me out of this . . . this . . . hellhole of mortal sensibilities!" he demanded, stomping to the door and back in a fairly good imitation of a caged beast.

I leaned my hip against the small wooden table in the center of the room. "And what, exactly, do you expect me to do? You're the one who had a hard-on of such extent it required a stone statue to relieve."

"Don't be idiotic," he snarled, pacing between the door and the far wall. "I wasn't screwing the statue — it was a matter of a simple incantation. I was trying to bring forth a Sybarite, if you must know, not that it's any of your business."

"You're kidding," I said, surprised. "A lust demon? What on earth did you want a lust demon for?"

Gabriel touched my arm and nodded toward the corner. A video camera was perched jauntily on the wall, its red light blinking as it obviously filmed us.

"Er . . . that is . . . never mind," I said, mindful of that fact. "I take it you weren't successful?"

"Do you see a small being with giant genitalia humping your leg?" he asked with an exaggerated arm movement.

"No, but it concerns me that you were even trying." I mulled over the idea of Magoth with a being wholly devoted to pleasures of the carnal sort.

"Does it really matter what his reasons were for being arrested?" Gabriel asked, glancing at his watch. "We have things to do, little bird. I believe it would be best if we were to provide bail for Magoth and conduct our discussion in a more appropriate location."

Magoth pounced on one of Gabriel's words. "Discussion? What discussion do you wish to have with me? I sincerely hope it is not that you regret spurning me for Manimal here, because much as I would like to see you grovel before me, I do not have time for the proper training that would be required to turn you into a suitable slave."

"Yes, I believe it is important," I said, answering Gabriel's question while ignoring Magoth's comment. I glanced toward the camera, picking my words carefully. "He shouldn't have access to the sort of . . . abilities . . . that would allow him to call a Sybarite."

Magoth's eyelids dropped until he was gazing at me through half-closed lids, a smug little smile playing with his lips.

"He knows that very well, so for him to even try . . . well, it says something isn't quite as we expected it to be."

Gabriel and I both considered Magoth, who had suddenly stopped pacing and had adopted an expression of almost angelic innocence.

"He certainly looks guilty," Gabriel observed.

"He does, which is why I still think we should leave him here. Perhaps a time out in a mortal jail is just what he needs to let us find out what he's been up to this last week."

Magoth snarled an oath that was not at all nice, lunging toward me.

Instantly, Gabriel was between us, blocking my view of Magoth as he growled in a

312

threatening manner. "Do not even think about touching May."

Magoth, to my surprise, didn't back down. Instead he took a step forward, until he and Gabriel were just a hairbreadth from each other, their gazes locked in a battle for dominance. "You think to threaten me, dragon?"

"You are in my world now," Gabriel reminded him, the air of menace surrounding him leaving little shivers skittering up and down my back.

Magoth didn't like being reminded he lacked power in the mortal realm. His eyes glittered like icy black onyx as he tried to stare Gabriel down. "There will come a day when you will be in my domain, and then we shall see who will reign supreme."

"I am not so foolish as to allow that to happen," Gabriel said, relaxing just a smidgen when I pulled his arm to move him back a few inches. "There is nothing in your domain that I would ever seek."

"You think not?" Magoth's eyes moved to me, his gaze striking me with such impact, I took an involuntary step backwards. "And yet, I can envision just such a scenario."

Gabriel growled again, a low, deep growl that was almost inaudible but caused me to shiver even more.

Magoth smiled and stepped back, lifting his hands in a show of surrender. "Such fun and games are enjoyable, but I really do have much I should be doing. If you could just see to my release, sweet May, we can all be on our respective ways."

"You know, something just occurred to me," I said pleasantly, tucking my hand in the crook of Gabriel's arm.

"You realize now that my body has much to offer you?" Magoth tipped his head on the side as he considered me. "This is true, but we must consider the effect that a dragon would have on our threesome. It might be interesting, though . . . the fire, the claws . . . yes, it could be very interesting."

Gabriel's lips thinned. I gave Magoth a look that told him I expected better. "As a matter of fact, it strikes me rather odd that you're here at all. Oh, I'm not talking about the fact that you were arrested making a lewd attack on a statue — that doesn't surprise me in the least. No, I'm talking about the fact that you're here *now*. As in, you haven't left."

"That is a very good point," Gabriel said, obviously understanding what I was trying not to spell out in front of a potential audience.

314

Magoth's face darkened. "There was a Wiccan here —" he started to answer, but I interrupted him with a pointed look toward the camera.

"You try my patience, consort," he said irritably, and waved one hand toward the camera. It dropped to the ground, the wires that had connected it to the wall still smoking.

"Oh, great; now the mortals are going to come charging in here to ask how you did that without even going near the camera. You know what that means, don't you? Either we're going to have to spend hours trying to explain that, or we'll have to fight our way out of here," I said, annoyed in my own right. "Which means we'll be fugitives from the mortal law."

"You worry too much about what insignificant insects think," he snapped. "If you cannot dodge the mortal police, you don't deserve to be in their world. In answer to your question, there was a Wiccan on the staff of the *préfecture.* She recognized me and saw to it that I was taken to this room, which, you have probably failed to notice, is bound in silver."

I looked around the room, frowning.

"I noticed," Gabriel said. "I can smell it."

"The famous dragon ability to smell precious metals . . . well, wyvern, in answer to your mate's question, *that* is why I have not simply destroyed these mortals as they deserve."

"Silver is poisonous to demons and demon lords," I said slowly, pulling a morsel of demon lore from the depths of my knowledge. "It's an important element in ritual acts of destruction, and can be used to confine them to locations if the boundaries are seeded with pure silver."

"Which, I can assure you, is accurate in this case." Magoth paced the edges of the room, glaring at the walls. "This room was clearly created by someone with a grudge against demon lords."

"More likely demons, since there are few princes who are able to walk in the mortal world," I pointed out.

"The important point in this lamentably long conversation," he said with a wicked look at me, "is that I be released. Immediately. If not sooner."

Gabriel and I exchanged a glance. The door behind us started to open, voices entering that questioned, in French, the status of the camera.

I threw myself at the door, slamming it shut. "We're not going to be able to hold it for long," I told Gabriel.

He braced himself against it as another attempt was made to open the door, pulling out his cell phone with one hand. He punched in one number and barked an order into the phone in a singsong language that I assume had Aboriginal roots.

"That should give us a minute or two," he said, grunting as he held the door firm despite some serious attempts on it. "Tipene will start a couple of fires in the station that will hopefully distract some of the people. Go ahead, May."

"Right, let's get straight to the negotiations," I said, my voice rocky as someone started pounding something large against the door. "We will agree to get you out of here if you help us with a situation in Abaddon."

"You need my help?" Magoth's frown cleared as he perched himself on the corner of the table, a slow smile lighting his face. "How very interesting. You desire a favor from me. This is highly unusual, and yet, oddly appealing. And what payment do you offer?"

"No favors, just a simple exchange of help," I said, digging in my heels and bracing as the door was continuously pounded.

He thought for a moment. "That is hardly fair. I do not know what situation you are referring to."

I glanced at Gabriel. The muscles in his neck stood out in cords as he strained to keep the door closed, but he managed a quick nod at my unasked question.

"There is a dragon in Abaddon, a wyvern named Chuan Ren. We want you to help us get her released."

"A dragon?" I could swear Magoth was sincerely surprised by that news. He spoke softly, as if to himself. "I have not heard that a dragon was sent to Abaddon, and surely I would have done so. Ahhh." He exhaled as his eyes narrowed. "That is what Bael was up to. He has been secretive of late, very secretive, and hinted once at an unprecedented event. It must be he who possesses the dragon."

"I don't know who has her, or what her situation is; I just know that we need her released."

He eyed us both as we were jounced on the door. The attacks on it were getting stronger, pushing us a few inches out each time. We wouldn't be able to last much longer. "This is not a fair trade of help. To free me is nothing, but to seize a minion of the premiere prince of Abaddon . . . *pfft.* That is a huge undertaking."

"She's a dragon; she can't be a minion," I

said, straining to hold the door. Gabriel labored beside me. "She's got to be held against her will, which should make her willing to cooperate with us."

"Still," Magoth said, idly trailing a hand down his chest. "It seems as if you ask more of me than I do of you."

"Fine; we'll do this by ourselves," I spat, turning to Gabriel. "We'll get that Guardian friend of Aisling to help us. There has to be some way to get Chuan Ren out of Abaddon. I'll just be sure to tell the mortals not to let Magoth out of this room —"

"You wound me, consort," Magoth interrupted, getting to his feet quickly. "Very well, I agree to your offer. Now, see to my release before I regret such generosity."

"Make it binding," I ground out through teeth clenched with the strain of holding the door.

"Your lack of faith in me is something we really will have to address," Magoth said with a look of pure scorn, but he casually reached behind him for the wooden chair, easily smashing it to smithereens on the table. He used a partially exposed screw to knick the tip of one finger, pursing his lips in a little pout as a bead of blood welled up on it, then milking it for a few seconds before strolling over to me. He touched the drop of blood to my forehead. "My blood seals the pact between us. Happy now?"

"Very," I grunted, wanting to wipe off the blood mark but not having an available hand to do so. I glanced at Gabriel.

"Shadow," he ordered, sweat starting to dot his forehead.

"I don't need to be protected from mortals," I said, intending to object to being kept out of the way.

"I have no time to argue about this, little bird. I can't protect you and Magoth together, so you must shadow."

"Don't think I'm going to let you get away with bossing me around the way Drake does Aisling," I answered, taking a step away from the door, shadowing as I did so.

The door exploded inward, but Gabriel is not a dragon for nothing. He moved so fast I could barely follow him as he snatched up a broken piece of chair, whirling around with it held like a lance. The police spilled into the room, guns drawn, but they didn't stand a chance against Gabriel. The wooden weapon he held spun and flashed in the overhead light, its movement almost immediately followed by the cries of those he'd wielded it upon.

I stood pressed up against the wall, watching with openmouthed amazement and appreciation as Gabriel single-handedly dealt with the group of seven policemen. He was grace and power personified, dodging, attacking, twisting around bodies as they crumpled to the floor, and yet I was willing to bet there wouldn't be a single fatality.

"Where did you learn to do that?" I asked, following as he jerked Magoth into the hallway after him.

Gabriel's dimples flashed for a fraction of a second. "I spent a few years in warrior training with a tribe in South Africa. Stay hidden, little bird, but remain close."

I did both, more to be able to watch Gabriel in action than to stay safe. It didn't take him much time to deal with the few remaining police officers in the hallways, and by the time we emerged at the front of the station, Tipene and Maata had cleared the rest of the way.

"Magoth!" shrieked Sally with joy, in her haste to get to him trampling a poor policewoman who lay prone on the floor. "I told you we'd get you out!"

"Really? I don't remember that," he said, stopping to give her a disbelieving look.

Gabriel shoved him toward the front door, handily knocking aside a policeman who had wandered in the entrance.

"Well . . . I would have said it if I'd

thought of it at the time," Sally admitted, dashing after them as Gabriel hustled Magoth out the door. He paused to look back for me.

There were enough lights on to make me visible, although I knew it would still be hard to see me. "I'm right here; don't stop," I told him.

He nodded and proceeded, our little group on his heels as he fought his way out onto the street. We attracted little attention once we had escaped the confines of the police station, and made it to the car quickly enough. I deshadowed but didn't relax until Tipene had clamped his foot on the accelerator, maneuvering with great skill around the wild Parisian drivers.

"So you're saying you lied to me?" Magoth asked Sally, continuing his conversation.

She smiled brightly. "As a matter of fact, yes."

He pursed his lips ever so slightly, his eyelids dropping to give her a seductive look. "Perhaps I was a little hasty in sending you to my sweet May. Any woman who would lie to a demon lord clearly has depths."

"Oh, I have many attributes," Sally answered, adopting a modest expression. "I always cheat at cards, I take every opportunity to use others for my own ends, and I make the most divine three-bean salad. I'm absolutely perfect for the job of demon lord, don't you think?"

"Such depths certainly deserve to be plumbed," Magoth answered with a leer.

I scooted closer to Gabriel, grateful the limousine he'd rented had enough room to allow Magoth and Sally to conduct their flirtation without being pressed up against me.

"Gabriel," I started to say, but stopped when Sally said brightly, "Are we going to have an orgy? I'd like to recommend Gabriel join us."

"There will be no orgy with Gabriel," I said, glaring at her.

She gave me a hurt look. "Sugar, selfishness is very unbecoming."

"I am not being selfish. Gabriel is my mate, not yours," I said, scooting over closer to him, clamping my hand down on his leg in a show of possession.

"But you have Magoth and Gabriel, and you want to keep them both to yourself! If that's not selfishness, well, I just don't know what is!"

I opened my mouth to argue that I didn't want Magoth at all, but decided that there were far more important things to address. "Do you think there will be any repercussion with the police about Magoth?" I asked Gabriel.

His fingers twined through mine where they lay on his leg. "I doubt it. They may have our names, but they pose no real danger to us. We will be able to avoid them without too much trouble. You have nothing to fear on that front."

His last sentence hung in the air with an unfinished sense to it that sent a little shiver of foreboding down my back.

CHAPTER NINETEEN

"I have a bad feeling about this," I said, frowning at the being that stood before us.

The demon made a face. "This was your idea, luv, not mine, so if you don't need me, you can just send me back. I've got things to do, people to torment, you savvy?"

"Someone has been watching far too much *Pirates of the Caribbean.*" Noelle, the Guardian Gabriel had called to summon a demon for us, stood on the far side of the living room, also giving the demon a jaded look. She was a pretty, cheerful redhead, a friend of Aisling's mentor, Nora. She'd summoned a demon for us quickly and with minimal fuss, keeping good control over it.

Valac the demon preened as we all eyed it. I had to admit that Noelle had a point — the demon looked as if it had been an extra in the movie, clad in leather boots, swash-buckling coat, sash, and tricorn hat, which sat atop ratty, nasty dreadlocks.

"That said, I think perhaps you may be right, May," Noelle continued. "Going to see Bael yourself sounds like a pretty bad choice. Magoth is one thing, but Bael . . . I just can't say I recommend that."

"It may be bad choice, but it's really our only option now that Magoth has done a bunk." I looked at Gabriel. He stood to the side, arms crossed as he watched me, his face unreadable. The dragon shard wanted me to leap on him, but I ignored the fires that threatened to burst out and thought instead of what I'd like to do to Magoth. "That bastard."

"He's still bound by blood to you," Noelle said, glancing at my forehead, where the blood mark still remained, and would continue to remain until his oath was fulfilled. "You could call him and he'd have to respond."

"We tried that. He was so obnoxious, we figured we're better off without him."

"Ah. That's not good," she agreed.

"Even Sally wasn't helpful — she just suggested we steal Chuan Ren back, and somehow, I don't relish that idea."

Noelle gave a delicate shudder. "No, I agree with you there."

"So all in all, we're better off without Magoth. Besides, he took Sally with him, and frankly, it's worth losing the dubious amount of help he'd give us just to get both of them off our backs." I took a deep breath and steeled myself for what was coming. "Ready, Gabriel?"

He wrapped an arm around my waist, the warmth of his nearness sinking deep into my bones. "Let's get this over with."

The dragon-heart shard wanted to make a fuss, so I nodded to Noelle. "Do it."

"Demon Valac, I command you to take May and Gabriel to Bael without harming either of them, after which, you will be released," Noelle said, giving the demon a piercing look.

It made a face. "A courier; that's all you wanted me for? Do you have any idea of all the work I have to do, of how late I'm going to be, just because you want a couple of dragons to go to Abaddon? I'm an important demon, you know! I'm third class!"

"I'm not actually a dragon," I told it, feeling it important to point out that fact.

"You're not?" it asked, looking surprised for a moment. It eyed me for a second. "You look like one. You smell like one. You sure you're not?"

"Quite sure. I'm a doppelganger!" I said, shaken more than I wanted to admit. A tiny little wisp of smoke escaped my lips, wafting in lazy curlicues in front of my astonished eyes.

I clamped my lips shut tight, panic rising inside me.

Gabriel's arm tightened around me. "This is not important, little bird. Let us be on our way. The sooner we have Chuan Ren, the sooner we can be done with Abaddon."

I wanted to argue with Gabriel that it was, in fact, very important to me, but he was right about getting the worst over with quickly. I allowed myself to give a mental grumble about Magoth going back on his word to help us after we had him released, but cut that short as Noelle ordered the demon to obey her command.

"Fine," Valac snapped, grabbing my wrist. "But the next time you need a courier, get one of the minor minions. I don't have time for this!"

The trip to Abaddon via demon often left me retching after being deposited there, since the act of being yanked through the fabric of being was such an abomination, it was literally sickening. But this time, rather than leaving us collapsing in a gasping, gagging heap, Valac deposited us both on our feet, feeling nothing more than a slight queasiness.

"I'll tell the master's secretary you're here,

but don't expect much. He doesn't see people without appointments," Valac said as it marched out the door.

"Are you all right?" I asked Gabriel. He looked remarkably well, considering what had just happened to us.

His eyebrows rose slightly. "Of course. Shouldn't I be?"

"Well . . ." I frowned, moving around him. My arms and legs felt fine, too, not at all resembling the normal trembling, weak appendages they usually were after being called to Abaddon. "It's just that normally the trip here is a bit hairy."

He shrugged. "Dragonkin don't suffer the way humans do. Should we seek an audience with Bael, or rely upon the demon to let someone know we're here? I'm inclined to do it myself. I don't think we can trust that demon."

I followed him as he left the room, wordlessly stomping out the little fires that broke out around me.

"Good evening," Gabriel said to a young man who stood in an elegant hallway, a notepad in hand as he checked off items on a list. "I am wyvern of the silver dragon sept, and this is my mate. We seek an audience with Bael."

The demon gave us a look that said it

wasn't too impressed with us. "I don't remember any business with the silver dragons on our calendar. May I inquire if you made an appointment through proper channels?"

Gabriel was about to answer when I stepped in front of him. "You may not," I said, simultaneously appalled at my rudeness and annoyed at an underling who thought he could push us around. "Tell Bael we're here, and we wish to see him."

The demon narrowed its pale blue eyes at me. "You are Lady Magoth, are you not? Very well, I will inform his lordship that you are here, but I feel obliged to point out that you are not very high in our favor at the moment."

"You can take that royal we and shove it up next to your head," I told the demon as it strode off down the hallway. The instant the words were spoken, I clamped a hand over my mouth, turning to look at Gabriel with horror-struck eyes.

He looked a bit surprised in return. "Are you feeling all right?"

I spread my fingers. "I don't know. I'm almost afraid to talk. Did I just say what I think I said?"

"Yes." His eyes were concerned as they examined me. "Perhaps it was the journey here that has discommoded you."

I shook my head. "I feel fine," I said through my fingers, too worried about what my mouth might say next to remove my hand. "Not sick at all, as I normally am when summoned, just kind of . . . feisty."

"Hmm." He watched me for another moment, then turned when the demon appeared at the end of the hallway.

"We will see you now," the demon said with condescension.

"I will speak for you if you wish," Gabriel said, his hand reassuring and warm on my back as we walked toward the double doors the demon had opened. "I do not wish to hurt your feelings, but if you are not feeling up to it, perhaps it would be better if I were to take the lead."

"Works for me," I said, dropping my hand and struggling to regain my usual composure as we entered Bael's study. He stood in a casual pose next to the fireplace, a sheaf of papers in his hand, his head bent as he read from them. An expression of mild interest was on his face as he glanced up. He looked different from when I'd seen him before, now he was sandy haired and freckled, with a long English face and washed-out green eyes.

The aura of power was the same, however,

making the air feel thick with static.

Gabriel bowed politely. "I am Gabriel, wyvern of the silver dragons. This is my mate, May."

"What business do you have with me?" Bael asked, addressing me. I gritted my teeth to keep from saying anything untoward.

"We believe that you have an associate of mine, a wyvern by the name of Chuan Ren. We would like to negotiate for her release —"

"I was not speaking to you, dragon." Bael interrupted, his eyes cold. "What business does Magoth's consort have with me?"

"I speak with my mate's consent," Gabriel said, moving to stand in front of me, effectively blocking Bael's view.

The air thickened as Bael set down the papers, turning to face us head-on. The sane part of my mind demanded that I instantly shadow, or better yet, retreat to the shadow world, but that part of me that was being taken over by the dragon-heart shard had me stepping around Gabriel, my head held high as I met Bael's intimidating gaze with one that might not be so potent, but was totally at odds with the normally humble attitude I adopted when around demon lords. "Gabriel and I are of one thought, so you may consider his words mine. We want to talk to you about releasing Chuan Ren."

Bael was silent for a moment.

"Do you deny having her?" I asked. Evidently he'd been rather secretive about her, and I wondered whether he was going to make us work just to get him to admit he had her in his possession.

Bael strolled over to a large walnut desk and pressed a button on a phone. "Dillard, fetch the wyvern."

I relaxed a smidgen, exchanging a relieved glance with Gabriel.

"What price do you demand for her release?" Gabriel asked Bael.

"She is not for sale."

"Everything has a price," Gabriel countered.

"True. However, in this case, the price is beyond even the capacity of a dragon," Bael said. "And since I know you will ask, I will say simply that it would involve the sacrifice of your mate."

"That is not an option," Gabriel said quickly, before I could protest.

Bael smiled, and I thanked every deity I could think of that we were immortal. "As I said, the price is beyond you. Still, I will allow you to see my newest acquisition, since I am certain you will ask for that, and I am, as ever, obliging. Ah. Here she is."

Chuan Ren entered the room. At least, I assumed it was her — she was of Chinese descent, tall, with straight black hair and eyes that burned with fury. She spat out something in Chinese that I assumed wasn't a wish for Bael's continued good health, but then she noticed us, and her ire focused on Gabriel.

"You!" she shrieked, lunging at him. "I should have known it was you behind this. You're always drooling over that simpleton Aisling, pretending to listen to Fiat, but lying, always lying."

"Hey!" I said, irritated on Gabriel's behalf. Rage was swift to fire within me, forcing me to fist my hands to keep the dragon claws from popping out. "Gabriel is not drooling over Aisling, and he does not lie."

She gave me a scathing once-over. "I do not know you. What sept do you belong to?"

"May is my mate," Gabriel said in a smooth voice, his face impassive. I gave him full points for maintaining such control in the face of the irritating Chuan Ren. I badly wanted to adopt my usual sense of calm, but it kept eluding me.

"A mate? This is not possible. You lie." She turned to Bael, who was leaning against the desk watching us with mild interest.

"This is some new form of torment you have devised? I will not forget it. You will be repaid in kind."

"*Tch.* Such is the gratitude for my magnanimity in allowing you to see your friends," Bael said.

"They are not my friends. Either kill me now, or leave me alone. I will not be abused in this manner! You shall be the first to feel the full weight of my revenge!" she shouted, her hair whipping around as she marched to the door.

Bael looked at us. "Are you sure it is *this* one you wish to have released? It was not, perhaps, a wrath demon or behemoth you were thinking of? Someone with a bit more charm and less lethality?"

Chuan Ren spun around at the door, and I think she would have made a rush for Bael, but his words sank in first. "You are here to see to my release?" she asked Gabriel in a slightly less hostile tone.

"Your son has petitioned us to that purpose," he said, glancing at Bael. "But it seems negotiations are at a standstill."

"You ask much gold for me?" she asked, marching back into the center of the room, eyeing Bael much as a cat would a comatose mouse. "You seek treasure of an unimaginable amount? Very well. He will pay it."

She pointed to Gabriel with the last of her words.

"Like hell he will," I muttered, stamping out the fire that broke out around me.

Bael said nothing but watched with raised eyebrows.

"Your mate is unlearned," she told Gabriel, a sneer on her lips. "Just like that fool Drake and his equally stupid mate."

"I'm not so unlearned as you think," I said, focusing long enough to light the ends of her hair on fire.

Gabriel nudged me. Sighing, I extinguished the flames, pain pricking my palms as the dragon claws tried to emerge.

"The price Bael has demanded is not payable in treasure and is not acceptable. I have hopes that we will be able to negotiate another one, however."

"Not treasure?" Chuan Ren looked scornfully at Bael. "What price have you put as my value, if not that of treasure?"

Bael toyed with a bone letter opener that had been lying on the desk. "My standard price for everything is always what would cost the person the most. In this case, it would be the sacrifice of the silver mate."

"Bah," Chuan Ren said. "We agree to the price. Take the female and let me go."

She started to walk to the door just like it

was a done deal.

"I do not agree to the price," Gabriel said swiftly.

Chuan Ren tossed him a crass word.

"You dare call my mate that?" I yelled, suddenly too angry to care if I was being politic or not.

She spun around. "You dare speak to one who is your superior? Begone, before I teach you how to properly address a wyvern."

"Newsflash — you're no longer wyvern. Someone else is leading the red dragons."

"May, that is enough," Gabriel said, taking my arm and tugging me toward him. He had an odd look on his face, a mishmash of amusement, caution, and wariness.

"What?" I asked him, wondering what that look was about.

His lips quirked. "You yelled. I've never heard you yell before."

"She started it," I said, pointing at Chuan Ren.

She spat out another word, this time directed at me, and with it, an epiphany came. The anger that had been steadily building within me flashed hot and pure, and before I could blink, I was across the room, slamming Chuan Ren up against the wall, my curved scarlet claws pricking deep into the white flesh of her throat. "I am the mate of the silver wyvern. You dare use that tone with me?"

Answering fire burned in her eyes as silver scales rippled up my hands and arms. She knocked me backwards, but I had a grip on her hair and took her with me, the two of us rolling in a ball of claws, fire, and painful blows.

She cracked my head into Bael's desk, causing me to roar in fury, fire erupting around us as I whipped my legs around, knocking her down. Her claws flashed silver in the light as she slashed at my face, but I was too fast for her, slamming my fist into her throat. She kicked me in my gut and blasted me with dragon fire. I was about to return the favor when Gabriel, who had been yelling my name, yanked me backwards, out of her grip.

I stood hunched over, panting fire, my entire being focused on destroying the female who threatened my mate . . . and as that thought coalesced in my brain, I froze in horror. What was I doing? I never fought unless it was a matter of life or death. I never yelled — a lifetime spent in Magoth's service had taught me the wisdom of keeping my temper under control. And now here I was, not only thinking, but *acting* like a dragon.

"I think I'm going to be sick," I murmured, turning away from the sight of Chuan Ren slowly getting to her feet.

"As amusing as this is, I do not have time for these games," Bael said. "You abuse my patience. Either pay the price I demand for the dragon, or leave."

"Your patience is going to be one sad panda if you don't release Chuan Ren to us," someone said, and with horror I realized it was me.

I clapped a hand over my mouth again as Gabriel shot me a startled look. I wanted to cringe before Bael and beg his forgiveness at the same time I had an almost overwhelming urge to punch him in the nose and set his hair on fire.

Bael looked at me with blatant surprise. "Does Magoth condone his consort acting in such a manner?"

I took a deep breath, got a firm grip on the horrible, out-of-control mess that was my emotions, and lifted my chin. "Magoth knows full well I'm here, and yes, he told me I had his approval to release Chuan Ren."

"Indeed." Bael's expression turned calculating. "I believe I underestimated him. He is smarter than I gave him credit for, inducing you to have him expelled from Abaddon so that he might regain his powers."

"What?" I shrieked, horror swamping me.

Gabriel frowned. "My mate does not seek excommunication of Magoth, only the return of the wyvern Chuan Ren."

"I beg to differ," Bael said mildly, still fiddling with the bone letter opener. "She has made a demand that I release a minion to her. Such an act consists of insurrection, and since she is Magoth's consort, it will be he who suffers the penalty. As any consort knows, that price is removal from Abaddon."

"Agathos daimon," I swore, a horrible vision before me, my skin crawling as the full extent of what Bael was saying was made clear. "Magoth would be expelled from Abaddon and released on the mortal world."

Gabriel's frown tightened a smidgen. "He's already in the mortal world. How could a permanent expulsion be any worse?"

Bael pressed a button on his phone, and immediately two demons appeared. He waved toward Chuan Ren. "Take her back to her accommodations."

"No!" she snarled, her eyes spitting fire as the demons approached her. "I will not stay here! You will have me released no matter what it takes!"

Gabriel and I watched silently as she was

hauled away, screaming and fighting every step.

He turned to me and cocked an inquisitive eyebrow.

I swallowed down a painful lump in my throat. "According to the Doctrine of Unending Conscious, if a prince is permanently expulsed from Abaddon, he loses control of his legions, his seat on the council, and his right to call on the ruling prince for help in times of need."

Gabriel's second eyebrow rose to join the first.

Bael smiled.

I slumped against the wall, battered, exhausted, and sick at heart. "But he would take with him a compensation for services rendered on behalf of Abaddon. In other words, Magoth would be unleashed on the mortal world with the full extent of his knowledge, abilities . . . and powers."

CHAPTER TWENTY

Fiat called a weyr meeting for that evening. This was a much smaller event than the previous *sárkány,* held in a private room at a dragon-owned restaurant. Aisling and Drake were present (the latter looking none too happy about his mate's presence), as were Bastian, Fiat, and to my surprise, Kostya and Cyrene.

"Mayling!" the last had called as Gabriel and I entered the room, about to run to hug me, but pausing with an odd look of incomprehension on her face. "May?"

"Hello, Cy. What are you and Kostya doing here?" I asked, pain twisting in my gut as my twin reacted to my now more-dragon-than-doppelganger self.

"Kostya is on probation. Or something like that. He has applied for formal recognition, and evidently one of the rules says he can't cause any trouble with any of the septs, so he's here to show there's no hard feelings between us and you."

The "you" stung. Cyrene had always spoken of the silver dragons as separate from me, but now I was clearly one of them.

I nodded, miserable, and followed Gabriel as he took his place at a long table. The *sárkány* was short, just long enough for Fiat to claim he had challenged and beaten the red wyvern, and he was now leader of that sept.

"Oh, yeah, I just bet it went that way," Jim said, leaning against Aisling's leg.

Fiat smiled. He was still blue-eyed, which made me wonder about wyverns and their respective eye colors. I made a mental note to ask Gabriel about it later.

"You cannot rid the weyr of us," Fiat told everyone present.

I said nothing. Gabriel had told Drake he wanted to have a talk with him and Aisling later, so I assumed we would use that time to explain what had really happened in Fiat's house.

"If there is no other business, we will consider this *sárkány* ended," Gabriel said after Fiat made his formal statement.

"I have a question," Cyrene said, raising her hand.

"You are not a mate, nor a recognized member of a sept," Fiat told her haughtily,

343

blithely ignoring the fact that he had been willing to recognize Kostya earlier. "You do not have a right to speak at a *sárkány.*"

"I am too a mate. Well, possibly am a mate. I just haven't been named such because Kostya isn't formally recognized. And he's on the list for that, so we get to be here and ask questions. Don't we?"

She asked the last bit of Gabriel.

He glanced around the table and, with a little shrug, said, "I don't see any harm in your request. The weyr recognizes your right to speak at the *sárkány.*"

"Thank you. My question is how someone who is one color can become another color. I mean, I know Drake did it, but Kostya says their grandmother was some special dragon, and that's how Drake did the change. But Fiat was blue and now he's red. Shouldn't that make purple?"

Aisling giggled. "I thought the same thing, but it doesn't quite work that way. As I understand it, dragons who are ouroboros are stripped of their septs, which means they're . . . well, kind of colorless, so to speak. So they can join another sept without having to go through the rigmarole that Drake's grandmother went through. Isn't that right, sweetie?"

Drake nodded. "Ouroboros dragons can

be taken in by any sept."

"Just as they can take *over* any sept," Fiat added with a smirk.

"Provided they actually challenge the wyvern for it," Gabriel said softly.

Fiat shot him a startled look, but Gabriel evidently had a reason for keeping mum about the true happening with regard to Bao. He simply met Fiat's gaze with a steady, knowing one of his own. I followed suit, saying nothing when the *sárkány* was declared closed, and the dragons rose to depart.

"Something is wrong with you," Cyrene told me in a quiet aside as coats were gathered and farewells were made. "You feel different. Are you all right? Is it something to do with Neptune?"

I shook my head, giving her a little hug that I hoped reassured her in ways my words could not. "No, silly, I'm not a water elemental. He can't really affect me."

"I know, but you seem . . . off. Is there anything I can do to help?"

"No, but thank you for being concerned."

"Now you're the one being silly. You're my twin; of course I'm concerned." She bit her lip, her eyes troubled. "May, do you ever wish I'd never created you?"

I frowned. "I told you decades ago that I

forgave you for binding me to Magoth —"

"No, not that. I meant do you ever wish I'd never created you to begin with?" Her hands fluttered in movements of distress. "That comes out sounding so wrong, but you know what I mean. Do you wish I'd left you to be born normal. Human. Mortal."

Emotions generated by the dragon shard swamped me. Rage, love, lust, joy, and sorrow, all mixed up together in a big jumble that left me wanting to cry to the heavens with the confusion of it all.

"May?" Cyrene's eyes grew big. She reached out a finger and touched my cheek, examining the wetness on the tip of her finger. "You're crying. You've never cried before."

"Yes, I have," I said, angrily scrubbing the tears from my eyes. "You've just never seen me. I cried when Pepper died."

"Pepper? Oh, your dog. That was . . . what, seventy-some-odd years ago?"

"I'm just a little emotional right now," I answered, taking a firm grip on myself. "And all philosophical debates about the existence of humankind aside, no, I'm not sorry you created me."

"All right." She watched me closely for a moment before giving a little shrug. "I just

346

thought that maybe this whole thing with Gabriel was getting to be too much for you."

"What do you mean?" I asked, startled. Had she put two and two together and figured out that I was slowly being turned into a dragon? Did she sense my conflicted emotions regarding Gabriel? Did she, too, mourn the loss of my being as the dragon shard took over?

"Just that you've never had a romantic relationship with a man before, and sometimes it takes a few tries before you get the hang of it."

I smiled. Oh, it was a grim smile to be sure, but there was a certain satisfaction in being able to force my lips into a smile. "I have no complaints about the romantic portion of my life whatsoever, so you can put your mind to rest on that matter."

"I'm glad to hear that," Gabriel said from behind me. His dimples were in evidence as he held out his hand for me. "I am loath to interrupt you ladies, but we have an appointment we must keep."

Cyrene watched as we left, her blue eyes filled with concern that, despite my efforts, was not alleviated.

"You are no doubt wondering why I did not speak up at the *sárkány*," Gabriel said a few minutes later when we were in his car, zooming through the streets of Paris.

"I assumed you had a reason for keeping mum about the fact that Fiat most decidedly did not challenge Bao for the right to rule the red dragons."

"You are as smart as you are beautiful," he said, his teeth flashing in a quick grin. "In fact, you are correct. I debated bringing the method of Fiat's coup to the attention of the weyr, but upon consideration, I decided little would be gained by such an act, and quite possibly much lost."

"Much lost?" I frowned. "I don't see what would be lost, except Fiat. Now you have him as a member of the weyr, with the potential to make serious trouble for you."

"You've met Chuan Ren," he said with a little quirk of his eyebrows. "Do you believe she will allow Fiat to remain in control of her beloved sept?"

A light dawned in the dim recesses of my brain. "Oh, I think I understand the devious way your mind words."

"Intricate, little bird. My mind is intricate, not devious."

I leaned over and nipped his bottom lip, stomping down hard on the dragon shard as it demanded I do much, much more. "It was meant as a compliment, I assure you. So you expect that if Chuan Ren returns to our world, she will take care of the problem of Fiat, leaving you blameless?"

He was silent for a moment, his fingers stroking mine in a gentle rhythm. "Why is it I can no longer read your thoughts, I wonder?"

"I didn't know you couldn't."

His silver eyes considered me gravely. "I've only just become aware of the fact."

"Does that have something to do with Fiat?" I asked, confused by the juxtaposition of subjects.

"In a way, perhaps it does. It is for your sake that I did not present the truth about Fiat at the *sárkány.* You are about to ask me why — I can sense that without reading your mind," he said with a brief dimpling of his cheeks. "Fiat in ostensible control of the red dragons, while not an ideal situation, offers, at least, some control in the form of weyr laws. Having been once removed from the weyr, he will be certain to follow the rules to the letter."

I shook my head. "As far as I see it, he violated the laws by simply hacking off Bao's head rather than challenging her as he should have."

His fingers curled around mine, and I allowed myself a moment to enjoy the sensation. I have always been a fairly tactile person, and holding Gabriel's hand seemed an intimate act, our fingers entwined much as our souls were. "That would be true if Bao was legally the wyvern of the red dragons, but with Chuan Ren alive, it's doubtful the control was passed over in a proper manner."

"So you're saying that Fiat, who wasn't technically the wyvern of the blue dragons despite claiming he was, took over for Bao, who likewise had moved into the wyvern spot when Chuan Ren was banished to Abaddon, but who also didn't formally challenge for the position?"

"Correct. Thus, at best, the punishment against Fiat would have been for the murder of a member of the red dragons. And although I am opposed to murder for any reason, Fiat would most certainly strike back should I present your evidence."

I searched his face, reading the truth in his eyes. "You're afraid he'd challenge you for me."

His fingers tightened. "I do not fear a challenge of *lusus naturae,* little bird. You are my mate, and I will not give you up to any other. But Fiat would seek you not for yourself, but for what you bear."

"The dragon shard," I said, closing my eyes for a moment as nausea gurgled around in my belly. "I understand your reasoning, but I don't see what will prohibit him from challenging you for me even if he is the red wyvern. The weyr allows those sorts of challenges."

"That's why I put that little worm in his brain," Gabriel answered, his voice hard. "Only a wyvern may. challenge for a wyvern's mate, and he is now aware that I know the truth about his method of taking control of the red dragons. He'll know that if he challenges me for you, I will simply reveal the fact that he is not a wyvern at all. Much as I believe he would wish to possess the dragon shard, he will value the position of wyvern more."

I looked at him with open admiration. "And to think I thought you were just an extremely pretty face attached to an incredibly hot body."

"Modesty has never been one of my strong points," he admitted, glancing out of the window when the car stopped in front of a familiar hotel. "We are here. Just when I was going to allow you to praise me more, too. Alas."

"I thought we were going to Drake's house to discuss all of this." I said as he helped me out of the car.

The smile he gave me was pure wolf.

"Drake asked us to come in a few hours, after Aisling has had time to rest. That gives us time to . . . *discuss* . . . things first."

CHAPTER
TWENTY-ONE

A little ripple of fire swirled around me, but I stamped it out immediately, not wishing to attract attention. "Gabriel, I don't think that's going to be such a great idea —"

"I have something I wish to show you," he whispered in my ear as we stood before the elevator.

His breath on my neck sent another wave of desire crashing through me. I fisted my hands to keep the claws from popping out, fighting the shard for control of my emotions.

Gabriel, Tipene, and Maata discussed Fiat as we made our way to the suite. I struggled with myself, part of me desperately wanting to have the *discussion* that Gabriel indicated, the other part sick at the idea of losing control.

"Pass the word through the sept to be cautious with regards to the red dragons," Gabriel told them as he led me to his bedroom.

"Explain what has happened, but remind everyone that the silver dragons' official stance is one of neutrality."

The bedroom door closed on Maata's acquiescence. I half expected him to pounce on me right then and there, but he dropped my hand and went over to a safe set into the wall, twirling the knob as he whistled softly to himself.

"Gabriel, I think we need to have a little talk," I said, preparatory to explaining my reluctance to engage in any lovemaking.

"Certainly, if you like. But my mother reminded me I was remiss in giving you a gift."

"What sort of a gift?" I asked, curious despite my better intentions. I peered over his shoulder as he shuffled through a couple of black leather boxes inside the safe. He pulled one out.

"Ah, there it is. It is tradition in my mother's family for the men to give their brides a necklet. This one was my great-great-grandmother's. I think you'll like it. It's gold."

He opened the case, and instantly the smell of the gold hit me. It was a hundred times more potent than the gold dust he'd used earlier, leaving me feeling as if I had been zapped with electricity, every hair on my head standing on end as the rich, sensual, intoxicating scent of gold permeated my pores. I ripped my clothing off, actually ripped it off, flinging myself on Gabriel as I snatched up the thin square plates that had been strung together in a tight choker of gold, rubbing it between us as my body turned into one gigantic erogenous zone.

"Gold," I said, making a little purr of pleasure as the metal touched my bared flesh.

Gabriel's smile was slow and knowing. "I thought you might like it, since you enjoyed the dust. Kind of makes you tingle, doesn't it?"

I licked him. "I want to rub it on you."

Instantly, he was naked, his eyes burning with a fire almost as bright as the one that he had started in me. "I'd rather you rub yourself on me. Well, perhaps both you and the gold."

"Mmm." I arched my back, trailing a red claw down his chest, the other hand dragging the gold necklet across his collarbone. I kissed the path the gold had followed, tasting both Gabriel and the arousing bite of gold. I wanted him, all of him, right then, and there was nothing or no one who could stop me. He was my mate, we had gold, and there was only one way things were going to end.

"Take me," I demanded, flinging myself on him and wrapping my legs around his hips. The impact of me slamming into him so unexpectedly resulted in him taking a couple of steps backwards until he bumped up against a table. He sat down on it suddenly, impaling me as he did so.

I squealed with absolute pleasure at the invasion, squirming against him, the sleek silver scales on his chest sliding against my own in a sensation so erotic, my mind was completely consumed with thoughts of nothing but joining body and soul with him, our dragon essences bound together until there was no discerning a difference.

The last little fragment of my true self gave a hopeless cry of defeat, checking the dragon shard for a moment.

"Mayling, don't stop now," Gabriel murmured, his mouth busy with my breast as I rode him, my hips moving in a rhythm that seemed to sing with the beauty of our act.

But it wasn't beautiful, not when it wasn't really me who was there with him. With a cry of pain that went soul deep, I tore myself off of him, backing away with my arms wrapped around myself.

"May?" Gabriel's face was a study in

confusion. "What's wrong?"

I sank to my knees, rocking with pain and regret and confusion, not sure of what I wanted anymore, not sure even of whether my thoughts were my own.

"Please, little bird. Tell me what I've done." Gabriel's hands were warm on my knees as I rocked silently, wishing things had happened differently.

"May. Please."

I couldn't ignore the pain in his voice. He thought it was something he'd done, and I couldn't let him continue to think that.

"Put the necklace away," I said, the scent of it driving me almost insane with desire.

He said nothing but returned it to the box, locking it away in the safe.

"It's the dragon shard," I said, looking up at him as he returned to me. My heart was so filled with regret, I thought it might break.

A little frown appeared between his brows. "You're still worried about that? I've told you that you will learn the ways —"

"I don't want to," I interrupted with a wail, taking his hands and tugging him down to me. "Don't you see? I don't want to be a dragon, Gabriel! I never did! But the shard is too strong for me. It's taking over, and every time we make love, it gains a little more ground. It's not going to take much more and it'll have taken over *all* of me!"

"It's taking you over?" He touched one of my scarlet claws. "You mean physically? That will end when the shard is placed in another phylactery."

"No, not just physically. It's taking over my emotions, too! Haven't you noticed? I can't believe you haven't noticed. Dear gods, man, I'm almost yelling, and as you pointed out, I never yell! Cyrene yells, but I don't."

He looked thoughtful for a moment. "You have been a little . . . er . . . passionate the last few days."

"I was passionate about you before the phylactery exploded. But the shard is doing more than just making me want you — it's changing my emotions, changing me, and Gabriel, what if I don't change back when the shard is gone? What if we can't get rid of it?"

He opened his mouth to protest, but stopped. "I wish I could assure you that your fears are unfounded, but I don't know the answer to your questions."

"You see?" I said, all but sobbing. "I can't make love to you, Gabriel. I want to, but not at the cost of losing the last little bit of me. I don't want to be a dragon. I may not be perfect, or even remotely close to that, but I was happy being me. I'm sorry. I'm really, really sorry."

He laughed, and for a moment I wanted to punch him. But then a tiny shred of common sense rose up to point out the unlikelihood of him mocking my concerns. "Mayling, making love to you will remain at the top of my daily list of things to do, but as I assured you once before, I am not a beast. If you require a little space to put things into perspective, then I will gladly give it to you." He glanced down at his erection. "It will not be easy, but if you wish to remain chaste for a bit, I will not force myself upon you."

"I didn't mean I was sorry that I couldn't make love to you," I said, forlorn knowledge making me want to burst into tears. I swallowed back a painful lump. "I meant I'm sorry that I can't be the dragon you obviously want."

"Now you are acting all too human, fishing for compliments," he said with a playful grin that faded when I didn't respond. "You're serious, aren't you?"

I nodded, too miserable to speak, my eyes on the carpet beneath my knees.

"May, look at me."

It took a bit of doing, but I managed to drag my gaze up to his.

"Before, when you started the mating dance, it was exciting to me," he said, and my heart turned into a leaden ball. "I would like to say I could have not responded, but that would be impossible. I am a dragon. You are my mate. You initiated a mating dance, and that delighted me. But that delight was nothing compared to what you mean to me. You are my mate, May, the being that is you, no matter what your form."

Unfamiliar tears pricked my eyes. I hated the dragon shard for making me feel so overwhelmed with gratitude, so vulnerable. "You wouldn't want me to be a dragon like you?"

"Not if you don't want it, no," he said, taking both my hands in his, kissing each finger. "You are happy as you are — were — and I have no complaints whatsoever about that state of affairs. So you can stop feeling guilty and unhappy, and instead tell me what your limit is."

"My limit?" I said, blinking away the last of the tears, my heart once again hopeful. Perhaps it was a sign I was all too human in that I sought reassurance that he treasured me for what I was, but if so, I embraced that humanity. "What sort of a limit do you mean?"

"How far can you go without the dragon shard taking control of you?" he asked, his thumbs rubbing across my fingers.

A little fire started at my knees.

"Ah," he said, looking at it.

I couldn't help but smile. "Just looking at you makes the shard kick into high gear, but I can keep it under control for the most part. It's just when we . . . er . . . that it takes over. And bringing gold into the equation is definitely out."

"Can I kiss you?" he said, bending forward to press a kiss of infinite sweetness onto my lips.

"Yes," I said, lifting my head in hopes he'd do it again.

"Can I touch you here?" He put his hand on my upper arm.

I nodded.

A little glint of wicked intent started to burn in his eyes. "What about here?"

His hand cupped my left breast. I sucked in my breath, arching my back. "Oh, yes."

"And how about this?"

His mouth closed over my aching nipple, his tongue a brand as it swept across my breast, causing my breath to catch in my mouth. My hands went to his hair, tugging on the soft dreadlocks as he kissed his way over to the other breast.

"That's . . . that's . . . that's really, really OK," I said, my eyes closed as I clutched him while he tormented my breast.

"Just OK? You wound my ego, little bird. What about the rest of your torso? Are you still firmly in control if I explore the sublime beauty that is your belly?"

Fire licked my flesh when he laid me back on the floor, his hair trailing down my sensitive breasts as he kissed a path to my belly button.

"The dragon shard wants me to roll you over and jump on you," I moaned as he nipped my hip.

"It shall have to want in vain. You are in control, not it, May."

"I know, but it's so strong, Gabriel. The need in me is so strong. It wants you."

"It only reflects your desires, which does much to assuage my male pride," he said with a deep chuckle that seemed to reverberate through me. His hands slid along my thighs, gently parting them. "Will it let me touch you here, do you think?" he asked.

His breath was hot on highly sensitive flesh.

"The shard can take a flying leap as far as I'm concerned," I said, my body tight with anticipation as I struggled to control the rising demands that built up inside me. I wanted to tease and run and play and do all sorts of things to Gabriel that seemed both foreign and yet so right. My fingers dug into the thick pile of the carpet as Gabriel's mouth touched me, the heat of his tongue almost causing me to lose the control I just barely held.

"Too much?" he asked, looking up at me.

"Almost," I said, my voice thick and unfamiliar.

"Do you want me to stop?"

I closed my eyes for a minute, concentrating fully on reining in the demands of the dragon shard. "No. I think I'm OK."

"You're more than OK, but that conversation is for another time. First we have this to explore."

Stars seemed to explode behind my eyes as he slid a finger into me just as his tongue made a swirling motion. The orgasm rippled through me, my fingers elongating as the red claws dug deep into the carpet.

"Keep ahold of the emotions the shard generates," Gabriel said, moving over me as he kissed his way upward. "Use it, but don't let it take over."

I struggled to do just that, the claws fading back into fingernails.

"Can you take more?" he asked, and I saw in his face just how much control he was wielding over his own needs.

"Let's try," I said, twining my legs around his as I dug my fingers into the thick muscles of his butt, pulling him where I wanted him.

"I'll stop if it's too much for you," he said, biting my neck with a groan when he sank into my body. "It may kill me, but I'll stop."

I held him tight to me as our bodies moved, praying I could do this without succumbing. The dragon shard wanted me to do more, to make Gabriel move faster, to satisfy urges that were too numerous to count.

It wasn't until his movements became more agitated that the thin control began to unravel. As the orgasm built up inside me, I flexed my inner muscles, urging Gabriel to finish before I lost it completely.

"Mayling, I'm trying to go slow for you, but if you do that, it will all be over," he said, panting as his chest rubbed against mine, his hips making long, slow movements that both thrilled and tormented me.

"Now!" I said, feeling the dragon shard take over as another climax crested. "For the love of the twelve gods, Gabriel, finish now!"

He shifted, his cry of my name echoing in my ear as his body elongated and changed, and within me, the dragon shard rejoiced and started forcing me to change with him.

"No!" I sobbed, clutching him as I fought back the need to answer his unspoken call.

Immediately he was back, his mouth hot as he kissed me, his body still trembling with little aftershocks of pleasure. "Do not fear, little bird. You did it, you embraced the strong emotions, and you did not change."

I clung to him as he rolled over, pulling me with him, mindless with pleasure on one level, but knowing just how close a thing it had been.

CHAPTER
TWENTY-TWO

Three hours later, we arrived at Drake's Paris house. "So, what exactly are you going to tell Drake and Aisling about Fiat?"

"What they need to know to help us with Chuan Ren."

I waited until we entered the spacious entrance hall, divesting myself of my coat before stopping Gabriel. "Are you sure this is a good idea, involving them in the whole thing? Drake isn't going to let Aisling do anything that will endanger her or the baby, and I just don't know that anyone else has the ability to help us. Maybe if I was to force Magoth to help us, threaten him somehow —"

He stopped me with a kiss so hot, it made me want to jump him right there, in front of everyone. "My fierce little bird. Just when I am convinced that you could not get along without me, your claws come out and I live in fear you'll fly away from me."

I stared at him for a moment, my fingers moving against my legs to make sure that the claws weren't evident.

The teasing light in his eyes faded when I didn't respond.

"There you are!" Aisling said, emerging from what I remembered as being the downstairs bathroom. "Drake's in the lounge. Come in and have a drink. I bet you could use one after having to sit through all that bull from Fiat. I know I could, but the best I'll get is juice. No reason you all should suffer, though."

"I'd like a stiff belt, too," Jim said, following her into the sitting room. "All that restraint you made me show has left a really nasty taste in my mouth. Scotch on the rocks, István. No, make that a double."

"You let your demon drink?" I said as Gabriel, his bodyguards, and I entered the room. Gabriel passed me a glass of dragon's blood, the spicy drink that only dragons could drink without lethal repercussions.

"Not after the last time when it got drunk and called up Whoopi Goldberg to demand airtime on *The View*," Aisling said with a dark look at her demon dog. "You'll have ginger ale and like it, buster."

"Bully," the demon muttered, glaring at

the bowl that Drake's bodyguard set in front of it.

"I don't want to seem rude, but is this a social visit, or are you going to talk dragon business?" Aisling asked, sighing as Drake stuffed a pillow behind her back. "If it's the former, no sweat, but if you're going to talk about Fiat or Kostya, I'd appreciate it if you can do it in the next twenty minutes."

"Why twenty minutes?" I asked, puzzled by such an odd request.

"Baby's right on my bladder," she said, patting her bulging belly. "You've got my undivided attention until she makes it impossible for me to sit still any longer."

"Oh, I didn't know you decided to find out the gender. A girl! How exciting," I said.

"Aisling is having a boy," Drake said, seating himself next to his wife. "Everyone knows that girls are nothing but trouble. We will have a son."

"Ha!" Aisling elbowed him in the ribs. "You are so delusional. It's girls who are easy, and boys who are trouble. We will have a daughter, a lovely girl who won't put up with any of the medieval bossiness you're sure to try to pull on her."

Drake sent Gabriel a long-suffering look that had me smiling. "I would caution you to wait before having children, but I suspect that May will do exactly as she wishes, including deliberately having a female despite the well-established fact that male dragons are much easier to raise."

"The father determines gender, which you well know," Aisling said complacently, beaming at us as we sat across from her. "So are we chitchatting or dragon talking?"

"Dragon talk," Gabriel answered, his gaze flickering to Drake. "There is a situation with regards to the red dragons."

"I suspected as much," Drake said easily. "Fiat's reappearance and claim are a bit too pat for my liking."

With admirable brevity, Gabriel recounted the experiences of Cyrene, Maata, and myself in Fiat's underground environs. By the time he was finished, Drake was pacing the length of the room.

"I've never seen people pace as much as dragons do," I was moved to say in an aside to Aisling.

She nodded. "It's all that pent-up energy — they have to move, or it manifests itself in fire, and frankly, I'd rather put up with a stiff neck from watching them march back and forth. Our fire-retardant bill is high enough as is."

"Why didn't you mention any of this at the *sárkány?*" Drake demanded to know.

Gabriel glanced to me. Drake stopped in midpace.

"Ah. The shard. Yes. I see you had little choice but to allow Fiat to continue unimpeded."

"I don't get it," Aisling said, looking confused. "But wait, potty break. Explain it when I get back."

Drake hauled her out of the couch and sent her on her way.

Jim watched me with an avidity that made me uncomfortable.

"Stop doing that," I told it.

It grinned. "You know the rules as well as I do — I don't have to do what you say."

I gave it a thin-lipped look. "All I have to do is tell Aisling —"

"Sheesh! No one can take a joke anymore," Jim interrupted, rolling its eyes. "Fine, I won't look at you. I won't touch you, and I won't sit on your side of the car, either. Happy now?"

I ignored the demon to watch Gabriel and Drake as the two men talked about what Bao, Fiat, and the mysterious dragon had possibly been up to. When I glanced back, the demon was staring at me again.

"Will you stop that?" I hissed through my teeth.

"Sorry. Can't help myself. I've never seen

anyone but Ash who lipped off to Bael and lived to tell about it."

"I didn't lip off to him," I said, moving uncomfortably in my chair.

"Back," Aisling said as she returned, patting Jim on the head. "What have I missed?"

"Not much. Drake and Gabe are arguing about what it means that Baltic has returned from the dead, István has gas, and May was being mean to me," Jim said, plopping down on her feet.

István and I both glared at the demon.

"I'm sure if May was mean to you, you deserved it," Aisling said with perfect composure.

"I didn't —"

She waved away my protest. "Feel free to ignore Jim when it's being an idiot."

"Hey! Sitting right here!"

"So that guy you saw really was Baltic?" Aisling asked me.

Gabriel returned to his chair. "We do not know. There seems to be some ambiguity about his identity. However, that has no bearing on the reason I have sought your help."

"Fiat," Drake said, nodding.

"I don't think so, sweetie," Aisling told him, watching me. "It's your demon lord, isn't it? You kind of glossed over how things went with him, but I assume it wasn't a roaring success."

"Far from it," Gabriel said with a wry twist to his lips. "We had thought to tackle Magoth again, but unless we have something to use as barter, he won't help us."

"And even if we had something, there's no guarantee he wouldn't just take it and leave us poorer for the experience, as we've learned," I added.

"What do you guys expect?" Jim asked, rolling its eyes. "He's a demon lord. Tricking people is part of his job."

"Jim has a point," Aisling said, looking thoughtful. "I suppose I could ask the Guardians' Guild if they could help with the situation, but they're not really happy with me ever since . . . Well, they're not happy with me."

"Was it me?" I asked, worried that I'd gotten her in trouble with her professional organization. "Was it summoning me so often that got you into hot water with them?"

Jim snickered. Aisling looked embarrassed. "Er . . . no. It was nothing, really, just a minor little thing that doesn't matter, or it wouldn't except the head of the guild might not consider a request by me for help to be awfully high on his to-do list."

"She turned him into a simulacrum," Jim told me in a confidential tone.

"A simulacrum?" I asked, astounded. "A living statue?"

"It was just an unfortunate accident," Aisling said, waving it away. "There was a kobold outbreak in London when we were there, and I convinced Drake to let me help take care of it, and somehow, rather than binding the kobolds so they could be sent back to Abaddon, I zapped Caribbean Battiste, the head of the guild, instead, and he was temporarily changed into a simulacrum. But I got it reversed by nightfall, so really, I don't see why everyone had such a hissy fit. It wasn't like it was permanent."

I looked at her with renewed respect. Anyone who had the power to change the head of a Guardians' order into a statue was potentially someone who was the answer to my prayers. "We need your help. I hope we can count on it?"

"With your demon lord? Absolutely," Aisling said at the same time Drake said, "No."

The two glared at each other.

"You are not going to get involved with another demon lord," Drake told her. "It is too dangerous."

Aisling opened her mouth to protest but closed it again without saying anything for a moment. "All right," she said finally, causing Drake to shoot her a look of surprise. "Maybe Nora was right and the baby is making my grip on my Guardian abilities a bit iffy. Magoth may not be much in this world, but he is still a demon lord, so I'm going to retract my agreement and instead offer Nora's services. I'm sure she'll be delighted to help you. What, exactly, do you need Magoth to do?"

"Nothing." Gabriel pulled me up beside him.

"I don't understand," she said, looking from him to me. "What am I missing?"

Jim snorted.

"Before Magoth left with Sally in tow, she pulled me aside and pointed out that Chuan Ren was a dragon," I told her.

"Chuan Ren? Well, yeah. But what does she have to do with Magoth?" Aisling asked, still puzzled.

"She doesn't have anything to do with Magoth — it was Bael who found her after you banished her," I said, exchanging a glance with Gabriel.

"Heh. They deserve each other," Aisling said with satisfaction.

Gabriel gave my waist a little squeeze of confidence. I took a deep breath and continued. "We knew that Chuan Ren was a dragon, of course, but my experience with dragons has been limited until the last two months, and it just didn't strike me that although everyone is treating Chuan Ren like Bael's minion, she's not. She can't be; dragons can't be servants of demon lords. It's just impossible."

Aisling nodded. "That's why we can't summon her, as we could a demon, not that I could think of a conceivable reason to even want to do that."

"Exactly. But it also means that we don't have to go through Bael to get her."

"Why do you want to get to her? I'm sorry," Aisling said, smiling. "The pregnancy is draining all my brain cells obviously, but I still don't see your point."

"If I say the obvious, will you banish me to the Akasha?" Jim asked, its eyes hopeful.

"Yes."

"Damn."

I leaned back against Gabriel, seeking strength. "The point is — and don't beat yourself up for not seeing it; I certainly didn't and I know Abaddon better than you — the point is that Bael is holding Chuan Ren against her will. She's his prisoner, not a minion. Which means the only way she can leave him is either for him to give her up or for her banishment to be reversed."

"A recall," Aisling said, enlightenment finally striking her. "Well, yes, that would work. I did banish her, so I have the power to recall her. But for one thing, of course."

My heart, which had begun to soar at the possibility of a solution to the problem of Chuan Ren, fell at her words. "What one thing?" I asked.

She shook her head. "I'd have to be insane to do it. I'm sorry, but I can't recall Chuan Ren. I sent her to Abaddon for a reason. She's just too dangerous to the green dragons. I really wish I could help you, May, but I can't."

CHAPTER
TWENTY-THREE

It took longer than I expected to recall Chuan Ren from Abaddon. The problem ended up being Drake rather than Aisling, the latter of whom, like any intelligent woman, immediately grasped the finer points of the argument Gabriel and I put forward.

"You know, that's not a bad idea at all," she said after Gabriel explained how we saw things. "It might work. If Chuan Ren wants out of Abaddon bad enough, she'll have to agree to ending the war with us; otherwise, *pfft.* Right back she goes. And you said she's not having fun there. Heh-heh-heh."

I watched Aisling chuckling to herself, not doubting for an instant that Chuan Ren deserved her time with Bael, but amused nonetheless. "We wouldn't ask you to reinstate Chuan Ren to this world without due cause, I assure you. But we felt this would solve all of our problems — allow me access to the red dragons' shard, end the war between your two septs, and take care of Fiat."

"I knew I liked you," Aisling said, giving me a nod of encouragement. "So all that remains is for me to recall Chuan Ren, and we'll see what she has to say. If she refuses to go along with it, we'll just dump her back on Bael's lap and figure out something else."

I didn't want to consider failure. There were no other options that I could see . . . other than allowing the shard to take me over completely.

"Right. Let's get started," Aisling said, trying unsuccessfully to hoist herself to her feet. "Drake, let me up."

"You are not going to recall Chuan Ren," her husband said, holding her back so she couldn't rise.

She shot him an annoyed look. "You're not going to pull any of that crap about it being too dangerous for me, are you? Because I can assure you that a simple thing like a recall is not going to go awry."

"Kobolds," Jim said, raising its brows. "Caribbean as a statue. 'Nuff said."

"Shush, you. Drake, stop giving me that obstinate look. This won't go wrong, I promise."

"You are not summoning Chuan Ren into

our house, where she can attack and possibly harm you," he said calmly.

"But you'll be here. And István and Pál, and Gabriel. Even May has a dagger! Chuan Ren isn't going to have the chance to get near me."

"It's out of the question." If I'd thought Drake had been stubborn before, I was to learn a new respect for the word. It took a solid hour of arguing before we finally came to a compromise.

"I don't see that this is any less dangerous than me just simply summoning Chuan Ren," Aisling said grumpily as she prepared to send Jim and me to Abaddon. "What if they're caught?"

"May has access to the shadow world, and Jim can be resummoned if it loses its form," Drake answered, his arm around her as he helped her to her feet after she'd drawn an emergency summoning circle on the floor.

"Oh, man! I just broke in this form, too! I'm gonna scream if I have to get another one!"

Drake ignored Jim's complaint. "If either of them is seen in Bael's domicile, they can take steps to protect themselves."

"You might just want to remind Gabriel of that fact, because he doesn't look any too happy about having May going to Abaddon without him," Aisling said.

She was right. Gabriel had put up a bit of a fuss when Drake first suggested the plan, saying it was too dangerous for me.

"I know my way around demon lords," I told him again, brushing my lips against his. His eyes were glittering, but it was the cold light of mercury rather than the usual white-hot heat. "And Jim's been to Bael's domain before, so it'll help me get around without being seen. We'll just pop in, get Chuan Ren to formally end the war and agree to the rest of our terms, and be back without Bael or anyone else in Abaddon being the wiser."

I thought for a moment that he wasn't going to respond to me, but that passed the instant the fire in me heard its answer in him. He hauled me upward as his mouth all but devoured mine, his fingers digging deep into my hips. Mindless of our surroundings, I wrapped my legs around him, twining my tongue around his as it did a fire dance in my mouth. Claws emerged from my fingers as the inferno within me spun out of control, sweeping us up until we were a firestorm of love, passion, and desire. The dragon within me roared to life, causing me to arch back from him as it transformed me.

"Holy Jehoshaphat!" Aisling said at the same time Jim demanded a video camera.

"Is she turning into a dragon?"

Gabriel pulled me back from the brink just in time. He let me slide down his body, his hands cupping my face, his eyes burning through straight to my soul. "You are my life," was all he said, but within those few words was a world of emotion. My heart sang as it heard the unspoken words, and slowly, bit by bit, I regained myself until once again I stood before him a woman.

One who loved him more than anything existence had to offer.

"I love you," I whispered, my lips on his.

His eyes shone, but all he said was, "Come back to me safe, little bird."

"That's a promise," I said, stepping backwards, my eyes on him as I reached out a hand.

Jim thrust its head under it. I grasped its collar, feeling a modicum of reassurance in not going to Abaddon alone.

"Seat backs and trays in an upright position, please," Aisling said, warding both Jim and me before she made a sweeping gesture that ripped the fabric of time and space. "Have a nice time in Hell."

"Famous last words," Jim said as we stepped through.

Gabriel said nothing, but the memory of his face remained with me as we went into the maelstrom that resulted in us falling into darkness.

"You OK, May? Hey, you OK? You hit your head or something?"

Pain from the front of my head ebbed, as did the darkness. I rolled over and found myself looking up the large black nostrils of a Newfoundland. "Yes, I'm all right, and, ow, yes, I hit my head. Oh." My memory returned as I sat up, blinking away the accompanying dizziness. "Where are we?"

"By the looks of it, some sort of linen closet. If I had to guess, I'd say we're in the basement of Bael's palace in Abaddon."

Gingerly, I felt the knot at the front of my head. "What makes you say that?"

"That," Jim said, nodding to a clipboard that hung on a nail next to the door of the large walk-in closet.

I got to my feet and examined it. "Palace" headed the top of the paper attached to the clipboard, followed by a summary of linens and textiles. "For some reason, I find it extremely odd that a demon lord would take the time to inventory sheets and towels," I said, replacing the clipboard.

"He's the premiere prince. You think they give that job to people who don't know how to micromanage?" Jim shook its head. "You have a thing or two to learn, sister."

"Don't call me that. How long was I out?" I asked, straightening my clothing and opening the door just enough to peek out.

"About three minutes. I heard voices outside, but they left."

We were speaking in whispers, the silence of Bael's palace oppressive enough to cause even our whispers to sound reedy and insubstantial. "I don't see anyone now. Are you sure you know your way around here?"

"Yeah. Been here a couple of times with my old boss, and Ash landed here once or twice, as well. We need to go up to Bael's dungeon."

"Up for a dungeon?" I asked as we slipped out of the room and, after listening intently for a few seconds to make sure no one was out there, made our silent way down the dimly lit hallway. "I thought they were normally kept in a basement."

"If it was down here, then Bael wouldn't be able to hear the screams of his captives as they're tortured," Jim pointed out.

I made a face at that thought, tempted to shadow since the light was dim enough that I might escape being seen should we run into someone, but Jim was highly identifiable. If it was found, Bael would know someone else was with the demon, and the hunt would be on. "Just get us to Chuan Ren."

We had a few close calls with servants and minions running around as they carried out Bael's commands, but luck, for a change, was with us, and we found Chuan Ren with only relatively little trouble.

"That's the only door with a guard. My money is on that one being Chuan Ren's cell. Ouch. Wrath demon," Jim whispered as we huddled together peering around a corner at a door in front of which a human-looking guard sat — a huge human-looking guard, one that, were it actually human, would probably be a multimillion-dollar star linebacker.

Jim eyed me as I sank to the ground with an inaudible moan of dismay. "*Agathos daimon*. A wrath demon."

"Yeah, nasty business. I don't suppose you've ever dealt with one before?"

I shook my head.

"I hate to say it, but you're on your own here," Jim said with sickening cheerfulness. "I might be able to harm a lesser demon, but a wrath? Nuh-uh. Those guys are death on two legs."

"I know," I said, thinking frantically while keeping an ear cocked for anyone who might choose to stroll down the corridor in which we crouched.

Wrath demons, for those of you who aren't bound to a demon lord, are the first lieutenants in a demon lord's legion of minions. If you think of the worst qualities of various mass murderers, psychopaths, dictators, and sadists, and roll them all together into one beefy package of just about indestructible bulk, you'd get a pale approximation of a wrath demon.

And lucky me, there was one standing between Chuan Ren and my future.

"There's only one way we're getting past that door, and that's to take out the wrath demon. Right. Jim, you're going to be the distraction."

"Me?" it yelped, its eyes huge. "It'll destroy my gorgeous form in about two seconds flat!"

"No, it won't. You belong to another demon lord, and you know the rules about demons destroying each other — it's grounds for extermination. Just pretend that Aisling is here, and she sent you down on some errand or other."

"That's a first-class demon!" Jim protested. "I can't talk to it! I'm only sixth class."

"There's nothing in the Doctrine that says you can't. Just come up with some story that will buy me a couple of seconds."

The demon made a face. "Even if I do come up with a story, it's not going to believe me. Bael wouldn't let me wander around without supervision."

"It doesn't have to believe you, it just needs to be focused on you for a few seconds while I slip past it."

Jim looked skeptical. "Wrath demons can see shadow walkers, you know. They can even see into the shadow world."

"But not very clearly. If you hold its attention, I can slip into the shadow world and get by it into Chuan Ren's cell."

"Get in, maybe," Jim admitted grudgingly. "But how are you going to get out?"

"I'll worry about that when the time comes. Can you find your way back to the linen closet once I'm in with Chuan Ren?"

"Yeah. Assuming Wrathy there doesn't squash me into an incredibly handsome black pulp."

"It won't. It won't know for sure that Bael doesn't have a reason for accommodating Aisling."

"You'll leave me," it wailed softly, giving me a pitiful look. "You'll go off and leave me alone here."

"Aisling can summon you at any time," I pointed out.

"Not if I'm imprisoned, she can't," Jim said, glancing down the hall to the cell doors. "No demon gets out of those cells unless Bael wants them out."

"Oh." I wanted to point out that the likelihood of Jim ending up in a cell was slim, but the worried expression in the demon's eyes stopped me. "Well, that doesn't matter. I promise I won't leave Abaddon until you're with me again, or safe, OK?"

"All right, but if you forget, I'm never going to let you live it down."

I patted the demon dog on the head. "I won't forget. Give me about five seconds before you distract the wrath demon."

"If I didn't know better, I'd say you were taking lessons from Ash on how to come up with a wacky plan sure to go wrong," Jim said as I shadowed and slipped across the hall to the far wall.

I crept down the hall until I figured I was just outside of the range at which the demon might see me, holding my breath as Jim sauntered around the corner, whistling a jaunty tune.

"Heya," it called to the wrath demon, who stood up and glared with suspicion at Jim. "How're they hangin'? Assuming you got yourself some, that is. I myself have a really nice package. Aisling, that's my demon lord, says that it's just lucky that I'm furry; otherwise, she'd have to put a pair of underpants on me, ya know what I mean? Heh-heh-heh."

I gave a mental eye roll at Jim's choice of distracting topic, and moved into the shadow world. I'd never been in the parts of the shadow world where it touched Abaddon, and was taken aback for a moment by just how radically different it was. Whereas the normal shadow world was a slightly off version of the real world, the Abaddon-tinged version was a dark place that seemed to be made up of the memory of nightmares, with objects twisted in a parody of the original.

The wrath demon, oddly enough, didn't look any different in the shadow world, although there was a black corona that surrounded it. I was careful to avoid touching that as I squirmed past it, opening the cell door that was locked in the real world.

Chuan Ren sat immobile, her back to the wall of a bare cell that consisted of a repulsive straw pallet, a bucket that was no doubt used as a latrine, and a battered tray of what looked to be raw entrails heaped in a repulsive blob.

I stepped out of the shadow world and was instantly slammed against the wall,

Chuan Ren's claws digging deep into my throat.

"You," she spat, her dark eyes glowing with a red light.

The dragon shard inside me filled me with instant fury. Scarlet claws burst forth from my fingers, the silver scales following immediately as they rippled up and over my arms. I fought not just Chuan Ren, but the shard itself, which desperately wanted me to fully shift into a dragon.

"If you kill . . . me, you'll never . . . get out," I managed to gasp out as Chuan Ren attempted to throttle me.

I didn't expect her to release me at that, but to my surprise, she did just that. Her hands dropped to her sides, allowing me to slide to the floor, my fingers back to being my own. I rubbed my neck, coughing and wheezing as I tried to get air into my abused windpipe.

"Gabriel said he would not free me," she said, suspicion thick in the air.

I nodded, clearing my throat a couple of times to make sure I could talk. "He can't buy your freedom. Bael guaranteed that. But we don't need to get him to give you up when you are being held here against your will."

She grabbed my collar with one hand and

hauled me to my feet, giving me new respect for her physical strength. "How?"

"Aisling will recall you. Since she's the one who banished you here, she can recall you without going through elaborate ceremonies, or getting Bael's permission."

"Aisling," Chuan Ren said, her lips curling as she all but spat the name. "I will see her dead for what she's done to me."

"I don't think so," I said, shoving her hand off me. "In fact, you're not only going to be polite to her; you're going to call off the war against the green dragons. Unless you like spending your time as Bael's guest, that is."

An interesting parade of emotions passed over her face. Fury, disbelief, and more fury were followed by suspicion, and finally a cold, calculating look that indicated she was weighing her need to leave Abaddon against her desire to continue the war.

I expected some sort of protest on her part, but once again she surprised me. I guess it was because she had been wyvern for so many centuries, and thus used to making decisions on the fly, but she took less than a minute to work through all of her anger and allow reason to take its place. "There's nothing to stop me from declaring war again," was all she said.

"That's between you and the green dragons, although I should mention that your son has promised us the use of the Song Phylactery in exchange for freeing you."

The air cracked with energy as she sucked in a huge breath. I thought for a moment she was going to blast me with a fireball, the dragon heart insisting that I take immediate action against her, but she released her rage before I could do anything. "Tell me what he agreed to."

I explained the terms of the agreement with Jian along with our reason for wanting use of it, and after a moment's thought, she nodded her head. "Red dragons always honor their word. When you have the other shards collected, I will provide you with the Song Phylactery so that you can re-create the dragon heart. But you will not have the shard until then."

"That's acceptable," I agreed, wondering about her lack of demand for its immediate return afterwards. "I'll need your formal acceptance of this peace treaty before I can tell Aisling to begin the recall."

She snatched the thick vellum and pen I pulled from my leather bodice, snarling under her breath as she signed her name to it, using the nib of the pen to nick her finger, and sealing the treaty with blood, as was customary in the Otherworld.

"Excellent. I think you'll find that this was the wisest choice."

Her look should have dropped me dead on the spot. I just smiled as I rolled up the treaty and tucked it away. "I have to go back to the shadow world to let Aisling know she should begin the proceedings. It shouldn't take long, although I do feel that I should point out that Drake will make sure Aisling is well protected, so if you're planning on getting the jump on her once you're back in the world, you'd better think again."

She said nothing as I stepped back into the shadow world, but I sensed a great many emotions burbling around under the surface.

I closed my eyes for a moment, focusing my thoughts on Gabriel, reaching out to find the essence of him that I knew would be waiting for me in the shadow world. There was much in the space where it touched Abaddon that left me shaking with fear, but slowly I began to feel warmth, a comforting glow that filled me with light and love.

"Gabriel," I said, the word whisper soft.

"I am here, little bird," was his answer, his voice distant. I couldn't see him any more than he could see me, but just hearing his voice gave me comfort in a comfortless place. "Is it done?"

"Yes. Tell Aisling that Chuan Ren signed the treaty."

"Has she agreed to honor Jian's promise?" his voice asked, echoes of it rolling around me.

"She has."

There was silence for a moment. "I have told Drake. Aisling will begin the recall immediately. May . . ."

His voice stopped, and I was aware of a sense of something troubling him.

"What's wrong?"

"Is Chuan Ren there with you?"

I looked behind me. The cell was represented in the shadow world by sooty archways that led into inky darkness. The ground was covered with glittering dragon scales. In the middle a silhouette stood — Chuan Ren.

"I see her, yes."

"There in the shadow world?"

"No, in the cell."

Gabriel was silent for the count of twenty. "Then who is in there with you?"

"No one. It's just you and me."

The sense of unease in his voice grew. "May, there is someone else here. I can feel the presence of another dragon. Come back to me now, little bird."

I looked around, but there was no sign of anyone else visible. "I can't. I have to go back and get Jim first."

"Come back now, May," Gabriel insisted, louder and more strident.

The worry in his voice sent a little skitter of fear down my back. There was only one other dragon I knew of who could be in the shadow world. "I promised Jim I wouldn't leave without it."

Gabriel swore softly to himself, frustrated at being limited to an insubstantial presence in this world. "Get out. Get out of the shadow world. It is not safe for you here."

I thought of the wrath demon standing outside, in the real world. "I don't think it's terribly safe for me out there, either."

"Much as it distresses me to speak the words, you are Magoth's consort. Bael cannot harm you without violating the laws he enforces. I can rescue you from him, May, but I cannot save you from whoever is stalking the shadow world."

He had a point, but I didn't particularly like it.

CHAPTER
TWENTY-FOUR

Gabriel was adamant about me leaving the (relative) safety of the shadow world. "I will remain here in an attempt to locate the dragon. If Bael finds you, demand that he contact me for a ransom."

"Gabriel —"

"Please, little bird. Do as I ask."

When he put it like that, I couldn't come up with a good reason for refusing his request, so with reluctance, I left the shadow world . . . but not until I'd slipped as far away from the wrath demon at the door as I could manage.

Luckily, Chuan Ren's cries as she saw me distracted the guard, which allowed me to shadow and race out of her cell even as she was beating it on the head and demanding that it catch me.

"Oh, man, you came back? I figured you'd ditch me. I gotta say, May, if I was in your shoes, I probably would have left me behind," Jim said as I scooted into the linen closet where it was hidden.

Its words may have been flip, but relief filled its voice, and it butted its head against me in a gesture of affection.

"I won't say I didn't consider it, but I do try to keep my promises," I answered, patting it on the head and suffering a couple of happy swipes of its large tongue. "Before you start celebrating, though, we have to get out of here."

"I thought you were just going to find a way out of Abaddon via the beyond, and let Aisling summon me," it said.

"That was the original plan. It's been changed due to some unknown dragon finding his way into the shadow world." I opened the door and peeked out. Although I hadn't encountered anyone on the way back to the closet, signs of occupation around us were audible.

Jim whistled. "Dragon? Are you sure?"

"Yes."

"Ah. Baltic," Jim said, nodding.

I glanced down at the demon. "Why do you say that?"

"He studied with a famous archimage named von Endres. Antonia von Endres, I think. Everyone knows that mages have the ability to overcome most types of magic,"

Jim said with complacence. "If it's a dragon in the beyond, it's gotta be Baltic. He's the only one who has the ability to get in there. Which . . . Oh, wow, that means he probably is hunting you."

"Me? I don't see why, unless it's for the shard, and if it really is Baltic, then that won't make sense since he was the one who stuffed the blasted thing in Kostya's lair to begin with."

"What makes you think that?" Jim asked with a little curl of its lips.

"Well, someone who had the shard to begin with must have done it, and who else would have taken it from Kostya only to return it?"

"Dunno, but I don't think who used to have it is as important as who will be trying to get it now."

"Good point. And the sooner we get out of here, the safer the shard will be. Do you know if Bael's palace has a physical manifestation in our world?" I asked Jim.

"Yeah. House in England. Aisling went to it once. I think there's also a London house."

"Which means there's probably one in Paris, too, if he's maintaining multiple entrances from the real world to Abaddon. Let's hope we can find it quickly, before we're spotted."

It took some time, but we managed to make our way up to a level that seemed to have access into the mortal world. One was blocked by a bevy of female demons sporting wicked-looking swords, and another bore curses and spells that made the portal glow with black light.

"Third time's lucky," I said softly as we crept down an empty hallway toward a promising door.

"The only luck in Abaddon belongs to the master," a female voice said behind us.

I spun around and beheld the sight of another wrath demon, this one wearing the body of a pretty, but muscular, dark-haired woman. It strolled toward us with apparent nonchalance, but there was no mistaking the fact that it was probably capable of breaking both Jim and me in half if it so chose, quite possibly both of us at the same time.

I resisted the instinct to shadow and stood my ground as the demon approached, absently noting that there was a huge sword strapped to its back.

"*Eep*," Jim said, pressing into my leg. "Wrathy at twelve o'clock."

"So I see. Good afternoon. I assume I have the somewhat dubious pleasure of addressing one of Bael's elite guard?" I asked with the formal tone that folks in Abaddon seemed to prefer.

"I am Jecha. The lord Bael wishes me to inform you that you are now his prisoner. Your attempt to free his prize has not gone unnoticed, and you will pay the price for your actions." A nasty smile curved the demon's lips. "I've never tortured a doppelganger before. This should prove to be enjoyable."

With calm disdain I looked down my nose at the demon, which, given that it was several inches taller than me, wasn't particularly easy, or I fear effective. "Do you know who you address, demon? I am May, consort to Lord Magoth, sixth prince of Abaddon. By rights, you should kneel in my presence, but I will be gracious and allow you to stand."

"Ten out of ten for style," Jim said sotto voce, rubbing its head on my leg. "But something tells me you're going to have to win the swimsuit competition to get the big prize."

The demon smiled even more. It caused a muscle in my cheek to twitch uncontrollably. "Effrijim, demon sixth class, speaks the truth. You, however, do not, doppelganger."

"What do you mean?" I asked, frowning. "I am Magoth's consort. Bael cannot order my torture without violating the very laws he upholds."

"You were Magoth's consort . . . but with your act of insurrection against Lord Bael, Magoth has been excommunicated from Abaddon." Evil amusement danced in the demon's eyes. "Which means that you're no longer a consort to a demon lord and, hence, are an interloper and a thief. Do you know how Lord Bael deals with such?"

Fear chilled me. Not a faint, worrisome fear, but the sort of freezing fear that slows your brain and locks your body into a statue of absolute, complete terror. Bael had kicked out Magoth?

"Jim?" I asked, blinding reaching my hand out for its head.

"Right here."

"You remember what Aisling said?"

"Yup."

I figured it hadn't forgotten that Aisling had commanded it to follow any and all of my orders without exception.

"Excellent." One part of my brain started back up, rather sluggishly, but enough to trigger self-preservation. "Destroy!"

A large, black furry shape lunged upward from the floor as Jim threw itself at the demon, taking it by surprise. The demon fell over backwards, immediately pulling the sword from its scabbard. I stomped down hard on its hand, causing it to scream in pain, Jim taking advantage of the distraction to clamp its teeth down on the demon's other arm. I snatched up the sword, intending to disarm it and escape to the shadow world, but wrath demons are not so easily taken advantage of.

It spat out a few words, and instantly the ground was crawling with imps, nasty rage imps whose bodies were covered with a type of acid.

"Go!" Jim bellowed as it flung itself off the demon and onto the mass of imps that had risen as one to strike me.

I didn't wait to debate the point, not while the wrath demon was preparing to spring at me. I twirled around and left that reality for the shadow world, the demon's heavy sword still clutched in my hand as I raced away until I was sure it could no longer see me.

Instantly, I was aware of two things: one was Gabriel's presence, and the other was that he was absolutely correct — there was another dragon there.

The man I'd come to think of as Baltic stood at the end of the twisted parody of Bael's palace hallway. He spun around when

I entered the shadow world, avarice chasing disbelief across his face as he saw me.

"You!" he said first, then seemed to scent the air. "You bear the dragon shard?"

He started down the hallway toward me.

"May!" Gabriel yelled; he was not visible to me, but I could feel his presence nonetheless. "What are you doing? Leave now!"

I spun around on my heels and bolted, not wanting to stay around to see what Baltic had on his mind. "I can't!" I yelled to Gabriel as I raced around tortured bits of masonry and metal, sliding down an incline to a pit, only to leap up the other side and through a shattered archway. This part of Bael's palace seemed to be in ruins in the shadow world, making it difficult to navigate. "Bael knows about the recall. He's kicked out Magoth, which means I have no status."

Gabriel swore again, this time more profanely, railing against the fact that he was unable to help me.

I hurdled a fallen stone pillar, quickly crawling underneath it to curl up in the inky recess it created, holding my breath as a shadow touched me briefly as it sped past.

"May? May!"

I waited until the dragon was well past me before emerging from my hiding spot, silently racing back the way I'd come. I assumed he could hear Gabriel and me talking, but the diffusing effect the shadow world had on sound made it likely he couldn't pinpoint my location based on it.

"May, answer me!" Gabriel roared, anger, frustration, and an impotent fury audible in his voice.

"I'm here. I'll find a way out," I answered, taking a different path from the one that led to Chuan Ren's prison. "Don't worry about me, Gabriel. This is my world. I know my way around it."

"Gabriel," a male voice called out, uncomfortably close. I swung around and raced in the opposite direction. "Gabriel . . . Tauhou? Wyvern of the silver dragons."

Gabriel spat out something in the language I recognized as Zilant, the tongue used by dragons centuries before English was adopted as a universal means of communication.

The voice chuckled, the sound seemingly coming from everywhere at once. "And this is your mate? How did you get around the curse, I wonder. It is of little matter. She is no longer yours."

A wordless roar met that statement, one not of pain, but of absolute, unadulterated rage.

I paused for a second, startled by the depth of emotion in the sound.

"Find somewhere to hide," Gabriel yelled suddenly. "I will find you, little bird. Hide yourself and wait for me."

I wanted to point out the obvious, that even if he did find me, there was little he could do to help me since he had no physical presence in this world, but there seemed little use in that. I concentrated on controlling my breathing as I dashed around the shadow version of Bael's palace, seeking a place well away from the mysterious dragon where I could hide, or a passage out to the real world.

Time seemed to blur as I searched. It had been hard enough to find an exit in Bael's palace, but here in the shadow world, where the fabric of being had been warped by association with Abaddon, it was a nightmare of endless onyx archways leading to nowhere, pits that opened at my feet, broken columns and walls, and twisted black metal that clawed at me as I raced past.

A faint lightening in the distance heralded what might be a passage out of Abaddon. I stood for a moment, catching my breath before making my cautious way toward it, struggling to control the emotions the dragon shard had stirred in my flight. The hand gripping the demon's sword was stiff and aching. I relaxed my fingers, flexing them to restore the blood flow as I listened intently for sounds the dragon was near. For the previous fifteen or so minutes I hadn't heard anything but the normal muted sounds of the shadow world. Perhaps I'd given him the slip.

I looked at the promising light on the horizon, weighing my need to save myself with Gabriel's request that I find a hiding spot and wait for him. I shook my head as I considered the latter. "There's no time," I argued to myself. "Even if he got someone to come into the shadow world to help me, it would take that person too long to find me. I have to get out of Abaddon."

"I agree. Abaddon is no place for you," a voice said behind me. I snatched up the sword, whirling around to face the man who emerged from the shadow of a half-tumbled wall. He glanced at the weapon held in front of me, one eyebrow rising lazily. "You have nothing to fear from me, mate."

"I'm not even going to point out how ludicrous that statement is," I said, both of my hands holding the sword so it pointed at his heart. Dragons might be hard to kill, but even they wouldn't run headlong into a sword. "I will warn you that I have no intention of being taken away from Gabriel, nor will I allow you to take the dragon shard."

The dragon ignored both the threat and the sword as he circled around me, eyeballing me from the top of my head to the toes of my boots. I kept the sword between him and me, turning as he made his objectionable examination. "You are not as finely made as my mate was." A slow smile made his lips quirk. "On the other hand, there is much pleasure to be had in taking the mate of a silver dragon again."

"I'm not Ysolde," I said, wondering if my stab in the dark was going to find its mark. "And Gabriel is not Constantine Norka."

He lunged at me, snarling out something I didn't understand. I slashed at him with the sword, amazed as the air in front of me gathered into a blue light that formed itself in a sword. "Do not think that because I will take you as mate means you will be anything but a pale comparison to her. You are merely a female, a means to an end, a lesser dragon and nothing more."

"I'm not a dragon," I growled, the tip of my sword cutting through the air as I waved it in warning.

He looked at my hands. My fingers were long, covered in silver scales, and tipped with red.

"Not normally," I added, moving slightly to the side. If I could get around him, I might be able to race toward the spot that I thought might be an exit.

The blade of light flashed in an arc directly at me. I swung my sword upward, intercepting it, bracing myself for the inevitable blow. I was no stranger to swordplay, having had years of fencing lessons at Magoth's behest, but there was a great difference between learning the style of fencing used by actors, and fighting for your life with a maniac dragon who apparently had powers well beyond what anyone thought. The impact of his sword on mine sent me to my knees, sparks flying from the blades as they screamed with the impact. I held on to the demon blade with all my might as Baltic — there was no doubt in my mind that the dragon before me was him — stood above me, his eyes dark and unfathomable as he crushed me into the ground.

"If you kill me, you'll destroy the shard," I told him, every muscle in my arms screaming as I fought to keep his sword from striking me.

"There's no one to stop me from taking it from your corpse," he said, spinning around, the blade dancing in the air as it descended toward me again.

I rolled away, hoping to get to my feet, but as I was in the act of rising, Baltic's sword of light flashed, knocking mine from my hands. I watched in horror as it spun through the air, seemingly in slow motion, the dim light twinkling down the length of its blade as it tumbled handle over tip. It made a perfect arc upward, a graceful movement that I watched with despair. It hung in the air for a moment, then began its descent, just as graceful, but with each flash of its blade, my hope evaporated more, leaving nothing but resignation.

Just as the sword was about to strike the earth, a shadow tore itself through the webbing between worlds. A woman emerged, holding a staff of shining gold, which she slammed down into the ground, the reverberation from which knocked the demon's sword backwards through the air, coincidentally sending me reeling against the wall.

The woman looked at me for a moment, silent but magnificent, a glorious corona of golden light emanating from her before both it and her crumpled and dissolved into nothing. A figure flashed through the mist she left behind, flying through the air and falling to the ground only to spring up again, the demon's sword held in his hand.

"Gabriel," I said, astonished.

Baltic froze for a moment, his gaze lingering on me for a second, and I feared for the space between heartbeats that he would kill me.

But as Gabriel stalked toward us, the demon's blade glowing brightly in his hand, Baltic turned from me and met him with a little salute with his sword.

"I forgot that your mother was a shaman," Baltic said, glancing toward the space where Kaawa had stood. "It must have cost her much to bring you here."

"Not as much as it will cost you," Gabriel said, answering the salute with one of his own. "I have seen paintings of Baltic. You do not bear a resemblance to any of them."

The dragon merely smiled. "Appearances, as the mortals are so fond of saying, can be deceptive. You intend to fight for your mate."

It was a statement, not a question.

"She is mine. I will not let her go," Gabriel said, his eyes lit from deep within.

My heart was overwhelmed with love and fear, not for him, but for myself. I knew that according to dragon dogma, a wyvern's mate could survive the loss of her dragon, but not the reverse. If Baltic killed Gabriel, though, the pain would just be too much to bear. I would live, but I would remain in the shadow world, hidden from life, bound to a love that would survive regardless of my wishes.

The dragon shard protested such a defeatist attitude, and for once, I welcomed the flow of emotions with which it filled me, easing the dagger from the sheath at my ankle, moving slowly and silently to a position behind Baltic.

"You make it all so easy," Baltic said, shaking his head a split second before he lunged at Gabriel, his sword leaving a little contrail of blue light as it flashed in a complicated pattern above and around Gabriel.

My admiration for Gabriel, already pretty high, rose even more as he easily parried Baltic's attacks with the sword of light. I knew from experience the sort of power the former wielded, and yet Gabriel didn't seem to be affected by them at all. The two men moved in and out of the shadows, in an elegant if powerful dance of light and darkness, Baltic's blade slicing through the air in quick, sharp movements, while Gabriel's responses with the demon sword seemed slower and more deliberate, but no less deadly.

I watched for an opening where I could make my own attack, but just as Baltic spun around a broken bit of marble, leaping over

Gabriel while slashing downward with his sword, a flash of red sprayed upward. Gabriel grunted and dropped into a roll, getting to his feet slowly, his shirt soaked with blood as his left arm hung at an odd angle. For a moment my eyes saw only the bone and tendons exposed by the blow Baltic had made, nearly slicing off Gabriel's arm, but then a red mist swept over my vision.

"May!" Gabriel yelled. "Get out of here. Find your way out to safety."

A horrible noised echoed throughout the shadow world, half roar, half battle cry. My body filled with fire, too much fire, bursting from me in an explosion of anger, fury, and retribution, and I realized with abstracted interest that it was me making all that noise. My body changed, lengthened, sinews and muscles increasing as the fine silver scales swept up from my limbs. I could taste Gabriel's blood, hear his labored breathing as he continued to fend off Baltic's increasing attacks, slowly trying to lead him away from me, fighting to the end to save me when it was himself he should be saving.

"May, you must leave!" Gabriel yelled again. "If you shift completely, I don't know that you can come back!"

No one harmed my mate and lived. That was the thought that consumed me as I lashed out at Baltic, striking him with blood-red claws and a razor-sharp whip of a tail, every atom of my being focused on the destruction of the dragon who hurt my mate.

The ground itself burst into flames as Baltic screamed in pain, his body shifting instantly into that of a dragon . . . but it was white, not black.

His eyes were the same, dark and menacing, filled with knowledge that went beyond that of even the oldest of dragons, and they held me in their grasp for a split second before his body twisted and I was sent flying, slamming backwards into a half-collapsed archway.

The blow left me dazed, watching with unfocused eyes as Gabriel's form shimmered for a second, then shifted into that of a powerful form that glittered as bright as his eyes. The dragons still held swords, one of Gabriel's arms limp and bloodied, but the wordless roar that was ripped from his throat promised more than retribution.

He drove the demon's sword deep into the chest of the white dragon, causing Baltic to shift back into human form. He staggered backwards a few steps, both hands on the hilt of the demon's sword, a look of amazement on his face. "A shadow sword?"

Gabriel looked startled for an instant as well, but that expression vanished when he returned to his human form. He snatched up the dagger I'd dropped when I transformed, stalking toward Baltic, his head down, one side of his body held higher than the other, his eyes burning with mercurial fire. "She . . . is . . . mine," he growled, and Baltic, staggering slightly, shook his head as if in disbelief.

"How can you know? It cannot be, and yet, this shadow blade is real. This is not over."

The roar that followed shook the shadow world. "She is mine!"

Baltic said nothing in response to that, just backed into the shadows and disappeared.

Gabriel stood for a moment, panting with the effort that I knew it took him merely to keep conscious, before turning toward me.

"Little bird," he said, and dropped to his knees.

I crawled over to him, noting with the same abstracted interest that my hands were no longer silver, but the normal freckled beige I expected.

"He'll be back," Gabriel said, gasping for air as I peeled back his shirt. "We have to get out of here."

He held his left wrist with his right hand, pulling it close to his body to keep the limb from dropping off altogether. I gritted my teeth against the gruesome sight that was his shoulder, ripping off my shirt to bind his arm to his torso, ignoring the little sounds of pain that escaped him. "We must leave, mate."

"We will," I said, cradling him to me as the loss of blood caught up with him. His head lolled back against my shoulder. I held him tight, weeping hot, silent tears from the lingering emotions left by the dragon shard.

CHAPTER
TWENTY-FIVE

"How's he feeling — good lord, May!"

A female voice pierced the haze that so often accompanies exhausted sleep. I pushed myself out of it, sitting upright, momentarily confused about where I was.

Aisling stood on the other side of the bed upon which I was lying, a startled expression on her face.

I followed her gaze to my hand, which had been resting on Gabriel's chest. It was covered in silver scales, the scarlet claws in stark relief against his skin.

"Wow. Half dragon, half girl. That's gotta be a moneymaker if you set up a webcam," Jim said, peering over the bed at me.

Panic gripped me as I tried to force the dragon part of me back. If I was starting to shift while sleeping, could it be long before the dragon shard took me over completely?

"Do not distress yourself," Gabriel said softly to me. "Relax, little bird. Take your time. Do not force the change."

It was easy for him to say; he wasn't the one losing himself, I thought bitterly to myself as I nonetheless followed his advice. I took a deep breath and tried to relax my tense muscles, gently but firmly pushing out the volatile emotions that so persistently held me in their grip.

"Aw, man! Now she looks normal. We aren't going to get rich that way," Jim said with disgust.

Aisling watched me for a moment. "I guess I should have been asking if you were all right, rather than Gabriel."

I pushed aside my own troubles to glance anxiously at Gabriel. Unlike the half-dead, unresponsive man whom I'd managed to drag to an exit outside of Abaddon, he looked positively brimming with health now, his color good, his breathing unlabored.

"Tipene is a good healer, but I wouldn't be here if it wasn't for May," he answered with a slight grimace.

Drake entered the room, giving Aisling a pointed look before pulling a chair over behind her and gently pushing her down into it.

"Are you still in pain?" I asked, quickly checking the bandage that was wrapped around his shoulder. "Do you want me to call Tipene?"

"No, that face was a reflection of my failure," he answered, taking my hand and kissing my fingers.

"Failure? What failure? You did the impossible, Gabriel — you saved me from Baltic when no one else could have," I said, relieved by the spark of sexual interest that lit in his eyes. If he was feeling randy, then he couldn't still be in much pain.

"You had to rescue me," he answered, disgruntled. "It should have been the reverse."

"If your arm hadn't nearly been hacked off, I would punch you in your shoulder so hard you'd flinch," I said softly.

He grinned, and instantly the dragon shard insisted I jump his bones.

"Honest to god, men," Aisling muttered, giving both Gabriel and Drake a dark look. "I understand protecting your loved ones, but this is just pure macho, and you both know it. Although I admit I don't understand the whole thing, since May was fairly incoherent when she called us. With worry, naturally, but still, you did promise to tell us what happened. Jim dished with a little of what happened after I summoned it back, but we want to hear the full story."

I examined Gabriel's face. There were

faint lines around his mouth that gave a hint as to how much pain he'd been in until I'd managed to drag him out of Abaddon, but otherwise, he looked up to a recap.

"Before we go into that, did you get Chuan Ren out?" he asked.

Drake nodded. "We did. She has left to go deal with Fiat."

"Deal with?" I asked, not easy in my mind about what we had unleashed, but knowing there was no other option. "As in kill?"

"Possibly," Drake said, his fingers caressing the back of Aisling's neck. I was struck once again by their bond, by the deep love the two shared. Would the dragon shard let me love Gabriel the same why? Or had it already changed me so that I would never have that kind of quiet contentment? The dragon emotions were so volatile, so explosive, so totally at odds with my normal, placid self, I couldn't help but mourn what couldn't be.

"He's got it coming to him," Jim said, plopping itself down on the floor. "I bet he would have had a blast in Abaddon. Not that Chuan Ren is much better. She killed her whole family, didn't she?"

"It's possible that Chuan Ren may attempt to kill Fiat," Gabriel said thoughtfully, his fingers stroking mine. "But it's also quite possible that the reverse may be true, as well. Fiat seems each day to become more and more unhinged. It would be madness to try to eliminate Chuan Ren, but if his ability to reason is gone, then he may try it."

"Which would be his own destruction," Drake said, nodding. "Chuan Ren is too strong to take by a coup. It will be interesting, however, to see what happens."

"I don't honestly care so long as she doesn't try to declare war again," Aisling said, patting her belly.

Drake smiled. "I believe Fiat will be the target of her spleen for a while. And after that" — he glanced at me — "we shall see."

"So what exactly happened after Bael chased you back into the shadow world?" Aisling asked, making herself comfortable.

I went quickly over recent events, recounting faithfully everything Baltic had said.

"You're sure he was a white dragon?" Drake asked, frowning.

I glanced at Gabriel, whose lips had thinned. "That's what I saw, but admittedly, I had just cracked my head on the stone wall and was a bit muzzy still."

"He was white," Gabriel agreed. "I was expecting black, not that he looked anything like the portraits of Baltic. Still, he might have changed his appearance. But he was white, Drake, white."

"Is there a white sept?" Aisling asked her husband. "Or rather, was there at one time?"

"No to both questions," he answered.

"This is really confusing, then," Aisling said, and I wholly agreed with her.

"It does seem somewhat conflicting," I said. "On the one hand, he didn't deny being Baltic, but he also said something about appearances being deceptive, and he was definitely not a black dragon. Which he would be unless he was made ouroboros, wouldn't he?"

Gabriel's fingers tightened around mine. "Yes. Baltic wasn't ouroboros."

"White's the opposite of black. Maybe he's the anti-Baltic," Jim said.

We all looked at it.

"What?" it asked, its eyes wide.

"Can there be such a thing?" I asked Gabriel.

His forehead wrinkled as he thought. "I've never heard of it, but then, I've never heard of a dragon having access to the beyond, or wielding a blade of light. That is the weapon of an arcane master, not a dragon."

"Baltic is said to have trained with an archimage," Drake said slowly.

"Which would explain why, if he was

Baltic, he responded so violently to the wrath demon's sword," Gabriel said, looking thoughtful.

"I know I'm going to regret asking this, but what is the big deal about a wrath demon's sword, other than it's obviously a badass weapon?" Aisling asked.

"Can't take her anywhere," Jim said, shaking its head.

"Quiet, demonic one. May? Do you know?" Aisling asked me.

"I know something about them, but not as much as someone more learned in Abaddon," I answered. "Wrath demons are the equivalent to wyverns' bodyguards. They are an elite corps, very nasty customers, kind of semi–demon lords used to enact only the most deadly of events. Unlike other minions, who rely upon their demon lords for their powers, wrath demons have the ability to use the dark power directly. They imbue that power into weapons, most preferring to use blades of some sort since it's hard to kill an immortal unless you can sever their head, or twain them in two, or something equally impossible to recover from."

"OK. But what does that have to do with this dragon?" she asked.

"A mage uses arcane magic," Gabriel

answered. "Part of that is based on the ability to manipulate light. Beings who use arcane powers are particularly susceptible to dark power."

"So when Gabriel skewered the dragon with the wrath demon's shadow blade — a fancy name for a sword imbued with dark power — it had an extra wallop," I finished.

"Ah. That makes sense. But it doesn't sound like this dragon is Baltic."

Drake rubbed his chin, his gaze sightless as he thought. "It is conceivable that the dragon was Baltic. The sword of light would fit that premise. We already know he's been able to go into the beyond at will."

"Oh! That's what I wanted to ask, but forgot. How did your mom get you in there?" Aisling asked Gabriel.

I wanted to know that as well.

"My mother has several dreamings, or aspects of nature. She sought aid from them to allow me access to the beyond. I fear that she promised them much in exchange for their help."

"So you showed up just in the nick of time, and rescued your damsel from the big bad dragon. That's really very romantic," she said, giving us both a gentle smile.

My gaze dropped as my fingers twined through Gabriel's. It was terribly romantic, but I found it impossible to celebrate when I stood on the brink of personal destruction.

"Isn't it?" Aisling asked, looking from my downcast face to Gabriel's, which reflected his worry. She sighed. "I'm missing something obvious again, aren't I?"

"Man, you are just asking for a one-liner, aren't you?" Jim said, standing up and shaking.

"Come, *kincsem,* you must have your rest," Drake said, gently heaving her to her feet. "I will take you home now."

"You're going to do some explaining, as well, like what exactly it is that has both of them so glum," she said, allowing him to escort her to the door. She paused there for a minute, looking back at me. "Before I forget, your twin was here, but she had to go. Something about a dirty stream. Or was it a hot springs? Whichever, she sends her love and says she hopes you're feeling better soon so you can help her clean."

I couldn't help but smile. That sounded just like Cyrene.

Aisling winked at Gabriel before turning back to me. "I may not be the savviest person on the face of the earth — one word, Jim, and it's the Akasha for you! — but I know a good thing when I see it, and you two definitely have it. I hope whatever it is that's troubling you can be easily overcome."

I waited until the door was closed behind them before meeting Gabriel's gaze. There was sympathy in his eyes, as well as warmer emotions, but there was also a tinge of pity that made me sick.

"Do not turn away from me," he said as I made a move to get off the bed.

"Don't," I protested as he pulled me across the breadth of his chest, his warmth and scent sinking into me. "Tipene said you shouldn't use your arm for another day just to make sure everything has healed properly."

He smiled against my lips. "It would be worth a little pain to reassure you that no matter what you are, no matter what happens to us both, you will always be my mate, and I will always desire you."

I gave in to the demands of my body and kissed him, my head spinning with the taste and feel of him. "I'm losing the battle, Gabriel. The dragon shard is just too strong."

"My fierce little bird," he said, stroking back a strand of hair from my face. "It is a battle, yes, but not one we will lose. We have one shard, Drake and Bastian will lend us theirs, and Chuan Ren has sworn to give us access to the Song phylactery. That leaves only one for us to find, and I have no doubt that the dragon we encountered has that. It just remains for us to put a few plans into place, and you will be able to bring the dragon heart together again."

I let his calm confidence soothe my frayed nerves, resting my forehead against his as I smiled. "And what will we do if we can't get that last shard?"

"Then we will both remain in dragon form, and I will make suggestive comments about your tail."

I couldn't help but laugh a little at the twinkle in his eyes. The dragon shard, to my surprise, allowed me to enjoy the moment without demanding immediate mating. "You already do make suggestive comments."

"Yes, but these will be very specific about what I want you to do," he answered, his lips hot on mine. "Don't worry about what we must face. You have fought the biggest battle of all, and won."

"Escaping Abaddon, you mean?" I asked, my hands unable to keep from stroking the heavy muscles of his bare chest.

"No." His tongue invaded my mouth, doing a fiery dance that was impossibly sweet and arousing at the same time. "You won the battle for my heart."

I froze for a second, not sure if he was saying what I thought he was saying, but it was there in his face and eyes, and I just wanted to purr with joy despite the coming storm.

"I love you," I told him, generating a little fire of my own.

"You see? How can our future not be a happy one when you love me as much as I love you," he said, his hands starting to roam.

I was just considering whether or not I could keep the dragon shard's presence minimalized so I could make incredibly hot, sweaty love to Gabriel when the door to his bedroom was thrown open with a vengeance that made me jump.

Magoth stood in the doorway, a gorgeous red shirt open nearly to the waist of his black leather pants. "I hope you're happy!" he said, hands on his hips as he glared. "I just hope you're both happy!"

"Magoth," I said, astonished to see him. "What are you doing? This is Gabriel's bedroom. Get out."

He stepped into the room, waving someone in. Three bellboys staggered in with a vast array of expensive-looking luggage. Magoth stalked into the room until he stood glaring down at both of us. "You just had to tell Sally what you were up to, didn't you? I told you not to, but did you listen to me? No, you did not, and the little backstabbing bitch ran straight to Bael with the details in an attempt to ingratiate herself, and what did he do but excommunicate me! Me, the sixth prince! I've been in Abaddon for more than a millennium, and poof! It's all gone, thanks to you, former consort."

"*Former* consort?" I asked.

The look of scorn he shot at me would have stopped a rhino in full charge. "You don't think I'm going to keep a consort who has me kicked out of Abaddon, do you? I'm divorcing you, May."

"But . . ." I looked at Gabriel. He appeared to be just as surprised by Magoth's sudden appearance as I was. "But what are you doing *here?* With all this stuff?"

Magoth plopped himself down in a chair and put his feet up on one of the suitcases, smiling. The mirror behind him shattered. "I'm powerless in both worlds until the excommunication has been finalized. So until my powers are returned to me, sweet May, you're back to being my servant."

"If you're no longer a demon lord," Gabriel said, a little frown between his brows, "then May is no longer your consort *or* servant."

"Consort, no. But servant . . ." Magoth's smile turned truly appalling. I wanted to throw something at him. "She was bound to *me,* not to my position, so she is most definitely mine to command again. And she can start by getting me something cold to drink. Something tasty. Champagne will do nicely."

I felt my jaw drop as the horrible realization sank into my brain. "You don't mean —"

"That's right," he said, leaning back, his hands behind his head as he gave me a sultry look. "Until my powers are returned, I'm staying with you. Shall we discuss the sleeping arrangements? I like boy, girl, boy, for aesthetic reasons, but if you absolutely insist, I can take the middle spot."

Gabriel and I exchanged identical horror-stricken looks.

"So much for a happy future," I said, sighing as I slumped back against the headboard.

ABOUT THE AUTHOR

Growing up in a family where a weekly visit to the library was a given, **Katie MacAlister** spent much of her childhood with her nose in a book. She lives in the Pacific Northwest with her husband and dogs, and can often be found lurking around online game sites, indulging in world building of another sort. To contact Katie, visit www .katiemacalister.com. Fans of the Otherworld are invited to stop by www.dragon septs.com.

We hope you have enjoyed this Large Print book. Other Thorndike, Wheeler, Kennebec, and Chivers Press Large Print books are available at your library or directly from the publishers.

For information about current and upcoming titles, please call or write, without obligation, to:

Publisher
Thorndike Press
295 Kennedy Memorial Drive
Waterville, ME 04901
Tel. (800) 223-1244

or visit our Web site at:

http://gale.cengage.com/thorndike

OR

Chivers Large Print
published by BBC Audiobooks Ltd
St James House, The Square
Lower Bristol Road
Bath BA2 3SB
England
Tel. +44(0) 800 136919
email: bbcaudiobooks@bbc.co.uk
www.bbcaudiobooks.co.uk

All our Large Print titles are designed for easy reading, and all our books are made to last.